# THE WIND MONKEY

# LEO BERENSTAIN

# THE WIND MONKEY

## & Other Stories

RANDOM HOUSE

NEW YORK

Library of Congress Cataloging-in-Publication Data
Berenstain, Leo.
The wind monkey, and other stories / Leo Berenstain
          p. cm.      ISBN 0-394-57557-1
          1. Indonesia—Fiction. I. Title.
PS3552.E6965W56    1991    813'.54—dc20    91-52819

Manufactured in the United States of America
The text is set in 12/13 Bembo
Design by J. K. Lambert
2 4 6 8 9 7 5 3
First Edition

*For my parents, and for Kania*

*The author would like
to acknowledge gratefully
the work of his editors,
Susan Kamil and
Karen Rinaldi.*

# CONTENTS

# THE WIND MONKEY

# THE PACT

The old three-story Grand Hotel of Cirebon, with its air-conditioned restaurant, attached discotheque, and broad white-pillared verandah, seemed to be itching for foreign tourists. That it was ready only for the more seasoned among them had been apparent from the first morning of Janet Riddell's stay, when she had informed the desk clerk about the lack of hot water for her bath. The young man smiling at her from behind the counter had been fully prepared.

"Oh, yes," he said in bold English. "You must waiting ten minute."

She answered in Indonesian, "But I waited fifteen minutes and it was still cold as ice."

The response, without hesitation, came also in Indonesian: "Oh, you need to wait maybe twenty minutes."

"I'll try again later," she said, aware that the argument she might have sought had been deftly sidestepped. Not even five months in Java had been enough to teach her all the applications of Indonesian "rubber time."

Now, settled in a wicker chair on the verandah, Janet gazed past the Grand's venerable pillars to the main entrance of the parking lot, where *becak* drivers lounged in their pedicabs under a massive banyan tree. The banyan's aerial roots hung motionless in the blazing north coast sun, as did the brightly colored flags that had been strung along Jalan Siliwangi a month earlier for Independence Day. During her week in Cirebon, Janet had grown fond of these flags. She had puzzled over the origin of their graceful shape— they were long and slim and vertically tapered, curved gently forward at their apexes as though bowing—until one day she had noticed the tops of the high bamboo tapered and curved just so.

"Hello, Miss. What you doing?"

Janet looked up into the bloodshot eyes of a slim young man with angular Javanese features. He had one hand on the back of a chair and another wrapped around a tall dripping beer glass. He was grinning down at her with the kind of lopsided leer she remembered from her college dating days. In his prefaded designer jeans and expensive white shoes, he was ready for the disco, which would not open for another three hours. Wonderful, she thought, already sloshed at three in the afternoon.

"I'm reading over some notes," she answered in Indonesian. She kept the notebook conspicuously open in her lap.

"Ah-h-h." The acrid smell of beer hit Janet in the face. "Are you a reporter?"

She marveled at the naïveté of this question she was asked

wherever she went. When was the last time a Western reporter had appeared in Cirebon? Ten years ago? Twenty? Fifty?

"I'm a travel writer," she said.

The young man set his glass down on the small circular table and slid himself into the chair next to hers. "May I join you?"

Janet conjured up her iciest tone of voice. "Only if you promise not to invite me to the disco tonight."

For a moment the young man stared blankly at her, struggling to conceal his astonishment at this Western brutality. He flashed a smile.

"Oh, I won't," he said. "I couldn't. You see, I'm here with my girlfriend. Look, here she comes."

What a relief, Janet thought as a petite young woman with almond-shaped eyes glided up to them and began talking rapidly in Javanese with the man. Her designer jeans matched his, and she wore a frilly pink blouse and high-heeled slippers of carved wood. Her fingernails and toenails were painted crimson. Now and then the young man would giggle and give her a little poke in the ribs and say to Janet, *"Cemburu."* Jealous. When the girlfriend had settled down, he told Janet his name was Prio and that he was originally from Magelang, in central Java. Prio was an engineering student at the technical college in Cirebon and was spending a few days at the hotel with Diah, a sales clerk at the Matahari Department Store downtown. He was obviously a student of means: the poor ones could not spend eight U.S. dollars a night on a cold-water double at the Grand Hotel.

Though Prio was too drunk to take an interest in anything but the sound of his own voice, Diah was sincerely curious about the foreign woman's reason for being in Java and asked about it as soon as her boyfriend lapsed into a stuporous silence. Janet explained that she was a Canadian and had been living in London and working for a British publishing house. She had written some travel pieces about Canada and the United States for British magazines; on the strength of these, her employer had contracted with her for a travel guide about Java. She was now at the end of an extended tour of the island for the purpose of gathering information.

The self-assurance and sense of purpose with which Janet spoke of this seemed so firm that anyone listening might have thought she had possessed these qualities all her life. In fact, she had been unable to decide on a career until, at age thirty, she had seized the present opportunity. At last she knew exactly what she wanted to do: write guidebooks. It was a career that would take her all over the world to write about all sorts of exotic places. She felt reborn. Not only was she free of romantic entanglements, having jettisoned old ones while making a solemn pledge to avoid any new ones that did not fit her globe-trotting life-style, but she was also rid of another old nemesis: the stifling fear of being tied to one place.

Diah, a native of Cirebon, asked Janet how much space she planned to devote to the city in the upcoming book.

"Well," said Janet, "Cirebon is quite interesting, of course: the sultans' palaces, the Islamic history, the mixture of Javanese, Sundanese, and Chinese cultures . . . "

She paused. Diah's question had struck a nerve. She recalled the first time she had passed through Cirebon four and a half months ago on the drive east from Jakarta, overjoyed at escaping the crowded capital for the countryside of emerald rice paddies and lavender volcanoes. Honking and swerving past water buffalo and barefoot children and old women bowed under heavy loads, her driver Ujang had expertly navigated village after village until one of these had swelled to form the outskirts of a city. She wanted badly to stop and explore this interesting seaport, whose endless sprawl of bazaars and low buildings scarcely hinted at its distinctive place in the history and culture of Java. But she denied herself and pushed on along the coast to the less intriguing cities of Pekalongan and Semarang, sensing she would need more experience and language to tackle the secrets of Cirebon. She would save Cirebon for last.

Though in the end she had left only a week for the city, she'd been certain that this was more than enough time to uncover a half-dozen interesting places that had yet to grace the pages of a guidebook. She visited and revisited every spot mentioned in the small library she carried with her, filling her notebook with details and nuances that had escaped other authors. She had captured the air of decadence that lingered around Gua Sunyaragi, the outlandish pleasure dome fashioned out of a limestone cavern by a wealthy nineteenth-century Chinese trader. She had paid special attention to the eclectic quaintness of the sultans' palaces, with their Javanese doors and pillars, French chairs and chandeliers, and walls studded with Chinese porcelain and delft tiles from Holland. The atmosphere at the holy tomb of Sultan Gunung Jati had been hardest to do justice to; nevertheless, in rereading her notes just now she had been pleased with the description of the cluttered tiered graveyard and the white-clad pilgrims bowing to the great old wooden door of the mausoleum they were forbidden to enter. But for all that, she hadn't found a single genuine novelty worth including in her Cirebon chapter. Proud as she was of the notes resting in her lap, she could not ignore the fact that they were a rehashing of what had been covered, however cursorily, elsewhere. And today was her final day in Cirebon.

Diah's voice suddenly brought her back into focus.

"I'm sorry, what?" Janet asked.

"I asked if you would rather not talk about your book."

"Oh, no, it's all right." Janet glanced at Prio, who was slumped in his chair with eyes closed, snoring loudly. "You see, I'm really not sure what to do about Cirebon. I'd been hoping to find some new places—places not in the other guidebooks—but I haven't. I was especially wanting to find some place with an interesting legend behind it." Raising her teacup for a sip of cold tea, she added in a half-joking tone, "You wouldn't know of any, would you?"

Diah screwed up her face and pondered the question. After a brief silence, she looked as if she were about to speak, then thought better of it.

"What is it?" Janet asked.

"Oh, nothing. I thought of a place with a legend, but then I realized it wouldn't be interesting."

"Why not?"

"Because there isn't anything there. Just a hill."

"Just a hill? With nothing on it?"

"Nothing. Only jungle and monkeys."

Janet sat straight up in her chair. "But jungle and monkeys *are* interesting," she protested.

Diah frowned. "They are? Why?"

"Because most of my readers live in countries without any jungles or monkeys."

Diah's frown gave way to an incredulous smile. "Countries without jungle or monkeys? How funny! Are you joking?"

"Not at all. And this legend—what is it?"

Diah shrugged. "I forget. I heard it when I was little. It's about where the monkeys came from. A lot of the old folks believe it, but we modern Cirebonese don't pay much attention to their stories."

"Where is this hill? What's it called?"

"Plangon Hill. About fifteen kilometers south on the

road to Bandung in the district of Sumber. It's near Panjunan Village. You can take the number six bus from Siliwangi and Veteran—it goes right by there."

Janet returned to her room for a few glorious minutes of
air conditioning before venturing out again. She was tired,
already drained by the heat and humidity. In five months'
time, she had wasted countless hours and a great deal of
energy tracking down leads like this that had not panned
out. Still, she had little in her notes about monkeys outside
the national parks; that made Plangon Hill a potentially
useful addition to her book. Exchanging her cotton skirt for
a pair of blue jeans and her sandals for tennis shoes, she
walked through the courtyard and out to the gateway of
the parking lot, searching for her pedicab driver. He was
standing expectantly beside his cab with a grin on his face.
Within a day of her arrival in Cirebon, Hadi had become
her personal pedicab driver, just as she had become his
personal gold mine—three months' worth of fares crammed
into one giddy week. After failing to persuade her that it
was beneath her dignity to ride city transportation and that
she should let him drive her out to Plangon (a three-hour
pedicab ride for a fare it would normally take him a month
to earn), he grudgingly pedaled her down Siliwangi to
where she caught the number six.

The ride to Sumber District took half an hour on the
Bandung-Trusmi road. The "bus," a pale-blue minivan,
contained a dozen passengers and air thick with clove-
scented cigarette smoke. At the outskirts of the village of
Panjunan, Janet got off and asked directions from an old
woman squatting by the road minding three little barefoot
boys who were playing tag. The boys pressed themselves
into the old woman's sarong and didn't resume playing until
Janet was well down the road. It was a paved road that
descended for a quarter of a mile before rising again along

the foot of a wooded hillside. She walked briskly, for the late-afternoon light was changing and she wanted to get some decent photos. Her heart stirred when she saw that the hillside was truly wild, cloaked in jungle. It was a striking sight after miles of neat, cultivated fields and little square yards with banana trees sprouting like huge weeds from the bare earth.

Several hundred yards from the edge of the village, she came to a whitewashed signpost bordering a dirt path that led up the hill into the jungle. The sign proclaimed the hill to be under the jurisdiction of the Department of Religion. To Janet's surprise and delight, it also informed her that she was about to ascend to the Makam Kramat Plangon— "Plangon Holy Grave." This was already more than she had hoped for. Still, there would have to be monkeys to draw the interest of her readers, for the grave site was obviously little known and hence unlikely to be even a fraction as impressive as Sultan Gunung Jati's. She walked a few steps beyond the signpost and peered up the path to where it curved and disappeared into the jungle. The path was rocky and cratered, strewn with large brown stones. The jungle was low and close overhead.

Having checked that her camera was loaded, Janet was about to start the climb when an old man wearing a felt hat with a narrow brim stepped barefoot onto the path from behind a broad-leaved shrub not ten feet from her. She wasn't afraid, for through the tangle of trees and lianas behind him she could make out a small house of plaited bamboo about thirty yards off in the jungle. It was obvious he lived there and thus had every right to be curious about her. He was, she thought, extremely picturesque. The felt hat was filthy and discolored, misshapen with age. Above gray trousers spotted with what Janet guessed was cooking oil he wore a zippered sweatshirt that might once have been green but was now no color at all. He was so grimy and tattered that he might have been one of the rag-clad psychotics she had seen wandering the city streets of Java. A frizzy salt-and-pepper beard covered his face; matted hair hid his ears. As he stepped toward her, Janet noticed that his right big toe was splayed so far inward that it looked like the thumb on a chimpanzee's foot.

"Good afternoon," Janet said in Indonesian. He returned this with a nod of his head and stood waiting. Remembering that this was the entrance to a holy grave site, she realized that he was the caretaker; as such, he was obliged to greet her, but was understandably shy, for it may have been many years since he'd seen a Westerner. She motioned up the path and told him she wanted to go to the top. He nodded again, turned, and padded up the path. The big toe of his splayed foot flapped and waggled as he dragged it over stones and exposed roots.

It was deliciously cool under the jungle canopy. Though it was not a high canopy like some of those she had seen in the national parks, the interlocking tree crowns were knitted together with vines and climbers so that in most places sunlight penetrated only the uppermost layer of foliage. Looking up and around as she walked, Janet could see the canopy's shell, splotched and streaked where it caught the slanting rays of the sun and turned them the color of honey. Lianas looped through the maze of branches; aerial roots bearded the forest edge. Strangling figs coiled woody tentacles around trees in whose crowns they had sprouted ages ago. Janet inhaled the rich mildewy smell, somehow corrupt and fresh at the same time, intensely fragrant after Cirebon. This place, she thought, was a time capsule, the way most of Java must have been less than a century ago.

The caretaker stopped walking and pointed off at the forest to her right. *"Monyet."* At first she saw only leaves and branches and lianas, but then her eyes found a cat-sized monkey with gray-brown fur staring at her from where it sat on top of a gray-brown boulder. It had bushy white whiskers and sad brown-and-yellow eyes. It seemed to be waiting for her next move, the way the caretaker had at the foot of the hill. Janet made a soft kissing sound that she had learned was a friendly gesture among these common *kra* monkeys. She took a step toward it, but the animal scrambled backward off the boulder and into the undergrowth, where it crouched, eyeing her.

The caretaker chuckled, displaying a mouthful of crooked teeth. *"Betina,"* he said. *Female.* *"Malu."* *Shy.* He reached into his pants' pocket, pulled out a peanut, and held it at arm's length toward the monkey. Janet watched the animal's anxious eyes as it crept forward to the boulder and halted. Again reaching into his pocket, the caretaker produced a handful of peanuts and passed them to Janet. He tossed the already proffered nut onto the path halfway between her and the kra. Comprehending his intention, Janet held out a peanut while the monkey darted forward to retrieve the one that lay on the path. Sure enough, the little animal crept right up to her and, after several moments of shifting its eyes between her face and hand, snatched the nut and scurried back to the boulder, where it sat regarding her as it husked and chewed the offering.

The path grew steeper as they neared the top of the hill. Janet's thigh muscles started to burn. She looked back once and saw to her delight that there were now three kra following them at a safe distance—the female, a juvenile, and a larger one that she presumed was a male because of its big squarish head and thick shoulders. This was wonderful! And they hadn't even gotten to the grave site yet! She flung some peanuts over her shoulder and clambered up the final stretch of path. On the hilltop was a flat grassy clearing that extended off to their left before sloping gently upward to a little brick building with a roof of corrugated tin. The structure, which she guessed was the holy grave site, was surrounded by a pair of concentric stone fences, and the enclosed grounds were tiered. To the right, another path, much narrower than the one they had just ascended, snaked off into the jungle.

The caretaker turned to Janet and said something she didn't understand. When she looked puzzled, he motioned toward the path into the jungle, then to the mausoleum. She nodded at the mausoleum, and he led her to it. The three monkeys—no, it was five now, she noticed—followed them, snatching at the peanuts she kept trailing behind her. Just to the right of the mausoleum's outer fence stood a magnificent banyan tree with a trunk like twisted taffy. The caretaker picked up a club resting against it—a club long ago worn smooth—and struck the banyan tree three heavy blows. A low booming sound reverberated over the hill. It was the kind of sound, Janet thought, that was sure to make even the most jaded, Asia-wise tourist catch his breath. She awaited the next part of the ritual, but the caretaker simply stood with the club at his side. There was a splash in the canopy far off to their left, then one behind them, one closer, another, and another. Soon the jungle all around was splashing and dipping and swaying as the monkeys came. The caretaker scattered peanuts over the clearing and around the mausoleum, and within seconds there were forty or fifty little gray-brown creatures chattering on the stone walls and chirping in the low trees.

What a find! An isolated hill on the outskirts of town, a miniature jungle, a holy grave with an old caretaker who conjured up monkeys with a summons from out of the distant past. *And no one knew it was here.* Clearly, the handful of foreign tourists that trickled into Cirebon each year didn't come here; it appeared that even Indonesians seldom visited. Her guidebook's readers would be pioneers!

Janet raced through a roll of film. Soon the caretaker's pockets were empty of peanuts and the monkeys had drawn back to the edges of the jungle, where they sat grooming one another and resting. Clearing his throat officiously, the caretaker gestured at the mausoleum and began speaking. He said something about long ago and brothers from Baghdad and the Sultan of Cirebon. Though Janet managed to catch isolated words and phrases, the flow of the narrative was past her before she could grab hold of its meaning. She realized why she hadn't understood his first words when they had crested the hill: he was speaking in the old Cirebonese language, a mixture of Javanese and Sundanese. Most likely, he had never learned much Indonesian. She let him finish his explanation, then asked in Indonesian where the monkeys had come from.

*"Orang-orang,"* he said.

"People," she repeated. "People brought them here? Who?"

The caretaker shook his head and said something in Cirebonese.

Janet said, "I don't understand. People didn't bring them here?"

Shaking his head again, the caretaker said, *"Orang jadi monyet."*

"You mean," she asked, "that a person became a monkey? People became monkeys?"

He nodded.

"How? Why?"

Patiently, he explained in Cirebonese. She couldn't get the gist of it, but it didn't matter. She stopped listening and looked around at the jungle and the monkeys and the walled mausoleum. Her heart gave a little flutter. It was too good to be true. The legend of Plangon Hill, whatever it turned out to be, would be quaint, colorful, *dramatic*. Clearly, she would have to stay in Cirebon another day to investigate the legend. She was so excited that when they reached the bottom of the hill she gave the caretaker a five-thousand-rupiah note, worth about two and a half U.S. dollars. The old man looked with surprise at the money in his hand. *"Terima kasih,"* he said, bowing.

A solitary cicada broke into raspy song. Within moments, thousands of cicadas on the hill had answered and the air was saturated with the sound. Janet turned and walked back up the road toward the village in the fading light.

On the next day, Friday, Cirebon baked once more under a brutal September sun. Janet hurried through her usual breakfast of watery orange juice, fried rice topped with a fried egg, and scalding coffee in an ordinary drinking glass. Carrying her briefcase, she walked down Siliwangi to the local office of the Department of Religion. There a middle-aged man in a government-issue batik shirt looked up from his crossword puzzle long enough to tell her politely that the story of Plangon Hill had not yet been written down. He had heard of an old tale associated with the place, but didn't know anything about it; maybe she should go to the local office of the Department of Education and Culture, down Siliwangi just past the train station. She walked briskly, waving off the pedicabs that came nosing up like curious sharks, and entered the little white building, the exterior of which was all Dutch windows and oversized pillars. The young man behind the desk wore the same style batik shirt and had the same knowledge of Plangon Hill as the previous official. Fortunately, he was more eager to help. On a sheet of paper he scribbled the name of Pangeran

Abdurachim Sanjayaningrat, whom he described as a distinguished local historian, with an address on Jalan Lemahwungkuk. Janet thanked him and turned to leave but stopped, staring at the paper in her hand. She wasn't sure whether the official had meant that Abdurachim was distinguished as a historian or just distinguished. The *Pangeran* preceding his name indicated that he was a prince or lord.

Turning back to the official, she said, "But he's called *Pangeran.*"

"Yes, Miss. He's the Sultan's brother."

"But is it all right? I mean, his house . . . it must be a mansion." She had never liked these intrusions and only yesterday had thought she was finally done with them.

The young man smiled. "Oh, no, Miss. Just an ordinary house." He added, "Though I'm certain that if it were a splendid mansion, Pak Rachim would welcome you just the same."

Half an hour later, she stood before the Prince's house. Her pedicab driver had gotten her to Jalan Lemahwungkuk, a midsized thoroughfare in an old commercial district sporting an assortment of sidewalk vendors, motorbike-parts shops, and general stores. Had it not been for the postman who happened by, however, she never would have found the house. He had drawn the piece of paper up to his nose, frowning and moving his lips as he read the address to himself. He then led her to a narrow alleyway whose entrance from Lemahwungkuk was little more than a cleft in the solid wall of shop-houses. The alley wound its way past chickens, goats, young children with runny noses, cooking hutches that reeked of coconut oil and peanut sauce, and ended at a cramped, boarded-up cul-de-sac. Pointing at the only house there, the postman handed back the piece of paper and disappeared down the alley.

From the general condition of the palaces she had visited

earlier in the week, Janet had already figured out that the Cirebon aristocracy had seen better days. Still, she could hardly believe that the tiny stucco house before her belonged to Pangeran Abdurachim. It was the kind of house a shopkeeper would own, or a leaser of pedicabs, or a small-time rice broker. On the verandah a very old and ordinary-looking male servant in an undershirt, sarong, and rubber sandals was sweeping with a rice-straw broom. Clearly, the postman had made a mistake. It had happened to Janet so many times already: an old man, embarrassed by his illiteracy, would gravely scrutinize an address and proceed to lead her in any direction but the correct one. But a postman? Not even Indonesian nepotism or bribery could land an illiterate a job as a postman. This fact kept her standing there long enough for the old servant on the verandah to notice her. He propped his broom against a wall and approached, bowing slightly and taking steps that got smaller the closer he came.

"Good day, Miss," he said in Indonesian.

With a sheepish grin, Janet handed him the paper, hoping he would direct her to the proper location. Instead, he nodded and with a graceful sweep of the arm invited her onto the verandah, where four rattan chairs were positioned around a low wooden table. Janet sat and rested while the servant went in search of his employer. She looked around at the verandah's peeling walls and cracked tile floor, across which columns of tiny black ants traced wavy lines. The tiles were a dirty tan, like those of the sidewalks of Cirebon. A bare light bulb dangled from the ceiling fixture above the table; a threadbare sofa languished in a corner. A small crowd of children and old women had collected in the cul-de-sac and now stood staring at Janet with expressions of wonder. She was beginning to feel uncomfortable, when all of a sudden they dispersed.

"Welcome," a pleasant voice said in English. A tall man of about fifty, with high cheekbones set in a long dignified face, came around the table and extended his hand as Janet rose. "Rachim," he said simply. She took his hand. It was satiny smooth. He wore a long-sleeved blue-and-red batik shirt patterned with fluffy rocks and clouds, and a sober but elegant charcoal-gray batik sarong. On his feet were leather sandals and on his head a *peci,* the white skullcap worn by those who have made the pilgrimage to Mecca.

"Janet Riddell," said Janet. "I'm very pleased to meet you, Pak."

"Oh, you speak Indonesian," replied Rachim with an ingratiating smile. "Please sit down. Pak Tua will bring refreshments in a moment. Actually, his name is Mursan, but I've always called him Pak Tua. You understand this expression?"

She nodded. *Pak Tua,* literally "Old Father," was a common nickname for elderly male servants in Java. Janet and Rachim chatted for several minutes about the weather, Cirebon, Janet's travels, and finally her book. She carefully avoided coming to the point, nor did Rachim press her to, for it would have been inappropriate before coffee was served. Rachim's manner, though outwardly formal, radiated an inner warmth. She began to relax as they talked. Surely he would solve the mystery for her, so that she could leave for Jakarta tomorrow, only a day behind schedule. That would allow her a full day's rest there before her flight home.

Pak Tua appeared with a plate of fried bananas and coffee in glass cups with plastic lids. When Rachim dismissed him with a nod, the servant left the verandah and walked quickly down the alley. Janet noticed his clean cotton shirt and traditional black Indonesian cap.

"Well, Miss Janet," Rachim said. "How may I help you?"

Briefly she explained. When she had finished, she saw that the warm, willing-to-please expression had gone from Rachim's face. He seemed to be looking past her.

"Plangon Hill," she prompted. "You know it?"

Rachim's thin lips pursed in apparent distaste. "Yes, I know it. That is, I know of it. I've never actually been there. Not many good Muslims have."

"Oh? Why is that?"

"There's nothing of any value to the faithful there. Please drink, Miss; don't wait for me."

"But it has a holy grave site," Janet said, "with a caretaker and a sign put up by the Department of Religion." She tried to sound merely curious and confused; to challenge the Prince would have been very rude.

Rachim said, "Yes, I know." He leaned back in his chair with a sigh, drawing up one saronged knee and clasping it with his hands. "The two brothers buried there came from Baghdad in the sixteenth century. They were involved in a heretical Islamic sect—Sultan Gunung Jati threw them out of his palace, in fact. Unfortunately, there are still only a handful of us Cirebonese Muslims who can distinguish pure from impure. Islam may be stricter here than elsewhere in Java, but it's still cluttered with ancient superstition and mysticism." He glanced from side to side as if someone might be listening, and leaned toward her, placing a hand to one side of his mouth in mock secrecy. "Even at the Department of Religion." He sat back in his chair and folded his arms. "You've already seen how the common folk kneel and pray to the spirit of Gunung Jati at the door of his tomb," he continued. "Idolatry, expressly forbidden by the Koran. And most of them pray not for spiritual purity but for money or a new chicken coop or a good rice yield. But at least they're in the right place!" His eyes sparkled for a moment in appreciation of his own wit. "No, no. Just because Plangon Hill has the tomb of a couple of Arabs on it doesn't make it holy. And places like that are full of old wives' tales. I'm afraid your monkey story is exactly that."

Rachim stood up stiffly, his expression pained. He put a hand to his lower back. Janet had noticed him fidget in his chair as if his back were bothering him. "If you'll excuse me for a moment." He went into the house and returned holding a thick paperbound book, which he handed to Janet. "I must go to the mosque now for the midday service, but I'll be back in an hour, if you'd care to wait. In the meantime, I think you'll find everything you need to know in this book. I'll send Pak Tua back from the mosque soon to bring you more coffee."

She started to say, "Oh, you don't need to do that," but Rachim had already passed from the verandah's shade into the patch of bright sunlight in the cul-de-sac. She watched him move swiftly down the alley, his sarong rippling across the backs of his legs.

Janet looked off into the glare of the noon sky, suddenly aware that she had been hearing the call to prayer for some time. She felt awful. It was Friday, of course, and she had arrived just as her host was preparing to leave for the mosque. No wonder he'd been fidgeting in his chair, sore back or no. And now he was going to give Pak Tua's sarong a tug right in the middle of prayer and send him running back on his knobby old legs to wait on her. She knew that researching a guidebook meant inconveniencing people from time to time, but this was well beyond the bounds of decency. And the Sultan's brother, no less!

She turned her attention to the book in her lap. It was

a typical government publication in a flimsy Plasticine bind-ing, but more scholarly than the usual fare, with copious footnotes and an extensive bibliography. It was a history of Islam in Java, written by her host and published by the Department of Education and Culture. Roughly forty pages of it dealt with the Cirebon area. It took Janet just ten minutes to determine that these pages contained no more information about Plangon than she had just gotten from Rachim. Well, not quite: they did assign names to the brothers from Baghdad—Syarif Abdulrachman and Syarif Kafid—and mentioned that they had come to Java with a younger sister, Siti Baghdad. The account also noted that the Sultan had dubbed them Pangeran Panjunan and Pang-eran Kejaksan, for the areas to which they were exiled when he banished them from the palace. She recalled that the present-day villages nearest Plangon were called Panjunan and Kejaksan. The odd thing was that the book didn't say anything about the brothers being heretics. Would the Sul-tan, she asked herself, have made heretics into lords? Not very likely, but then again, there had to have been some good reason for their expulsion. It was an interesting little mystery. But what did it have to do with people turning into monkeys? That, after all, was why she had come to see Rachim. She tightened her grip on the book. He had given it to her knowing full well there was nothing in it about the monkeys. She slammed it shut.

Calm down, she told herself. Perhaps Rachim didn't even know the monkey legend and out of embarrassment was pretending it beneath his dignity to discuss.

She was still in a nasty mood when Pak Tua returned, however. Out of breath and with a thin film of sweat on his brow and upper lip, he stepped toward her out of the sunlight. He gathered his sarong in front of him with one hand to keep it from brushing against her while he retrieved the cups and plate. She felt a pang of guilt on noticing that Rachim's coffee was untouched, for it suddenly dawned on her that he was fasting until sundown. He had had Pak Tua bring him coffee in order to keep her from realizing what an imposition she was making on him. How could Indonesians be so maddening one minute and so endearingly considerate the next?

As she waited for Pak Tua to bring more coffee and bananas, Janet softened her assessment of her host's behavior. Perhaps he had only been defensive about the old folk superstitions of a modernizing nation. Or, in his current financial state, he may have resented sharing the title "Pangeran" with Arab immigrants who had been lavishly supported by the Sultan even after their removal from court society. Or he may simply have been unwilling to discuss monkeys at all since, in the eyes of his religion, they were as vile and unclean as dogs. In any case, she, a guest in Rachim's country, had no right to be impatient with him. Besides, it would be stupid of her to risk alienating someone who might still prove useful to her. She decided that on Rachim's return she would veil her disappointment like a true Javanese.

"May I ask you something, Pak?" she asked in Indonesian when the servant returned to the verandah.

With a polite smile, Pak Tua folded his hands against the front of his sarong.

"Do you know the story of the monkeys of Plangon Hill?"

His smile froze.

Janet said, "I've been looking for the story in this book that Pak Rachim said would have everything I needed to know, but it isn't here."

"I see." Pak Tua's smile relaxed again. The ambiguity of the situation had been resolved. "It would be better, Miss, if you waited for Pak Rachim to discuss the matter." He turned to go, then stopped. "Have you asked the people at your hotel—which is it?"

"The Grand. Yes, but without success."

Pak Tua nodded, excused himself, and trundled off into the house.

Twenty minutes later Rachim, walking stiffly, emerged from the shaded alley into the sunlit cul-de-sac. He smiled when he saw her, as though glad she was still there. Janet smiled back. How was it, she thought again, that Indonesians could make you feel so ungrateful even when they let you down?

"I hope the book has been useful," Rachim said. He lowered himself carefully into a chair.

"Oh, yes, of course, Pak. But I'm a little confused by one thing: the information about Plangon Hill seems a bit . . . incomplete."

Rachim brushed ants away from the fried bananas. "Do you know this is the last day of Maulud, the month of the birth of the Prophet?"

"Yes, Pak. In fact, that's one of the reasons I waited until now to come to Cirebon."

Rachim nodded. "That was very clever of you. You are obviously doing your job well."

"Thank you, Pak. But I feel I would be doing it even better if I could learn the story of the monkeys of Plangon."

"Yes, I understand, Miss Janet. That is why I mentioned Maulud. It is one of the two holiest months in Islam, of course; only Ramadan is as holy. Thus, it would be improper for me to discuss the burial place of heretics, especially one crawling with unclean animals. If it were just a day later—"

"Maybe I could come back tomorrow," Janet interrupted. "I could delay my departure a day."

"I'm sorry, Miss; I won't be here tomorrow. I leave before dawn to pay a visit to an Islamic school in Tasik-malaya."

"How long will you be gone?"

"At least three days." His eyes searched hers. "Maybe more."

She sighed. "Well, maybe I should go back to Plangon tonight and have the caretaker repeat the legend to me in Cirebonese until I get the gist of it."

Rachim stiffened. "Oh, no, you mustn't do that. It really isn't safe, especially for a woman at night. If you must go back there, at least wait until morning."

It was clear to Janet that the conversation had gone as far as it would. She thanked Rachim and made her way back down the dusty alley, shooing the goats that nuzzled her legs.

❧

It was nearly five o'clock that afternoon when the message arrived. The young man from reception brought it to her on the verandah, saying that one of the room boys had been summoned out to the street to fetch it. Janet unfolded the sheet of notebook paper and read the penciled block lettering: *MAU BICARA SAMA MISS SEBENTAR—I want to talk with Miss a moment.* It was signed MURSAN.

He was waiting for her near one of the parking lot entrances; she could see him talking with the pedicab drivers under the banyan tree. When he noticed her approaching through the parking lot, he walked slowly down Siliwangi and stopped at the corner of the low stone wall that enclosed the grounds of the big mosque next to the hotel.

"Good afternoon, Miss," he said pleasantly when she reached him.

She sat down on top of the wall and crossed her ankles,

smoothing her skirt across her lap. "Good afternoon, Pak. What's the news?"

"The news is fine, Miss."

The old man had bathed and put on a clean brown-and-black-checked sarong and a beige cotton shirt. There was a furtive look in his eyes.

"Are you comfortable here at the hotel, Miss?" he asked.

"Yes, very comfortable."

"It's nice to have a breeze like this when dusk finally comes, isn't it, Miss?"

"Yes, it is."

He took a step toward her. "I wanted to tell you"—his voice lowered—"that Pak Rachim is the strictest Muslim in Cirebon. Even stricter than a Palembang Arab. He's been that way since he was a young man. He was twenty-four and had gone into business with a monopoly from the government on the import of refrigerators and freezers, and gotten rich quick. Then, all of a sudden, he started reading the Koran every day and going to mosque and praying all night and fasting, and before we knew it he had given away everything to the mosque and moved into the little house on Lemahwungkuk. For nearly thirty years he has lived a simple holy life. Every day he earns more merit in the eyes of Allah than I have in a lifetime."

He paused. This was Janet's cue. "Does that mean, Pak, that you are not such a good Muslim?" she asked.

Grinning, the old man nodded. "Yes, Miss; I'm afraid that's true. But, you know, Pak Rachim has never married—he could never support wives and children, and a man of his standing could hardly allow his wives to support him. He owns no livestock or fowl; he doesn't even own a fraction of a hectare of farmland." He pulled a *kretek* cigarette from the half-squashed pack in his shirt pocket, smoothed it straight, and lit it with a match, cupping his hands around the flame. "I have only one wife, Miss, but I have seven living children and twenty-three grandchildren, and none of them has ever been given a monopoly on the import of anything. I'd like to be as devout as Pak Rachim, but what can I do? Every chance I get I try to earn a few extra rupiah any way I can. On my time off, instead of reading the Koran or praying, I sell *martabak* in front of the main post office; and sometimes, when I don't have money for flour or cooking oil for the martabak, I even collect cigarette butts to sell the leftover tobacco."

Janet looked at Pak Tua. He was about to come to the point.

"You see, Miss Janet, I'm a bad enough Muslim—and a poor enough one—that I'm willing to help you even on the last day of Maulud. I will tell you the story of Plangon Hill."

"Including the part about the monkeys?"

"Oh, yes, especially that."

Thus the old man began his elaborate tale. He told how the Arab brothers and their sister had come to Java across the sea with three ships and an entourage of twelve hundred men, traveling throughout Sundaland before finally settling in Cirebon at the court of Sultan Gunung Jati. As he spoke, he warmed to the legend, embellishing it with details of the making of the ships, of the wealth, weapons, sacred books, and varieties of incense they carried, of each failed attempt to convert the Sundanese people of the Priangan to Islam (that would come later), and of the architecture, regalia, and rituals of Gunung Jati's palace-city. Janet began to feel drowsy as the old man droned on in the dusk. Did he think he would be paid by the word? Her mind drifted in and out of the story. For a while she dwelt on the lush wall of *petai* blossoms lining the street, their deep blood-red almost black now against the salmon-colored sunset. She took in the multitude of smells—simmering coconut milk, frying shrimp chips, smoking charcoal. She heard an insistent tinkling that reminded her of gamelan music: sidewalk food vendors tapping spoons against glasses, producing a distinctive rhythm for each food and drink. Pak Tua's voice grew urgent, as if he sensed that her mind was wandering.

"Though the Sultan disagreed with the brothers on some of the finer points of doctrine, that was not why he banished them and their sister from the palace." He paused for dramatic effect. "It was only because of the sister. You see, Siti Baghdad wasn't just lazy about religion, nor was she merely an infidel. Much, much worse than that: she was apostate. First she removed the veil that had covered her face since early childhood, and danced to the music of Sundanese harp and flute. Then she started drinking *tuak,* eating pork, wandering the lanes that surrounded the palace with a dog cradled in her arms. The Sultan, and no doubt her brothers as well, hoped she would come to her senses and see the error of her ways. But soon people noticed that the deep black eyes of the beautiful young Siti Baghdad had taken on an evil cast, and it was rumored that she had begun to dabble in the black arts. One night, she was caught by the palace guard at an old *dukun*'s home in one of the poor kampongs of the city. She had gone there to ask the dukun to put a curse on another beautiful woman of the palace. The ritual employed the urine of the dukun's pet monkey, which had years before been a rival whom the dukun had turned into a monkey during a sorcery skirmish. Upon hearing what had happened, the Sultan was furious.

"So it was that Syarif Abdulrachman and Syarif Kafid were banished to Panjunan and Kejaksan respectively, and became the lords of those places. Siti Baghdad, however, disappeared and was not heard of again until her death many years later in Indramayu. By that time, both brothers had died and been interred in the tomb on Plangon Hill, which had been Syarif Abdulrachman's favorite resting place in life. The sister's body was brought back to Cirebon and also buried at Plangon, but in a humble, lonely grave on the other side of the hilltop, so as not to defile the holy tomb of her brothers.

"At the time that Siti Baghdad was buried on Plangon Hill, it was still customary for people from the area to visit the hill from time to time to pay their respects to the remains of their old lords. But now they stayed away. Why? They were afraid that the new, unholy grave there might be a doorway into *dunia gaib.* You know *'dunia gaib,'* Miss?"

It was dark now. A nearby streetlamp blinked on and Janet saw that the telephone wires along Siliwangi were dense with swallows.

"No," she said. "What is it?"

"It's the *other world:* the hidden world unseen by men, where range the demons and evil spirits that have opposed the Mahakuasa—The Great Power—since the beginning of time. To open the door to that world, Miss, is to turn one's back on the Mahakuasa."

Janet felt a thrill along her spine. Pak Tua had used, in place of *Allah* or *Tuhan,* the ancient term that the Javanese and Sundanese had used before becoming Hindus and Buddhists and long before ever hearing of Muhammad.

"Well, rumors soon arose about the powers of the hill. One night a local cloth seller was seen going there, and soon afterward he became the most successful cloth seller in all of Cirebon. On another night, it was said, a poor herbalist went to the hill; within a week he was in charge of the Sultan's apothecary. Stories like these multiplied over the years, and before the passing of a single decade it was general knowledge around Cirebon that the unholy grave on Plangon Hill was indeed a door to the other world and that, moreover, the hill's caretaker was a *juru kunci*—a *guardian of the key*—a man who can unlock the door to the other world.

"Here is the way it works, Miss. A person goes to Plangon Hill and is met at the entrance by the caretaker, who takes him to the summit and asks him which way he wants to go—to the nearby holy tomb or off through the jungle to the unholy grave on the far side of the hill. In other words, to the world of the pure and holy or to the *other world.*"

Janet's eyebrows arched. "So that's what he meant when he pointed off into the jungle and then to the holy tomb?"

"Yes, Miss. He asks it of everyone, no matter where they're from or what they look like. It is often said that one can never tell who will turn up seeking his fortune on Plangon Hill. Nobody, of course, knows this better than the caretaker."

"Go on, Pak."

"Well, Miss, if his caller seeks the other world, the caretaker assumes the role of the guardian of the key and leads the supplicant down the winding path through the jungle to the unholy grave. There, overlooking Cirebon, the caretaker builds a fire and prepares to summon a spirit. He uses incense, fresh eggs, a cheroot, and flowers of seven colors that he mixes with the strong-smelling leaves of the *padan* tree and wraps in a banana leaf. With these things and with the secret words that he recites in Old Cirebonese, the caretaker unlocks the door to the other world. It is then that he summons the evil spirit with whom the supplicant makes his pact. For twenty years of wealth and comfort, the supplicant must spend twenty years as a monkey living on Plangon Hill; for thirty years of wealth, thirty as a monkey, and so on. When the pact comes due, the man's body dies and his soul lives on inside the body of a kra at Plangon. Outwardly, he is a monkey—chatters like a monkey, eats like a monkey, scratches like a monkey—but *inside* he has all the thoughts and feelings of the human being he once was. To remind him of his bargain, during each Maulud of his human life he feels his tailbone begin to grow. And if by the end of Maulud he has not returned to the hill to have the caretaker cut it off, he becomes a monkey on the following day, regardless of how many years of wealth he has enjoyed."

Pak Tua lit another kretek and drew deeply on it.

"And that," he said, "is where the monkeys came from. There weren't any on Plangon Hill until twenty years after Siti Baghdad's burial. So they say."

Smoke from Pak Tua's cigarette drifted down Siliwangi, scenting the warm night air with clove. The swallows had quieted in the petai trees and on the telephone wires. A pedicab slowed alongside them, its driver standing as he pedaled, arching his eyebrows at Janet. Across the street came the pushcart of the ice man, his spoon clinking against glass.

Janet smiled. "That's a wonderful story." She held it in her mind like a precious gem. Within minutes it would be preserved in her notebook in words as close to Pak Tua's own as she could render it. "Do you believe it, Pak?"

Pak Tua chuckled. "Well, Miss," he said, "Pak Rachim says none of it is true—that is, the part about the other world and men being turned into monkeys. He says the old Cirebonese beliefs are wrong, that they oppose the teachings of the Prophet and should be left in the past where they belong."

"Do you agree with Pak Rachim?"

He shrugged. "Pak Rachim is the wisest, most learned man in Cirebon. It is not my place to agree or disagree."

"But most Cirebonese of your generation believe, don't they, Pak?"

A smile. "Oh, yes, Miss."

She slid down from the stone wall and drew a ten-thousand-rupiah note from her skirt pocket. It was far too much, but the legend had turned out even better than she could have hoped. And it was her last piece of research. "I enjoyed your storytelling, Pak," she said, handing him the money.

The old man stared at the note in his hand for a long moment. He looked up eagerly. "Maybe Miss would like to go to Plangon Hill tonight? It's the last night of Maulud; perhaps some rich man has put off having his tail cut until the last minute."

"But he wouldn't let me watch, would he?"

"No matter, Miss. We can hide in the jungle; it grows close around the unholy grave—at least it used to when I was a boy. You would see every detail of the ceremony; it would be just what you need for your book. And you could give me money to take to the caretaker beforehand so we wouldn't be 'discovered.' "

Janet was tired and had already scheduled an early departure the next morning for Jakarta. She had been savoring the idea of relaxing at the hotel that evening, perhaps even celebrating the successful conclusion of her work with a bottle of champagne. But how could she turn down such an opportunity? An eyewitness account of the Plangon tail-cutting ceremony, which had probably never been seen by a foreigner, would lend her book a rare mystique indeed.

"Pak isn't afraid to go to Plangon at night during Maulud?" she asked.

Pak Tua pawed the dust with a sandaled foot. "A little. But for you, Miss, I'll do it."

"How much for the caretaker?"

He glanced at the sky. "Ten thousand, Miss."

She smiled, wondering how much of that the caretaker would actually get. "And how do we get there?" Ujang, her driver, was still on the road from Surabaya; she was certain, though, that Pak Tua already had someone in mind for the job.

"My friend Marto owns a truck, Miss," he said. "He'll take us there and back for ten thousand. But first he must take me there right away to pay the caretaker: that's another five thousand."

"All right, Pak." She had no energy left for haggling. "Anything else?"

"Possibly, Miss. Marto has a flashlight, but it might need new batteries. Two thousand, maybe."

She gave him ten thousand for the caretaker, two thousand for batteries, and five more for gas, saying she would pay Marto the rest of his share when he had gotten her back to the hotel. Pak Tua would call for her at nine. She realized she had set a bad precedent by giving him so much for the legend, but there wasn't a damn thing she could do about it now except submit to a gouging. It was just past six when they parted, Pak Tua to his pedicab, she to her room to fetch her notebook.

Pak Marto's truck was an old Datsun pickup that had seen better days. It rattled and lurched over the potholes on the road out of Cirebon, its weak headlights aided by a bright moon. Marto, a thin, wiry man, had put on a clean T-shirt for the occasion. He was a Sundanese from Bandung, who had lived in the Cirebon area for some years. He conversed with Pak Tua in Cirebonese as Janet, wedged between them on the seat, gazed out into the darkness.

On this last night of Maulud, the village of Kejaksan was

dense with celebrants thronging the lanes and paths. Men
and boys, women and girls, strolled arm in arm in twos and
threes, making the rounds of friends' and relatives' homes
where the day's fast was being broken. The festivities would
continue into the early morning hours. Kerosene lanterns
burning low in sitting rooms flickered past the truck. Janet's
eyes were drawn to the yellow glow of dozens of lanterns
illuminating a makeshift stage of bamboo poles and sawn
planks where a puppet show was in progress. The tinkle of
the gamelan was like rainfall as they passed.

Pak Tua had decided to approach Plangon the long way
around from Kejaksan so they would not be seen in Panjunan, so close to the hill. At last Marto pulled off the road
a good hundred yards from the Plangon entrance. Swirls of
gnats and mosquitoes filled the headlight beams as the engine growled and sputtered. "Kill it," Pak Tua told Marto
and reached for the flashlight. The engine gave a final
wheeze; the headlights blinked off. They sat for a moment
in the moonlit darkness, hearing the chorusing of frogs from
the ditch across the road. Pak Tua got out and helped Janet
down from the cab. He held on to her arm and trained the
flashlight on the ground in front of her as they moved down
the middle of the road. She was aware of the hill, a shade
darker than the night sky, rising on her right, its outline
softened by the contours of the jungle. Pak Tua swept the
flashlight beam over the sign when they reached the Plangon path. The caretaker's house, which had seemed so hidden earlier in the daylight, was like a beacon now with its
dim lantern. Pak Tua waved the flashlight back and forth.
They waited.

"He must be at the top with someone," Pak Tua said
finally. "Tonight he'd be watching the entrance closely for
visitors; he would have come to greet us by now. Let's go."

The jungle canopy overhead turned the path into a black

tunnel. Janet tried to keep her eyes on the flashlight trail but couldn't help glancing at the forest, where moonlight seeped in through gaps in the canopy. Weird even in daylight, the strangling figs seemed to tighten pythonlike around their victims; aerial roots that had made her think of beards earlier were now quivering tentacles, and lianas slithered through the canopy like hunting snakes. From time to time Janet touched Pak Tua's arm for reassurance and reminded herself that the legend of Plangon Hill was not literally true. Still, when the old man switched off the flashlight as they neared the top, she had a fleeting vision of monkeys creeping silently toward her through the jungle. She remembered the bushy-cheeked female perched on the boulder, staring at her as if she were an interloper. But surely the monkeys were all asleep now, safely huddled against one another or wedged into the crooks of branches.

They reached level ground. Pak Tua again switched on the flashlight and ran the beam across the clearing and up the little rise to the mausoleum. His lips moved. "Allah," he whispered. "Allah." The "bad" Muslim hedging his bets, thought Janet. He leaned toward her and said softly, "Good. He must be at the unholy grave. Stay behind me, but hold on to my hand."

The path that curled around the hilltop was a mere foot wide and crisscrossed with rattan vines. Janet caught an ear on one of the vines and needed help detaching herself from its fishhook barbs. When she saw Pak Tua's hand tremble as he held the flashlight up to her wound, she realized how frightened the old man was. He tightened his grip on her wrist as they picked their way along the trail. Soon an orange glow flickered through the jungle ahead. Pak Tua switched off the flashlight and stopped.

"What's wrong, Pak?"

"Nothing, Miss, nothing. I . . . I haven't been up here since I was a child. And never, *ever* at night, Miss." He glanced around at the jungle, then back at the beckoning glow. "He's made a fire, Miss; he's unlocked the door to the other world. You will see the tail-cutting; yes, you will surely see it now."

They reached the edge of the clearing. To their right, the vegetation thinned until it broke off where the land fell away into a wide ravine. To their left, at the jungle's border, a fire crackled and popped, casting its light over a large banyan tree, at the foot of which lay an odd, lopsided mound of stones. Janet realized that this ignoble structure was the grave. It looked as though it might once have been level, but the thrusting roots of the banyan tree had changed that long ago. Though two men squatted before the fire, it was the grave that first drew Janet's attention, for sitting atop it, his pelt the color of river mud in the firelight, was a large male kra. He was still, as though waiting for something to happen. Then she saw the rest of the monkeys. Sitting on the ground in the clearing and perched on branches at the jungle's edge, they formed a loose circle around the two men and the fire.

The old caretaker, a sheathed parang tied at his waist, was silhouetted against the firelight with his back to Janet. The other man, on the caretaker's right, wore a hooded cloak that gave him the appearance of a pilgrim. Janet saw that the caretaker had set out a series of props for his sorcery, and she realized that the monkeys were waiting for him to leave so they could rifle the props. Their patience gave them a startling look of reverence, as though they were participating in the ceremony, perhaps communing with their future comrade. This impression was heightened by the behavior of the supplicant, who kept glancing nervously at the furry creatures all around him. He looked in Janet's direction, the firelight full on his face, but turned back to the fire without having seen her.

Just then Pak Tua gasped. He rose and stood staring, mouth open in shock. It hit Janet even before she turned back to the clearing: the supplicant was Rachim.

When she looked again, Rachim was on hands and knees in front of the fire with his forehead pressed to the ground. The caretaker stood, parang drawn. He raised it above his head, the tip pointing skyward, and began to chant in a guttural voice that sounded barely human. Immediately the monkeys answered. When Rachim heard this, his whole body started to tremble. The caretaker brought his parang down until the flat of the blade rested against Rachim's upthrust buttocks.

Suddenly something moved just above Janet's head. She whirled instinctively and found herself peering into the wide eyes of a monkey—a yearling no bigger than a kitten—clinging to the upper bole of a sapling. With a screech of fear the monkey clambered up into the jungle canopy; instantly, barks of alarm rang out all around the clearing. The caretaker shouted, "Who's there?" and strode toward their hiding place, his right hand clutching the handle of his parang, his splayed foot flapping awkwardly. Pak Tua hissed, *"Aduh!"* and drew his own parang. *He kept all the bribe money,* Janet thought in a panic.

The caretaker was almost upon them when a commotion at the fire made him stop and turn. Rachim was on his feet, cowering as he stumbled backward toward the ravine. "No!" he cried. "Don't leave me, Pak! The monkeys!" The big male had climbed down from the mound and was strolling inquisitively toward Rachim. The other monkeys followed, beckoning with soft calls. In the firelight, Janet could see Rachim's face clearly as he stared down in horror at the approaching animals. All of a sudden the big male ambled up to Rachim and grabbed a handful of his cloak. Screaming, Rachim teetered at the edge of the ravine. The caretaker let out a bellow and ran toward him, brandishing his parang and barking orders at the monkeys, who scattered with a volley of alarm calls. But Rachim could not regain his balance; with a shriek, he vanished into the ravine.

The jungle was quiet again. The caretaker stood at the edge of the bluff, peering down into the darkness where Rachim had fallen. He disappeared down the slope. Sheathing his parang, Pak Tua kicked off his sandals and followed.

It was some time before Janet could summon the nerve to move. Heart pounding, she walked to the edge of the bluff and looked over. Far below—much farther than she had imagined—she saw figures huddled around the pinpoint of light from Pak Tua's flashlight. What a fall! Could Rachim have survived it? She heard faint voices down in the ravine. They might be discussing a rescue strategy— perhaps he was alive. Then it occurred to her: was she herself in danger? She had uncovered what was apparently the best-kept secret in Cirebon—there would be a scandal, and she did not trust the caretaker. Pak Tua was no murderer, though. She decided to stand her ground if the old servant reappeared with the caretaker; if the latter came up alone, she would run. Finally, the talking stopped. She stepped back into the clearing to wait, suddenly aware she was shivering in spite of the heat.

The two men crested the bluff and came toward her, breathing hard from the steep climb. A smile of recognition flickered across the caretaker's face when he saw her. Pak Tua's face was gaunt as he spoke.

"He's dead, Miss. Split his head open on a rock."

When traffic slowed to a standstill just before they reached Kandanghaur the next morning, Ujang lowered his window to question a boy walking past from up the road. He raised it again and turned toward Janet in the back seat.

"Accident, Miss. A bus and two cars. Maybe an hour."

She nodded and slid farther down the cushions, letting her head loll against the back of the seat. She was horribly tired. An hour's wait would be all right: the air conditioning was working—Ujang knew to leave the car running so long as there was enough gas to get them to the next Pertamina station—and she could catch up on some of the sleep she had missed last night. For that matter, Ujang could catch up on *his* sleep. The poor man had reached Cirebon from Surabaya at four in the morning and slept in the car until six.

Ujang had been Janet's regular driver for intercity trips ever since she had arrived in Java. Over the long months of travel, he had become her friend and confidant, entertaining her with stories, teaching her Indonesian, explaining the sights, listening to her problems and frustrations. With a wife and four children in Bogor, he needed more work than she could give him; nevertheless, she paid him well for his time, and though he seemed to find enough work between trips, he always showed up again on schedule. She was especially thankful that he had made it to Cirebon on time, for she sorely needed his company now.

It was Plangon Hill that was bothering her. She wasn't surprised at being upset; the problem was that something about her own role was troubling her, something she couldn't put a finger on. It wasn't that Rachim's death had shocked her, though it had, and it wasn't that she felt guilty about his death, because she didn't. True, it wouldn't have happened had she not gone poking around up there at night. But it wasn't she who had tried to hoodwink the caretaker, nor was she the source of Rachim's fatal fear of monkeys. Yet, she felt restless. Although restlessness had plagued her all her life, this was somehow different. Maybe talking with Ujang would help. She had just been telling him what had happened at Plangon, but was now suddenly too sleepy to continue.

*The braying of car horns that had been pressing in on her gradually drifted far away. She found herself lying in bed in her room at the Grand. She could still hear traffic noise in the distance; it was annoying her, keeping her from getting to sleep. She could hardly afford to lose sleep tonight, when tomorrow would be such a full day: in the morning a jetliner was coming to pick her up at the hotel and take her back to London; then, in the afternoon, she had to begin writing a guidebook about Java.*

*She let her head fall sideways on the pillow and a large rectangle of light floated into view. Of course: she'd left the bathroom door open and the honking was coming in with waves of mosquitoes through the transom window that would not close. She got out of bed and shut the bathroom door. No, she was wrong: there wasn't any honking after all, only Muzak from the speaker on the wall outside her door. She had forgotten to call the front desk before going to bed. They always let it play at night until she called to tell them she wanted to go to sleep.*

*For some odd reason, Pak Tua answered the phone this time.*

*"Good evening, Miss," he said. "How may I be of help?"*

*She asked him to turn off the Muzak.*

*He said, "Of course. But you'd better not go to sleep yet, Miss—you have a visitor."*

*"Oh, no, absolutely not. I'm going to sleep."*

*"Sorry, Miss, he's already on his way. He says he has something very important to ask you."*

*She stood naked next to the bed, hearing the drone of the air conditioner in the sitting room. She tried to remember where her robe was but couldn't. Her guest would be there in a matter of seconds. This Indonesian custom of arriving unannounced was simply perverse! The face-saving humility of it—the implication by the guest that his visit was unworthy of the host's preparation—would not do her much good now.*

*There was a soft tapping at the door. She went into the sitting room and switched on the overhead light. She regarded the familiar things: the rough gash where the air conditioner had penetrated the old Dutch masonry, the ugly brown paneling, the incongruous Dutch masters print of peasants and cottages on a lakeshore. Then everything was a blur: her eyes had filled with tears. They spilled down her cheeks, dripping onto her bare shoulders and breasts.*

*It was the same everywhere she stayed in Java: after only a week, this room, this hotel, was home. Home happened quickly here because one needed it so badly. Outside was a world that suddenly seemed more alien than when she had arrived five months earlier with her suitcase and a phrase book. Tonight she had seen a man die—a man she knew—and she knew why he had died, and it was not the kind of reason people died where she came from. Racing to catch up with the past, Rachim had gotten himself caught somewhere between the ancient and the old and had been left behind to twist in torment, untouched and untouchable by the present. She understood, and she didn't. Time was so different here—so much longer, so much deeper. It filled her with wonder and, at the same time, with an unaccountable longing. And these and the room and Cirebon and all of Java were making her cry now, on the night before the jetliner was to come for her.*

*The tapping came again. When she opened the door, she found herself looking across the courtyard full of frangipani and fan palms to the servants' quarters. Waiters and room boys lounged on the verandahs, their cigarettes weaving firefly patterns in the darkness. She could hear grumbling about the Muzak having been turned off, but not one of them commented on the white lady standing naked in her doorway.*

*Suddenly she felt a light touch on her shin. Sitting on the welcome mat and looking up at her with hazel eyes was a large gray-brown monkey. She knew instantly it was Rachim.*

*"Good evening," said the monkey.*

*"Good evening," Janet replied. "Please come in and sit down."*

*Arching his tail regally, the monkey strolled into the room and hopped up onto the desk. Janet shut the door and turned to face her visitor. The hazel eyes fixed on hers, held them.*

*"I have something very important to ask you," the monkey said in flawless English.*

*"What is it?"*

*The monkey selected an orange from the bowl on the desk and began peeling it with his teeth.*

*"Are you ready to go home?" he asked.*

*She was about to answer, "Yes, of course," then remembered this was supposed to be an* important *question, not chitchat. She felt herself drifting off again; the monkey was looking at her now from across a great distance. She wanted to stay and talk with him, but the room was narrowing into a long tunnel and he was getting farther and farther away. . . .*

Just then there was a roar. Janet opened her eyes to see a large truck grinding past.

"Where are we?" she asked Ujang, sitting up.

"Coming into Bekasi, Miss."

"So we're almost there." She rubbed her eyes with the heels of her palms.

"Yes, Miss. You slept more than three hours."

She looked down and ran her hands over her lap, grateful that her flowery dress hid creases. Squinting into the glare, she lifted her sunglasses to massage the bridge of her nose. Her stomach was queasy from the dream.

So it was almost over. She would overnight with an acquaintance in Cengkareng, so close to the airport that it would feel as if she were already on her way home. But it wasn't ending the way she had thought it would. She had pictured a final week in Cirebon as rounding out the trip, bringing a sense of closure to her book and to her whole experience of Java. And when, finally, she had happened upon Plangon Hill, that hope's fulfillment had seemed imminent. Plangon was the perfect place to complete her catalog of exotica. She had wanted to stick a pin through it and fix it there, like an exotic moth, on the map of her experience.

She saw what was happening. Five months ago she had come to Java relishing the sense of freedom it gave her to know that in a fixed period of time she would be gone and done with the place, and for five months she had maintained a comfortable, conversational distance from Java. Now Plangon Hill had seduced her. On the eve of her departure, she had finally become intimate with Java. Her restlessness was different from the usual desire to get away: this time, she wanted to get closer.

*No,* she thought, *absolutely not.* She would have to put it out of her mind. *No more love affairs that did not fit into her plans.*

"Miss?" Ujang said. "You didn't finish telling me about Pak Rachim."

"Oh. Where did I stop?"

"When they told you he was dead."

She looked out of the window distractedly. "Well, Pak Tua and I left right after that," she said. "The caretaker was to go back down and cover the body with something, then send someone from his household to the police. On the way back to the hotel, Pak Tua told me what the caretaker had said down in the ravine. When Pak Rachim was a brash twenty-two and fed up with the poverty of the sultanate, he went to Plangon one night and made a thirty-year pact with a spirit from the other world. Not long afterward, a distant relation who had risen rapidly in the Ministry of Trade offered him a major import monopoly for a percentage of the take, and he was suddenly wealthy. But at age twenty-four he truly received Islam and realized what a horrible sacrilege he'd committed two years earlier. He donated all his wealth to the mosque and from then on lived the holiest life in Cirebon, hoping Allah would forgive him his great sin. Because he fancied himself a devout Muslim, he knew he was forbidden to believe in the power of the unholy grave or the existence of the other world. He kept trying to convince himself that his getting rich after making the pact was just a coincidence. But twenty-nine years later, with only one year of the pact left, he was still returning to Plangon Hill at Maulud to have his tail cut."

Ujang shook his head. "So Allah never forgave him."

"According to Pak Tua, Allah made him pay with continual anguish for twenty-nine years, but finally forgave him and intervened to release him from the pact. His death proved it."

"How?" Ujang's tone was skeptical.

"The pact was for thirty years, not twenty-nine. Pak Rachim didn't violate the pact: there was still an hour of Maulud left last night when he died. So the pact had to have been nullified; otherwise, Pak Rachim wouldn't have been allowed to die. And only Allah can nullify a pact between man and the other world. Right?"

Ujang nodded, tentatively at first, then more firmly. "So they say," he said. "Yes, all right. It makes sense."

The outskirts of Jakarta began to glide past. Hawkers of

soft drinks, cigarettes, and newspapers waded into the street against the tide of slowing traffic.

Ujang said, "That will make a wonderful story for your book, Miss."

"I don't know," Janet said. "I don't think I could do it justice in a guidebook."

"Save it for another book, then, Miss. But you'll put Plangon Hill in it, of course."

Janet sighed. "Of course. Though it seems a shame to send a bunch of tourists there to disturb the old ways."

Ujang shook his head. "Oh, no, Miss; you mustn't feel that way. Tourists won't disturb anything. Why, Pak Tua and the caretaker could run Plangon tours with hired men to fake the tail-cutting ceremony on weeknights. On weekends, the real supplicants could come." He laughed. "Nobody would disturb the old ways!"

Janet laughed too. Sometimes it seemed that Java's every moment contained all of historical time. She would miss it.

Ujang said, "My uncle Yulfian especially would love to hear that story. The one who has the middle school in Bogor—you know, Miss?"

"Oh, yes. Yulfian."

"You still haven't met him, have you?"

"Not yet. Maybe next time."

"Oh, but you must tell him about Plangon, Miss. He's like Pak Tua and the caretaker: he believes in both the old gods and the new. But he's much younger than they and very modern—you would like him. His wife died last year of leukemia and his kids are both away at university in Bandung, so he really enjoys company. We could go there now, Miss."

"Oh, no, Ujang," she said. "I've got to get to Cengkareng."

"But your flight isn't until tomorrow afternoon, and his school is only an hour from here. I could have you back by dinnertime. And if you wanted to stay over, I could bring you back tomorrow morning. You could talk with Uncle about teaching English at the school: the salary would be low, but it would be very little work."

"But I'm leaving the country tomorrow."

Ujang chuckled at the note of irritation in her voice. "Of course, Miss; I meant the next time you come to Indonesia. When will that be?"

"I'm not sure," said Janet. "Most likely, my publisher will send me somewhere else to start all over again, and then somewhere else, and so on. Not for a long time, I suppose."

Ujang waved away a boy selling slices of jackfruit in plastic packages. "Teaching English would be easy, Miss," he went on. "You could write lots of books at the same time." He paused. "When you come back, I mean."

Janet smiled. Ujang, the matchmaker. This was likely the best part-time job he had ever had. Not that she doubted that he truly cared about his uncle. She pictured the broad tree-lined streets of Bogor at the end of the smooth ride on the toll road into the mountains. It rained there every day at three, like clockwork. It would be nice to stay for the afternoon downpour: from Yulfian's verandah she could watch the steam rising as the sun came out again.

Ujang was coasting in traffic, drifting across lanes.

"Well, Miss? The turnoff is right here; you could sleep another hour."

So many times in the past five months she might have chosen flogging over an extra hour in the car. Now she marveled at how little resistance she felt to the idea.

"All right," she said after a moment. "Bogor."

She settled back against the seat as Ujang, waving off

traffic with rapid gestures of his right hand, angled across one more lane and completed his turn. She closed her eyes and let her arms go limp. Her palms rested on the warm Naugahyde to either side of her.

Another hour's sleep. Somehow, Ujang always seemed to know just what she needed.

# STANDBY TIDUR

We got to the site of the Hash Run at about four in the afternoon. Thirty or forty expats and a few middle-management Indonesians were already there in their running shorts and tank tops, waiting for the weekly race to start. They stood around the beer truck, chatting and joking, while their kids chased each other off the dirt road into the *alang-alang* grass. An amah who was minding one of the kids didn't know what to do. Clutching her sarong with one hand, she darted into the fray and grabbed at her charge with the other. *"Jangan!"* she cried—*Don't!* —as the drivers, grouped in a cloud of cigarette smoke near the cars, laughed at her.

These races were organized by Union Oil. Like Huffco Oil and the French company, Total, Union had its own private compound for employees in Balikpapan. The compound, overlooking the city from a hilltop called Pasir Ridge, was a little patch of Southern California in East Borneo, with modern homes and apartments, a recreation center, and a school. The day before a Hash Run, a couple of expats would venture out of the compound to find a likely spot at the jungle's edge on the outskirts of town where they would mark a main route and a lot of dead-end branch routes to confuse the runners. Everybody would collect there after work the next day for the run. It was a diverse group: executives, technicians, geologists, teachers, housewives—mostly Americans, many of whom were Texans, but also a few Brits and Aussies, and, of course, the French from Total.

When I visited the Ridge, I usually stayed with the Bakers, Americans who taught at the school. I would come down every four or five months from Sangatta, where I worked as a technician for Schlumberger, a company that made and operated oil exploration equipment. Sangatta was a kampong—a small village—with a big Pertamina Oil installation extending from its outskirts into the surrounding jungle. The only other expat up there was the Aussie technician I lived with. We had an air-conditioned trailer with a cold-water shower and a Javanese babu from the kampong who did the cooking and cleaning. The Balikpapan expats would always ask me how things were going "up in the jungle." They thought of Singapore as civilization and Balikpapan as the boondocks; Sangatta was "the jungle." To me Sangatta was the boondocks and Balikpapan was civilization. On Pasir Ridge I could bowl and play pool at the rec center, even watch first-run American movies three nights a week. Once a month there was a theme party. (On this particular night it was the annual Octoberfest.) I went to cocktail parties and heard all the expat gossip and came out to these Hash Runs—to socialize, not run. What I most looked forward to on the Ridge, though, were the hot showers. I never felt really clean from the cold ones up in Sangatta, though they were certainly better than sluicing yourself with cold water from a big square tub the Indonesians call a *bak mandi.*

For this week's run, we were next to a kampong that had popped up on a recent clearcut. A good distance up the road was the jungle, colored a pasty gray-brown by the exposed tree trunks, with a wavy ribbon of dark green along the top where the tree crowns were. Ron Baker, who was in charge of the run, had driven me directly there from the airport. All day I'd been thinking of a hot shower, but I was going to have to wait until after Hash.

A few minutes before the race was scheduled to start, Tim Lundgren's car came up the road from town. As the kampong people lining the road turned in sequence to watch it go by, I felt a corresponding wave of tension run through the expats around me, as though there were some kind of scandal afoot. This was puzzling. Tim Lundgren was not the kind of guy to cause a stir. He was a shy, withdrawn young bachelor, who was rumored to spend most of his time in the paleontology lab.

When Tim's car pulled to a stop, his driver got out and opened the door for him—something Tim ordinarily did for himself. Tim got out unsteadily. Blinking, he held on to the car door as he scanned the crowd. I'd been to several parties with him and had never seen him drink more than one beer, but I could see now that he was dead drunk. After a while, he climbed back into the car. The driver must have been worried about him, because instead of joining the other drivers, he got back in the car and lit up a *kretek.* I noticed then that the driver was Linder, whom I knew far better than the others. Before driving Tim, Linder had driven for the Redfields, who loaned him to me for a couple of trips up to Samarinda. He was a peaceful, soft-spoken guy, and I was happy for him that he had been reassigned to Tim, who had a reputation for being courteous and considerate to Indonesians. Unfortunately, at that moment Tim was embarrassing him.

Ron Baker brought his whistle to his lips and blew two blasts. Fifty or sixty bodies of all shapes and sizes went jogging up the dirt road toward the jungle, some of the kids racing ahead, their parents yelling at them to wait up. The two Indonesian wives who "ran" actually walked arm in arm, chatting and laughing as though out for an ordinary afternoon stroll, daintily sidestepping the muddy spots in the road. They were notorious for refusing to follow trails into the jungle. Instead they would rest for a spell at the end of the road before walking back.

"What's with Tim?" I asked Ron. We had settled into lawn chairs in the back of the beer truck. He handed me a bottle of Bintang, raised his hand in a "wait a second" gesture, and looked across the road. Tim Lundgren was climbing out of his car again, this time before Linder could get the door for him. He weaved toward us, holding up his Hash ticket. He looked awful. His face was covered with a careless stubble and his blond hair was long and curlicued in back. I was surprised to see he had his running suit on. With a forced smile, he leaned against the tailgate of the truck and asked me how things were going "up in the jungle". His speech was slurred. Ron invited him to sit out the run with us in the cool of the beer truck, but he declined.

"Colonel Noto show up today?" he asked.

Ron said, "Haven't seen him."

Tim stared with hooded eyes. He tossed his head and said, "No big deal, catch him later."

He trotted off toward the jungle with heavy steps. He was a sight: a pear-shaped body bouncing along with fleshy limbs pumping and a bald spot gleaming in the sunlight. The kampong people stared after him as if he were some rare creature that had wandered out of the jungle.

"You think he ought to be running?" I asked Ron.

He shrugged. "What am I supposed to do—tell him he's too smashed to run?"

I asked him again what it was all about. He looked out to where the sun was beginning to gild the crowns of the coconut palms in the kampong. "Trouble in paradise," he laughed. "Actually, it's not funny. This Indonesian colonel is fooling around with Tim's wife."

"Tim got *married*?"

"Three months ago. Teenaged kampong girl who used to hang out at the Benakutai. Contract marriage."

I was stunned. Tim Lundgren was the last guy on the Ridge I'd have expected to take a contract wife. That kind of thing was common for the Texans who left their wives and kids in the States. But shy, straitlaced Tim Lundgren? I just couldn't picture him with one of those girls in spike heels and miniskirts who were always hanging around the bar at the Hotel Benakutai, swizzling margaritas bought by leering oil men. It was also hard to see him paying some poor kampong family a lot of money for their blessing on a temporary arrangement with a teenaged floozy they'd already written off as unmarriageable. That was how it worked. Once a girl started hanging around the Benakutai, she was considered lost. Contract marriage was usually just a way station on the road to prostitution.

According to Ron, Linder had suggested a contract marriage to Tim and found the girl for him. Her name was Ayu. She was Balinese, eighteen, and exceptionally good-looking. I tried to visualize Tim and his mocha-skinned, non-

English-speaking "bride" sipping cocktails in a Pasir Ridge living room with all the teachers and research scientists: I saw downcast eyes, frozen smiles, much throat clearing. Not because she was Indonesian—the teachers and scientists were less bigoted that way than others on the Ridge—but because she was a contract wife. The Texans wouldn't have batted an eye at that, but Tim's crowd considered it unconscionably sleazy. To further complicate matters, Ron said, Tim was being taken for a ride by this young lady. Despite her tender years and kampong background, Ayu had managed to reverse the usual direction of exploitation in contract marriages. She was ignoring Tim even as she spent a hefty portion of his paycheck on clothes, jewelry, cosmetics, and the salon. Apparently, she had big plans and Tim was just a stepping-stone. A few weeks ago she'd stepped to a much bigger stone.

"Have I met this Noto?" I asked Ron.

"Do you remember the army officer who said hello to me at the airport?"

I did. He must have been near sixty but, apart from the wavy silver hair, looked forty-five. And a real dandy he was, strutting around in his immaculate uniform. I recalled the young lady on his arm and realized with a sinking feeling that she was the beautiful Ayu. Actually, *beautiful* was hardly the word for her. She was breathtaking: about five-four with a waist you could wrap your hands around and satiny coffee-and-cream skin and a classic Balinese face that could make you cry. She was wearing a sheer black calf-length skirt with fishnet stockings and open-toed heels and a red brocaded jacket. With her raven hair pulled tightly back under a false bun, she was a combination of modern and traditional. You could picture her dancing the Ramayana ballet on delicate bare feet to rapt audiences at eight, then showing up in high heels at the Benakutai at eleven to turn the oil men into drooling jackasses. I realized just how hopelessly in over his head Tim was.

"Pertamina sends Noto here two months ago to run the commissary," Ron continued, "and I'm thinking, What's a guy like this doing in charge of asparagus—in fact, what's he doing in Balikpapan period? Then I hear he's one of the big shots from the BULOG scandal."

I said, "Fill me in; I'm from the jungle, remember."

"They were taking Bank of Indonesia credit they'd gotten at three percent and putting it into private banks at ten to fifteen percent, with the idea of withdrawing the money at the last minute to make whatever purchases it had been earmarked for and pocketing the interest. But three of the banks collapsed before they could get the money out, exposing the whole thing. The government made an example of a couple of them; the rest were sent away to places like this to lie low for a while. In six months the whole thing'll blow over and Noto will be outta here. In the meantime, he's living like an old-style Javanese king in a mansion that belongs to the Governor. And the only asparagus he ever lays eyes on are the choice stalks that somehow find their way from the commissary storeroom into his own kitchen before any of us can get a crack at them. Last week an accountant from the Jakarta office discovered that six thousand frozen chickens are missing since Noto took charge. But what can anybody do? The man's too big. On top of it all, he's made it his pet project to monitor the Indonesianization program here and report to Jakarta. He's interviewed all of us. Claims we're moving too slow, says middle management ought to be fifty-fifty expat-Indonesian already. Even told Tim he should hire an Indonesian assistant for the paleo lab."

"What did Tim say?"

"That he didn't think there were any Indonesian paleon-tologists."

I laughed. "But Noto paid him back."

"Swept the lady right off her feet. Only a matter of time before she skips out on Tim. All this via the drivers' grape-vine, of course; Tim won't talk about it. Which suits me fine, because then I don't feel obligated to tell him things like I just saw his wife at the airport with Noto."

"Where were they headed?"

"Probably Singapore for clothes shopping. He's got a private plane."

The kampong people began talking rapidly and rubber-necking at something up the road. Little kids on their fathers' shoulders pointed and laughed. Ron stuck his head out of the truck and glanced at his watch.

"Here comes Jacques," he said. "Right on schedule."

I hopped down from the truck and stood watching the tiny red, white, and blue dot bobbing against the jungle in the distance (Jacques's running suit was fashioned after the French flag). Behind me someone yelled, "Tuan! Tuan Mike!" I turned around. Linder had spotted me but didn't dare cross the invisible barrier that excluded drivers from the area around the beer truck. When I reached him, he smiled a big gold-toothed smile and grasped my hand. He was more comfortable with me than with the Ridge expats. As an outsider I could be confided in, and I worked every day with Indonesians and spoke the language fluently.

When I asked him how he was, his smile lost its luster. He took my arm and steered me over to a roadside spot clear of alang-alang grass. He was thin and wiry, an old Buginese sea hand from Sulawesi, who had gone to sea as a youngster despite having been raised in the interior. His parents had been servants for a Dutch official and were enamored of everything Dutch: hence the name Linder. His skin was dark and leathery from years of exposure hauling timber from Borneo to Jakarta, and his hands were as coarse as the rigging of the Buginese schooners he had crewed on. When he wasn't smiling, his Fu Manchu mustache made him look sinister, befitting a descendant of the famed pirates of the Indonesian archipelago. He was wearing gray slacks and a robin's-egg-blue shirt open at the collar, revealing a glossy scar that ran from the base of his neck toward his left nipple. His forearms bore other scars he'd gotten in knife fights back home across the Makassar Strait and up the Borneo coast in Samarinda and Tarakan. The big one on his chest was special to him, a mark of loyalty to a former boss. An ethnic Chinese businessman had hired him as a night watch-man when he was down and out in Samarinda, and one night he chased and stabbed to death a burglar and got slashed in the struggle. I believed he had killed other men, too, though the burglar was the only one he'd told me about, and then only because a couple of beers made him wax sentimental about his undying loyalty to his old boss. I'd heard Buginese were like that: if you treated them right, they'd kill for you, no questions asked. I also knew that, unlike the Javanese, they didn't mind if you were direct with them. So, right off, I asked him what was wrong.

He said, "Have you heard about Tuan Tim's wife and Pak Noto?"

I told him I had. He was squinting into the sun, and then he moved into my shadow and lit a kretek.

"It's bad, very bad," he said. "Very hard on Tuan. He's crazy in love with her. Every day, when I go back to the house from taking him to the office, she gives me the day off or sends me on some long errand, then sends the babu to the bazaar. Today I told Tuan about this and he ordered me to watch the house if she sent me away. If she went out

I was to follow her and report to him about where she went and with whom. I was frightened: what if Pak Noto found out I was spying on him? He's a Javanese colonel; I'm just a Buginese driver."

He smoked quietly for a time. I looked back toward the truck and saw that Jacques was back, walking in circles with a towel around his neck and a beer in his hand. More runners were visible up the road and the kampong people were talking and pointing again.

I said, "So, did Linder do it?"

"Yes. Had to—Tuan Tim has been good to me. I parked around the corner and watched. But after a while I fell asleep. When I woke up, two hours had passed. I didn't know if Bu Ayu was still in the house or not. Nori the babu came by on her way back from the bazaar, and I asked her to come back out and tell me if Bu Ayu was there. She wasn't. I rushed to Tuan Tim's lab and told him. He was drunk. He said some bad things in English; he was very angry. He asked me why I hadn't followed Bu Ayu. I was ashamed, so I said, 'Standby *tidur.*' That only made him angrier and he stopped talking. He brought a bottle of whiskey with him in the car."

"Standby *tidur*" is a Balikpapan drivers' expression for napping while waiting for the next assignment, a practice that employers don't mind because drivers often have to wait around for hours with nothing to do. It was *not* an accurate description of what Linder had done, however. He'd said it to save face, which must have been infuriating to Tim under the circumstances. But the very fact that he had used the term inappropriately was both an admission of guilt and an expression of regret, and I hoped Tim would leave it at that.

I told Linder what I'd seen at the airport, so he wouldn't have to worry about a confrontation between Tim and

Noto for a few days. He received the news with downcast eyes. A pained look crossed his face.

"It's gone too far," he said. "Now I must do something I don't want to."

My stomach turned over. I pictured Noto's crumpled body lying on one of the mansion's priceless carpets, his silver hair flecked with red and his uniform stained crimson. For a moment I was speechless.

I leaned over and whispered, "Linder—whatever you do, don't kill him."

He gave me a puzzled look. "Kill who, Tuan?"

"What did you mean about doing something you don't want to?"

"Ask Tuan Mike for money."

I gasped in relief. We exchanged reassuring pats and embarrassed laughter. I forced myself to look stern and asked, "What do you need it for?"

Linder looked away. "The kampong headman and the head of Civil Records haven't been paid yet for Tuan Tim's marriage."

"Why not?"

"I used their share to pay the *dukun.*"

I winced.

"Not for me, Tuan," he said quickly. "For Tuan Tim. To make him fall in love with Ayu. Tuan, I may not have been to Mecca yet, but I am Muslim enough to know that these contract marriages are not right. This is the first one I have ever arranged. I did it because I like Tuan Tim and know how lonely he is; many times I've seen the way he looks at women—as if they are all across a wide river and he without a prahu. I told myself, If I do this thing, I must make certain that it will grow into a true marriage. So I paid a very good dukun to make Tuan Tim fall in love with Ayu. I took things that belonged to Tuan and brought them to the dukun so he could cast his spell. I had no money for a spell on Ayu, but I didn't think it would be necessary—all these young kampong girls fall in love with their contract husbands, you know, unless they're very shrewd. And who expects kampong Balinese to be shrewd?" He shook his head in disgust. "What has happened to Tuan Tim is my fault."

"It's not Linder's fault," I said firmly. "Tuan Tim would have fallen in love with the girl anyway."

He shook his head. "Thank you, Tuan; you are very kind. But I know I am to blame. That's why I might ask Tuan for additional money to pay the dukun to reverse the spell. Unless Tuan would be angry—then I wouldn't ask for more."

I sighed. I had already given too much money to guys in trouble up in Sangatta and felt like a sucker. I asked, "How were you planning to get the money for the officials when you first spent it?"

"I thought that when everything went well and Tuan Tim was happy and relaxed, I would tell him I was robbed on the way to pay the officials. But things never went well."

I asked Linder how much he needed for the officials.

"A hundred thousand," he answered. It was almost fifty dollars.

"And the dukun?"

"Also a hundred."

"Why so much?"

"Taking off the spell will be harder than casting it, Tuan," he said. "It's a very strong one. Believe me; I've seen its effects."

I told him I'd think it over and give him my decision the next day. We shook hands and parted. I'd always liked Linder, but at that point I wasn't inclined to be the fall guy for him to the tune of two hundred bucks.

I made my way through the crowd of sweaty, beer-guzzling runners. Everyone seemed to be back, but for some reason they hadn't started the chugging ceremony yet. After each run, first-time and last-time runners had to chug bottles of Bintang while everybody else crowded round and chanted. Ron Baker was leaning against the truck, peering up the road at the jungle. The sun was an enormous red disk pressing down on the canopy.

"Tim's not back yet," Ron said uneasily when he saw me.

"Should somebody go look for him?"

He swatted a mosquito. "Guess I'm in charge. I'll get one of these kampong guys who knows the jungle and have Linder drive us up there."

I went to tell Linder. He seemed frightened. He'd been watching Ron talk to a cluster of kampong men, one of whom had already been singled out by his peers: a stocky middle-aged man with a square jaw and well-muscled arms and shoulders. According to Linder, his name was Karto and he wasn't afraid of the jungle because he'd worked for the logging company that had done the clearcut where the kampong was now. After Linder started the car, he reached through the open window and grabbed my arm.

"May I ask for your help once more, Tuan?"

"Yes?"

"When we get Tuan Tim back and I must take him home or to the hospital, Tuan Mike will please come with us?"

I hesitated. I was already beginning to hallucinate the hot shower I'd gone five months without.

Linder said, "I feel something bad is going to happen, Tuan. I don't want to be alone with Tuan Tim."

Looking into his eyes, I realized it wasn't Tim Lundgren or Colonel Noto he was afraid of. What "bad things" had Tim said to him back at the lab? I agreed to go with him.

Linder pulled the car alongside the knot of kampong people, and Ron and Karto squeezed into the front seat.

Karto waved to his friends and family as the car churned off up the dirt road. Linder was driving so fast that the back of the car gave a jarring hop at each rut and the three heads inside bounced in unison.

I looked around at the crowd. They had partitioned themselves neatly along professional and regional lines: Texans with Texans, techs with techs, teachers with teachers. The handful of Indonesians, after spending a few dutiful minutes mixing with the expats, had gravitated to their highest-ranking countryman and were politely posing questions and comments for his consideration. Everybody had expected to be home before dusk and hadn't brought any insect repellent, so there was a lot of flailing and slapping. The kampong people, superstitious farmers and traders, were hushed as they watched the road. To them anyone foolish enough to enter the jungle at dusk was asking for trouble.

The soft glow of pressure lamps was beginning to suffuse the kampong when headlights finally appeared far up the road against the darkened jungle. The white disks approached in stops and starts as Linder took the ruts more cautiously. Everybody had retreated to their cars to wait, and now they all piled out again as Linder pulled up next to the beer truck. There were cheers and applause from the kampong people as Karto hopped jauntily from the front seat. A little girl, probably his daughter, squealed with delight. Ron emerged from the back seat, motioning the crowd to move back. He announced that Tim was all right but wanted to be taken straight home. Karto was all puffed up and strutting. Barking "Tuan Mike! Tuan Mike!" he motioned me forward like a traffic cop and helped me into the back seat. He closed the door and leaned in through the window. "Not hurt, Tuan," he said. "Just lost." With a pat on the front window he signaled Linder to get going. We cruised through the crowd of expats and along the line of kampong people straining through the dark to see in.

It was well into durian season—durian being a foul-smelling fruit that Indonesians love—and when the season starts you keep smelling vomit, then realize it's durian. Now I smelled durian and realized it was vomit. Tim, covered with it, sprawled on the back seat breathing heavily.

I kept to my side of the seat and breathed through my mouth as we sped into town. Linder leaned on the horn to alert pedicab drivers and kids on bikes. He was too upset to drive at a safe speed, so he took a roundabout route of untraveled side streets full of pushcart peddlers, lottery outlets, and cracked pavement. We climbed toward Pasir Ridge along Jalan Minyak—Oil Street—with the huge shapes and flares of the refinery looming against the sea sky, and wound our way up the Ridge to the main gate of the compound. The uniformed guards waved us through. We passed the rec center, which was already lit up for the party later. The pool area was decorated with streamers and balloons and a huge banner over it that read OCTOBERFEST '83. The pool itself was like a kaleidoscope, with all the colored balloons reflected off it. Indonesian servants were standing around, looking stiff and out of place in lederhosen and little green oompah caps.

We pulled up in front of Tim's house. The verandah light was on, but it was dark inside except for the babu's quarters around back. When I told Linder to help me get Tim inside, he looked back at me as if I'd ordered him to defang a cobra.

"I must go *inside,* Tuan?"

I realized he had never set foot inside an expat's home. He had always been a driver, never an indoor servant. I wasn't sure I could handle Tim alone, so I insisted. When we had hauled Tim out of the back seat and gotten his arms around our necks, he opened his eyes partway like a basking lizard and inspected my face with great seriousness. "Who're you?" he croaked. I identified myself. His face went through a series of contortions, as if he remembered me and was trying to think of a civil response. His face went slack again, the mental effort apparently too great for him. "Fuck you," he said, and looked away. Linder giggled in embarrassment. Tim said, "Fuck you, too, Linder."

We got him across the verandah and into the living room—the front door was open—and Linder steadied Tim while I found the switch to the overhead. A chain of quiet, mouselike noises moved toward us from the back of the house. The kitchen door opened a crack and the old babu peeked in. She was a tiny woman with an oval Javanese face and slate-gray hair drawn back into a bun. She slipped into the room and stood in a half crouch, one hand still grasping the doorknob, the other clutching something against the front of her sarong. When Linder motioned her away, she crouched lower and held out an envelope. Linder motioned again, but Tim had already noticed her.

"C'mere, Nori—gimme that."

Still crouching, she averted her eyes and inched forward with tiny steps. She put the envelope into Tim's hand and bent deeply at the knees in a kind of curtsy, placing her left palm against her right biceps muscle. I had to suppress an urge to laugh at her doing all these obsequious Javanese things for a man who was completely gassed and smeared with puke.

"Who's it from?" Tim demanded in Indonesian.

Nori's answer came out in a whisper. "Pak Noto's driver brought it, Tuan."

With heavy-lidded eyes Tim regarded in turn Nori and the bulging envelope.

"Pak Noto can go fuck himself and so can his driver."

He staggered backward, tugging ineffectually at the corners of the envelope. Linder placed an armchair directly behind him so that the backs of his legs found it, and he sat down heavily. He handed the envelope to Linder to open for him. When Linder gave it back, Tim pulled out a letter. He unfolded the letter and stared blankly at it for a time. Finally he read it aloud. It was in English, which for Tim must have been the ultimate insult. Ayu hadn't even bothered to write it herself.

*Dear Mister Tim:*
*I regret to tell you I cannot be your wife any longer. I am sorry. I send Edi to collect my things.*
*With respect, Ayu.*

Slouched in the chair with his legs stretched out in front of him, Tim stared at the letter. Except for his bloodshot eyes and the mess on his shirt front, he might have been relaxing with the afternoon paper after a jog. He tried to push the letter back into the envelope. It wouldn't go. He peered into the envelope, then turned it upside down. A wad of crisp hundred-thousand-rupiah notes fell into his lap, slipped through, and scattered on the floor. It looked as if there was a good five-thousand-dollars' worth.

"Well, well," Tim said softly.

He looked up at me with a nasty little smile.

"I guess the Indonesianization program is right on track, eh? They just move in and take over whenever it suits 'em."

His eyes surveyed the room and came to rest on Linder.

"State capitalism at work—right, Linder?" he said in English, louder. "Maybe *you'd* like *my* job, huh? Tomorrow, you can go into the lab instead of me. That'd be a kick, wouldn't it?" He raised his voice another notch. "And I didn't even get a chance to tell Colonel Fat Cat and his little bitch what I think of them."

He kept staring at Linder. He was shouting now.

" 'Standby *tidur,* ' my ass! I ought to have you fired, you son of a bitch! *You lazy little brown son of a bitch!* "

He lunged at Linder and keeled over. Linder darted forward and caught him on the way down, softening his fall with a forearm. We got him into the bathroom and undressed him. I sat him down on the little shelf in the stall shower and turned the water on. He was crying. Linder wanted to stay with him, but I told Linder to wait in the living room. I left Tim slumped against the blue tiles, brushing the water from his eyes and snorting like a seal after a long dive.

I phoned the Bakers to send Popo, their driver, to pick me up, and told them to have him wait for me until I came out. I figured I'd be stuck here until I was sure Linder wasn't going to retaliate, and I wanted Popo within shouting distance. Linder was sitting in an armchair, staring straight ahead, shoulders hunched. He looked like a man who'd taken a punch to the gut. I'd already decided to give him the money for the local officials, and seeing him sitting like that made me want to offer him the rest. If he would still take it.

"Linder," I said. "Those things Tuan Tim said just now—he didn't mean them."

Linder's face tightened. He sat motionless for a full minute. When he finally spoke it was with a measured formality, as if he wanted to make it clear that he had made his decision and would never again mention the incident.

"Tuan Mike is right," he said. "It was the whiskey talking. Without it Tuan Tim never would have said those things."

I let out a long, slow breath. "Does Linder still want the money for the dukun as well as the officials?"

He looked up eagerly. "Yes, Tuan."

I told him he would have it the next day.

"Thank you, Tuan."

He managed a weak smile. He promised to drive me anywhere I wanted to go on his next day off. I said fine and told him to leave Tim in the shower for fifteen minutes in case he wasn't done vomiting. We shook hands. He was already loosening up a bit but was still very shaken.

"Tuan?" he said. "I've been thinking about that money for the dukun."

"And?"

"He said he would try to reverse the spell, but he wasn't hopeful about the outcome. He thought it would be better if I found another wife for Tuan Tim and we made him fall in love again, but that we should be patient and wait a month after Tuan and Ayu break up and that I should make a more careful choice. I told him no, I didn't want to risk it again. But now I'm thinking about it, and I'm thinking that Tuan Tim really needs a wife. What do you think, Tuan?"

His eyes looked tired.

I said, "I think your dukun is very wise."

He nodded. "Thank you, Tuan. This also means that the fee will be less and Tuan won't have to spend as much."

I heard Popo pull up in front of the house. Linder and I said good-bye and I headed for the door. Before opening it, I peeked back into the living room from the foyer. Linder was in the armchair again, his arms on the armrests and his head turned so that I could see his face in three-quarters view. He was sitting the way you'd sit on a car seat that is too hot from the sun—as if he were trying to minimize the contact between his body and the chair—and he was perfectly still. Despite his lack of swagger, I had often pictured Linder in his younger days, perched high in the rigging of a Buginese schooner, swaying dangerously with the bloated sails. Now I looked at him sitting there in this strange house, enduring this job that must have seemed to him like an eternally uncharted sea, and I was struck by his courage. The sour feeling in my stomach—from having been an easy mark—lessened.

My skin tingled at the thought of a hot shower, but I stayed, watching Linder. He seemed to be staring at the window. Then I realized he wasn't looking at anything: he was listening. I listened too for a moment but didn't hear anything.

I slipped out and walked to the car. Popo came around to the passenger's side to open the door for me. He got back in and we drove off into the warm, humid evening. We were passing the rec center with its multicolored balloons and servants in lederhosen when it occurred to me: Linder had been listening to the shower, marveling at the steady hiss of hot jets against tiles, so different from the cool, rhythmic splash of water sluiced from a *bak mandi.*

# ACHMAD

It rained that day in late October just before he met Achmad, a long-awaited rain that everyone stopped to watch with pleasure. At last the northeast monsoon drifted into Jakarta on the heels of the long dry season. Along upscale Jalan Thamrin, steel-and-glass skyscrapers turned dark; in crowded kampongs the first rain pelted drainage ditches and tin-roofed hovels. For a moment it gave an expatriate the welcome illusion of a cooler climate.

On that morning off, Paul Hersey sat in the air-conditioned restaurant of the Sabang Hotel, reading the papers and talking with the waiters. By lunch the waiters were too busy to chat, so as soon as the sun broke through again he ventured into the steamy afternoon for a stroll to Sukarno's Independence Monument. Passing the park where the homeless slept in rags and tattered sarongs under shade trees, he heard the rattle of a Vespa approaching. Over the traffic noise on Jalan Merdeka Barat, the driver shouted the most familiar English phrase in Indonesia:

"Hello, Mister!"

Paul half turned his head to give the midday greeting in Indonesian and kept walking. He had no desire to practice English with the man. The driver revved his engine and pulled up alongside.

"Where are you from?" the driver yelled.

*"Amerika Serikat."* Paul kept walking.

"Wait, Mister!"

"It's hot," said Paul, again in Indonesian. "If you want to talk, you'll have to keep up."

*"Mau ke mana?"*

"To the *monas.*"

"Please get on; I will take you."

"I never ride motorbikes."

The young man kept coasting, touching his feet to the road for balance. He looked comical, his helmet askew and fastened with a badly frayed strap. During Paul's first visit to Indonesia, he wouldn't have given this young man more than a vague nod of the head, much less invited him to follow along. But Paul had spent nearly all his time then with Western-educated Javanese who were either Christians or only nominal Muslims. Now, after two years with the embassy in Saudi, he had been transferred back to Indonesia to investigate ties between its Muslim opposition party and the Arab world. Since his arrival five days earlier, he had been trying to get a feel for the range of Muslim public opinion about the desirability of such ties; he had already interviewed a Minangkabau cabbie, a Makassarese hawker, and a *bajai* driver from Palembang. The Vespa driver— polite but more assertive than most Javanese or Sundanese—

struck Paul as possibly Sumatran and therefore likely to be a devout Muslim.

When they reached the bank of food stalls near the entrance to the monument, Paul bought a bottle of sweetened tea from a vendor. Shyly declining a drink, the young man removed his helmet and placed it on the seat of his Vespa. He had a large round head and wore a wispy mustache. His thick, wide-hipped body looked soft underneath a gray shirt and brown trousers. Paul noticed that the nails of his pinky fingers were long, extending a full inch beyond the fingertips, and guessed correctly that he was a student or low-ranking civil servant. Achmad was from Riau in central Sumatra; he was twenty-three, a graduate student in economics at Universitas Indonesia, and had lived in Jakarta for a year and a half.

"And does the university provide you with housing?" Paul asked when the young man seemed unsure of what to say next.

"Yes, but we have to pay and I can't afford it," Achmad said. "I live with my sister's family in east Jakarta. I hate it there."

"Trouble with your brother-in-law?"

"No. With my sister. She resents that I'm even poorer than she and have to live with her. I never ask her for money, not even for a pack of *kreteks*."

"And your parents?" Paul asked. "Still in Riau?"

"Mother came to Jakarta with me; I lived with her until she died last year." Achmad's smile went flat. "Papa died in Riau eight years ago."

Paul said, "It must be hard, still being a student with your parents gone."

"They were just poor farmers. I came here on a government scholarship, but it isn't enough. I just got a new job and hope to make enough money to pay for my examination next week. If I pass, they'll advance me to candidacy for my *Doctorandus.*"

Achmad worked for a local agency, tracking down Arab businessmen and diplomats who were interested in hiring Indonesian servants. Paul had stumbled upon a potentially useful contact.

"Yesterday was my first day," said Achmad, looking exasperated. "I went to seven hotels and talked to thirteen Arabs. Nothing."

Despite the young man's plea of poverty, Paul expected that Achmad would ask for money only after trying to further ingratiate himself with his potential patron. Achmad probably also wanted to practice his English, a common desire among Indonesian students, and for the sake of flattery was letting Paul show off his Indonesian first. Paul was more inclined to give him money than an English lesson in exchange for information, but that was something they could deal with later. It would be very impolite to come to the point before chatting for a while.

Achmad was delighted when Paul invited him into the monument. "Oh, thank you, Tuan!" he said. "Are you going to the top? I've never been up there." Only to the historical museum in the basement, Paul explained. "Wonderful!" cried Achmad. "I've never been *there,* either. ... In fact, I've never been inside the monas at all. Isn't that remarkable?" Paul thought Achmad's round face would burst from grinning. He bought both tickets, for which Achmad thanked him profusely, and together they descended the dimly lit stairs.

The museum was a vast, stuffy room ringed with dioramas depicting scenes that began with Paleolithic times and ended with the attempted coup of 1965. As the two men viewed the displays, they chatted about Paul's work in Saudi, a place that held a special fascination for Achmad as the faraway land to which he prayed five times a day, and about Paul's plans for the next two years in Indonesia. Achmad expressed admiration at Paul's having persuaded the State Department to send him out a week ahead of his family, before the house in Kebayoran Baru was ready, so that he could reacquaint himself with the city and the language. The young man also praised Paul for staying at the Sabang, which was owned by a devout Sumatran Muslim and where most guests were Indonesian, instead of at one of the hotels more commonly frequented by Westerners.

They moved to a diorama representing the Taman Siswa movement of the 1920s: rows of students at their desks and a teacher standing at a blackboard. When Paul had finished reading the legend aloud, his companion gave a cry of astonishment.

"What's wrong?" Paul asked. "Is it my Indonesian?"

"Oh, no—I mean, yes," said Achmad. "That's just it: it's wonderful. Your accent is lovely; I could listen to it all day. Please, read more."

Paul looked at Achmad. The young man's smile was not the obsequious one Paul was used to seeing on the faces of Indonesians who wanted money or favors. There was a disarming sincerity about Achmad. He might be an interesting interview, Paul thought.

"Achmad," he said, "would you mind meeting me again later to talk about your religion? It would be like an interview. I'll pay you, of course."

Achmad's eyes widened. "No, Tuan, of course I would not mind; I'd be honored. But I wouldn't think of taking money from you."

The refusal of payment, Paul suspected, was etiquette: Achmad would behave differently when the time came. It was a perfect trade. Paul would get his interview and Achmad would get his examination money without having to beg for it.

"Let's have dinner tonight," Paul suggested. "Know any good food stalls near the Sabang?" He suspected Achmad would feel out of place even in the Sabang's rather shabby restaurant.

Achmad glanced down at his scuffed shoes and asked softly, "You really wouldn't mind eating with a poor man?"

Paul asked him to come to the Sabang at six. They could go for an early evening stroll, a common Indonesian practice, and eat before seven. A touch of panic came into Achmad's eyes and he shifted uneasily on his feet.

"Is that too early?" Paul asked.

"No, no," Achmad laughed. "Just the opposite. You see, I must eat a few minutes after six. Would you mind?"

Paul realized then why Achmad had refused a drink in spite of the heat: he was fasting until sunset. Paul was accustomed to dealing with the Javanese, many of whom did not even bother to fast during Ramadan, the holy month of fasting. Today—an ordinary Monday—was apparently included in Achmad's personal fasting schedule.

Paul was in the shower at five-thirty when he heard a loud knock on the door. He pulled on his robe and opened the door.

"Achmad," he said. "I wasn't expecting you until six, down in the lobby."

Achmad smiled. "I hope it's all right I come early. I so much enjoy talking with you."

"Sure, fine. But I'm not ready yet—you'll have to wait while I dress. Please come in."

"It's all right I come to your room? You're not angry?"

"No, of course not. Have a seat."

Paul took his clothes into the bathroom, toweled off, and

dressed. When he came back into the room, the television was on. Achmad said quickly, "It's all right I turn on the television? It's my favorite program: the story of an Indonesian student in Japan. He's very lonely there, very homesick. Everything is strange."

Achmad turned to look out of the window at the charcoal-gray Bank of America building across Jalan Haji Agus Salim. He might have been listening to the wail of the muezzin coming from the loudspeakers of Istiqlal, the huge mosque behind the Independence Monument. He got up and switched off the television.

"It's almost six," he said. "May I use your room to pray?"

Paul realized that it was the obligatory six o'clock prayer that had made Achmad come straight upstairs instead of waiting in the lobby. He asked Achmad if he wanted to be alone.

"It doesn't matter who is present," Achmad said. "Whenever I pray, I am alone with my God."

After careful appraisal of the room, Achmad took an old copy of *The Jakarta Post* from under the night table and spread it out on the carpet. Ceremoniously removing his shirt and shoes and socks, he placed them in a neat pile under the coffee table and went into the bathroom. When he came out, his hands and feet were still damp, though he had dried his face thoroughly. He stood with feet together on the newspaper and glanced up at the ceiling to locate the little red arrow painted there. Turning to face the west wall, toward Mecca, he brought the palms of his hands together in front of his face.

Dusk was turning to evening. The sun went down so fast it seemed to leave an afterimage of dusk before Paul's eyes. He could see Achmad clearly in the darkened room. The young man stood motionless for a time. Then he went through an intricate series of gestures and positions, alternately standing and prostrating himself with forehead to the floor, spreading his arms wide and bringing his palms together again. As Paul watched the young man pray, he felt the great gulf between them. The prayer was infused with passion. He remembered that the word *Islam* means "submission," and it occurred to him that the rigid form of the prayer ritual had evolved expressly to channel that passion.

Halfway through the prayer, Achmad's posture changed. Tension gripped his entire body. He clenched his fists and raised his face heavenward as if to confront some obstacle that had come between him and his God.

What seemed an elaborate prayer lasted only a few minutes. There followed as long a period of recovery, or renewal, during which Achmad remained motionless with eyes closed, returning from a faraway place. His muscles relaxed, his eyes opened, he exhaled slowly. Without looking at Paul, he switched on the lamp and began clearing away the newspaper. It was a while before he again acknowledged Paul.

They ate at a food stall at the corner of Haji Agus Salim and Kebon Sirih, a spot that in typical fashion had been bare pavement that afternoon but was now a jumble of crude picnic tables and benches under a bamboo-and-canvas tent. Achmad said it was famous throughout Jakarta for serving "Arab" food, which turned out to be "lamb," which was really mutton. They washed down the *saté* kabobs and peanut sauce with weak sugared tea. After dinner they walked and talked. When Paul brought up the Muslim political party, he was disappointed to find that Achmad was completely apolitical; after a few perfunctory questions, he dropped the subject. They went down Jalan Sabang through puffs of smoke from sidewalk saté vendors fanning charcoal grills, then over to Jalan Jaksa on their way to Merdeka Selatan. Along Jaksa were the cheap hostels on the verandahs of which lounged the young suntanned tourists in their singlets and shorts and rubber flip-flops. Achmad cast a stony glance at one of the tourists as they passed.

"I suppose you don't approve of their dress," Paul said.

"Of course I don't," replied Achmad. "Here only laborers and pedicab drivers dress like that. How can I respect these foreigners? They must be crazy or immoral. But you are different, Paul: well dressed, your hair and mustache properly trimmed. I'll bet your wife is a beautiful woman. Do you have a picture of her?"

Paul did have a snapshot in his wallet but had left the wallet in his room, where it was safer than on the Jakarta streets. They were walking up Merdeka Selatan and could see the Independence Monument to the north, its gilded flame gleaming in the floodlights. In front of it was a row of billboards sporting lurid ads for kung fu movies. As they turned onto Haji Agus Salim, Achmad gave Paul a sidelong glance and said, "I think you should know I'm not a homosexual." He asked about gays in California. Paul had mentioned having grown up in California.

"And you live in San Francisco?" Achmad asked.

"I used to live close to San Francisco."

"But you're not a homosexual? Excuse me for asking, but I must be sure."

"No."

"Oh, I'm glad." Achmad sighed. "Please forgive me. I used to know a Dutchman who had been to San Francisco; he said everyone there is homosexual. That's why I asked about your wife."

"I understand," said Paul. "Do you have a girlfriend?"

"Oh, yes." Achmad took out his wallet and produced a snapshot of a young woman with a rather plain face. "My girl," he said.

"She's very pretty."

"No, she's ugly." He put the photograph away.

By the time they reached the Sabang, Paul was ready to pay Achmad for his time, despite having learned nothing useful from him. Not only was it the fair thing to do, it was also the surest way of indicating that he didn't want to continue socializing. But, although the young man was only a student, Paul worried that paying him there in the Sabang's parking lot in front of the doorman and the hotel cabbies would embarrass him. It ought to be done properly in private. He looked out at the traffic, still heavy on Haji Agus Salim. "The streets will be much clearer in an hour," he told Achmad. "Why don't you join me for coffee in my room?"

Achmad switched on the television as soon as they got there. Paul sat on the bed with the pillows propped against the wall and Achmad sat in the armchair, watching the national news. The coffee arrived and Paul served it. He asked Achmad if there were classes the following day.

"There's one at seven in the morning," Achmad said. "I have to do some reading for it tonight."

"You look tired. If you want to leave, don't let me keep you."

Achmad sipped his coffee, holding the cup with his little finger extended so the long fingernail wouldn't get in the way. "Oh, no, I can stay a while longer," he said. "I'll start studying around ten and go until midnight. From midnight until four-thirty I will pray. Then I'll sleep until six."

The news ended and the telecast cut to a montage of nationalistic scenes and national scenery to the strains of children's voices belting out a patriotic song modeled on the "Marseillaise." There were shots of the Independence Monument (without kung fu billboards), soldiers marching past a reviewing stand, factory workers, farmers in the fields, a barefoot man in a felt hat carrying baskets suspended from a shoulder pole. Achmad watched this last solitary figure move along a dirt path beside glistening paddies. His face had become grave.

"Is something wrong?" Paul asked.

Achmad hung his head to one side and looked out at the lights on Haji Agus Salim. "Sad," he said. "My father died eight years ago and I'm still sad."

There was an awkward silence. Paul said, "That's a long time. A long time to be sad."

Achmad started to cry. He cried silently but without making any attempt to hide his grief. Paul leaned over and rested a hand on his shoulder. Achmad vacillated between regaining control and breaking into sobs. He was still crying softly when he reached up to take hold of Paul's wrist and kissed the back of his hand with great tenderness, pressing a smooth cheek against it. Soon the tears subsided and he wiped his eyes on his shirt sleeve. He looked up.

"Are you angry with me, Paul?"

"It made me very uncomfortable."

"I'm sorry." Achmad looked away, his tone of voice very formal. "Please accept my apology. I would never have done it had I thought it would offend you. Now I'm ashamed. Among my people it's all right to do that with a close friend. And I must keep reminding myself that we've only just met—in so short a time you already seem like part of my family."

Paul looked away in disbelief. He realized now that Achmad was gay, and for a moment he felt deceived. But when he looked back at the young man sitting miserably with his head in his hands, he knew that neither the shame nor the story of his father's death was a lie: Achmad had not consciously set out to seduce him. Recalling the remark about a Dutchman, Paul pictured Achmad drawn again and again to men beyond the boundaries of his rigid world, struggling even then against the forbidden impulses.

The young man stood up. "I'd better go before it rains. It's a long ride—nearly an hour. And what about tomorrow?"

"Tomorrow?"

"Will you have time to see me tomorrow?"

"I . . . I don't think so." Paul started to reach for his wallet and stopped. After what had happened, paying Achmad might embarrass him further. "If I do have time, I'll give you a call," he lied.

Achmad's face brightened. "Yes, fine—at the office before four in the afternoon." He handed Paul a business card with glossy cobalt-blue lettering. "Brand-new today," he said proudly. "To impress the Arabs." He gave a broad smile as if nothing had happened, and reached up to grasp Paul's shoulders. "Please don't tell any of the hotel people about tonight, about my kissing you and saying you're like part of my family. They're mostly Javanese and Sundanese and might not understand."

From his window Paul could see Achmad ease the Vespa out of the parking lot into traffic, then pick up speed and turn the corner at Kebon Sirih. A few minutes later there was a crack of thunder and it started to pour.

The next morning Paul got up at seven, showered, and had a big breakfast of papaya and fried rice at the hotel. There was a lunch appointment with a fellow political officer at the American club in Kebayoran Baru, but the morning was free. Feeling tired, he went back up to the room to doze and watch CNN, which the hotel got by satellite. He had been lying in bed for a while watching the news when he felt a chill. He got up and turned off the air conditioner. His joints felt as though the bones were being twisted out of their sockets. He phoned the front desk to tell them he was not to be disturbed by anyone until further notice, and crawled under the covers. For the next ten hours, he lay in bed shivering, sweating, moaning feebly, dozing. In fleeting lucid moments he tried to imagine what he had caught. He had had all his shots and figured it was some kind of nasty flu that he could wait out without having to be hospitalized. Finally, around seven in the evening, he reached for the phone and mumbled to the receptionist to call a doctor. Five minutes later the phone rang.

"Mister Paul?" a voice said on the line.

"Yes."

"Are you all right? I hear a big noise."

"I dropped the phone. Who is this?"

"Dr. Subamia. You are sick?"

He felt encouraged: the doctor's English was good enough that he might have had some Western training. Paul described his symptoms.

"Sounds like typhoid fever," Subamia said.

"But I had that shot."

"Maybe paratyphoid. Hard to tell the difference."

"I had that one too."

"Oh, well. Not to worry. I come quick. Lie down, keep warm."

"I *am* lying down," said Paul. "I can't get up."

"Oh, good. I mean that you are lying down."

"Yes, fine. See you soon, Doctor."

"Yes. Good-bye."

Half an hour later Paul heard the scrape of a key in the lock, followed by an urgent rapping.

"Hallo! Yoo-hoo, it's Dr. Subamia!"

He was about forty, tall for an Indonesian, with bushy eyebrows and a head of thick, curly hair that spilled over his collar. His short-sleeved cotton shirt and gray slacks were neatly pressed; on his feet were dark-brown leather sandals. He put his bag down on the coffee table and stood smiling with arms folded.

"I let myself in by the key of the room boy," he confided. "I didn't want to make you to get up."

The doctor took Paul's pulse, then popped a thermometer into his mouth. "Lots of perspirations, yes?" He dabbed at Paul's brow with a forefinger. "Body very hot?" Paul nodded. Subamia retrieved the thermometer and scrutinized it with a frown. "Yes, yes. I think it is typhoid. Maybe paratyphoid. And there is diarrhea?"

"No," said Paul.

"You are sure?"

"I'm sure."

"Oh, well. You will soon have it."

"How do you know that?"

Subamia shrugged. "Because I give you now medicines that will cause it." He grinned. "Are you a Christian?"

Paul said he was. Having no religion was something few Indonesians could comprehend.

"Catholic?"

"Protestant."

"Oh, Protestant. Yes, excellent. I am Catholic." The bushy eyebrows arched. "So here we are: two Christians surrounded by Muslims." He chuckled. "May I see your health card?"

"It's in the flap inside my briefcase," Paul said.

Subamia brought it over to the night table and held it up to the lamplight, nodding gravely as he examined it. "I see," he said. "This explains our sickness. You had a typhoid injection."

"I told you that on the phone."

"Yes, but you were supposed to have *two* of them."

It seemed the typhoid immunization had recently been

changed from a single injection to a two-shot series. The government nurse had neglected to tell Paul to come back for the second installment. To this, Subamia just shook his head and smiled.

"They can put a man on the moon, but they can't put the typhoid vaccine into you! Oh, well. Turn onto your side, please. I must give an injection into your rump."

After the injection, the doctor counted out dosages of four kinds of pills into Ziploc plastic bags and made Paul take the first dose in front of him.

"Good," said Subamia when Paul had swallowed the last pill. "You will feel much more better in an hour, even maybe to get up and walk about. But do not go far from the toilet. Not to worry: the diarrhea will go away when the medicines are all gone. Well. I go wash up now." He disappeared into the bathroom.

Paul was lying on his back, relishing the thought of a quick recovery, when the door to his room slammed open and Achmad burst in. The young man strode to the foot of the bed and stared down at Paul, his face twisted by fury and despair.

"I called and called!" he blurted out. "They kept saying you were ill and could not be disturbed, but I didn't believe them—I thought you just didn't want to see me again. All night I thought of you, Paul. I almost forgot the three o'clock prayer, and afterward I couldn't sleep." He moved closer to Paul. "But you are sick, after all! Don't worry, my friend—I'll get a doctor. I'll nurse you back to health. . . ."

With a muffled cry, Achmad fell to his knees and took Paul's head between his hands. Paul tried to pull away from the kiss, but he was too weak and it grazed his cheek. At once, Subamia was at the bedside. The doctor's voice was icy as he addressed Achmad in Indonesian.

"I am treating Tuan right now, Mas. I must ask you to leave."

Achmad bolted upright, his eyes darting from Subamia's face to Paul's. His mouth opened as if to say something, but he thought better of it. He turned to Paul, who saw that he was trembling.

"Good night, Tuan," the young man said in a husky voice. "Until we meet again."

Achmad walked swiftly from the room.

Subamia leaned down to straighten the bed sheets. His lips were pursed and a muscle in his neck kept flexing. He closed and fastened his bag.

"Well," he said. "You must take the medicines again at midnight; I'll tell the hotel to telephone you. Tomorrow morning I telephone to see how you are doing. The bill is sixty dollars."

"Do you want it in rupiah?"

"Do you have American dollars cash?"

"Yes. Please bring me my briefcase."

When Paul had paid him and thanked him, Subamia moved slowly toward the door, then turned to Paul again. His gaze was cold. "May I ask you something, Mister Paul?"

"Yes?"

"After I leave, do you want that man to return?"

Paul pictured Achmad, hurt and shamed, riding his Vespa home to a two-room shack in east Jakarta, and felt a twinge of guilt for having failed to heed the obvious signals.

"No," he told Subamia. "I'd rather not see him again at all."

Subamia nodded approvingly. "All right. I tell the hotel people to watch out for that man. I think maybe he is a lot of trouble for everyone. No morals or religion, yes?"

"No," Paul corrected him. "He's a devout Muslim—*santri.*"

The doctor's eyebrows arched again. "Being santri must be very difficult for a man with his . . . needs. Yes?"

"Yes," Paul replied. "It must, indeed."

"Well, then. I call you in the morning. Don't forget the medicines. Sleep well."

Paul soon felt well enough to get up and walk to the bathroom. After sleeping soundly from midnight to four, he was awakened by the call to prayer from Istiqlal Mosque. He lay looking out at the hotel's gaudy neon welcome sign; he hadn't bothered to close the curtains. The soft crackle of tires floated up from the wet parking lot below and faded away. He glanced at the luminous dial of his alarm clock on the night table and thought of Achmad not having slept yet, praying in his sister's house in east Jakarta through the long hours, alone with his God and the memory of his father, listening to them both. Answering them.

# THE WIND
# MONKEY

When he felt the prahu finally ease out into the current, Richard Freeman leaned back against his pack and glanced over his shoulder at the swaybacked plank antique that served as Sangatta's landing platform. The villagers loitering there had watched with amusement as he lowered his five-ten, 160-pound frame into the slender craft. His embarkation was always something of a show, especially coming after Burhan's. The boatman's wiry little body never caused the slightest tilt of the prahu as he readied it for his boss.

Seeing the American look back, one of the men on the landing waved and called, *"Selamat jalan!"*

*"Selamat tinggal!"* Freeman yelled over the motor's rattle.

He turned back upstream. It was midday. They were headed for Mentoko, the tract of forest where he did his research. He pulled his peaked cap down on his forehead to block the glare and settled in for the long ride.

*A blessing on your going. A blessing on your staying.*

Freeman smiled. For all its frustrations, Indonesia paid rich compensation: resonant phrases, the warm smiles of the people, the bottomless well of hospitality. He was lucky such things made his day-to-day troubles bearable, for in eighteen months' time in the country he had had his share of troubles. He had been warned as much by his graduate adviser, Ray Brock, an old hand at zoological fieldwork. At their last meeting the professor had swung his feet up onto his desk and fixed Freeman with a look that said, "Now I'm going to tell you something that won't start sinking in for six months." Then, stroking his salt-and-pepper beard: "Remember a couple things while you're over there, Dick. First, the Indonesians won't understand what you're doing. It won't even occur to the Jakarta bureaucrats who sign your permits for Borneo that you're going to live way out in the forest, and the villagers who know it won't understand it. Your hired men will cut your trails and haul your supplies and collect data on your monkeys, but they'll never understand why you're paying good wages for it. Second, Indonesians just aren't precise about the same kinds of things we are. The Indonesian words for *science* and *magic* have the same root. *When* in future time is the same word as *if*. You'll ask someone when the boat is supposed to leave or the papers are supposed to be signed, and he'll say *besok,* but he won't mean literally *tomorrow,* like it says in your dictionary; he'll mean *maybe tomorrow or the day after,* or even *next week.* You'll get so damned frustrated you'll start to hate zoology. You'll want to chuck it and come home."

Freeman was skeptical. "I could never hate zoology. It's the only thing I ever wanted to do."

"Oh, you'll hate it," Brock said, smiling the little smile he reserved for graduate students not yet thirty. "I promise."

"So what do I do then?"

"Relax, have a cup of coffee, let it pass. Be Western whenever you can get away with it, but learn to be Indonesian when you have to."

Freeman watched the muddy riverbanks slide past. The shacks and floating outhouses of the kampong were beginning to scatter. Beyond a row of coconut palms and papaya trees, children ran and skipped home from school down the path that paralleled the river, their shoes dangling from their hands by the laces. The prahu left the kampong behind and entered the forest. Freeman unbuttoned his damp shirt and scanned the riverbanks. The Sangatta River never widened beyond thirty-five yards, and he could occasionally catch a glimpse of a sambar deer or a bearded pig drinking at the water's edge before it dashed off into the tangle of creepers and vines that linked the low-hanging trees. Now he saw only a facade of dark foliage stretching from one bend in the river to the next. The great canopy of interlocking tree crowns spread beyond, studded with enormous bird's-nest and staghorn ferns, draped with woody lianas that looped through it like Brobdingnagian cables. Here and there a towering *meranti* or *tebu hitam* pierced the canopy's ceiling to spread its massive crown thirty yards across the sky.

Gazing at the forest, Freeman slipped into one of his frequent meditations on patience and flexibility. Though he realized that any kind of doctoral research required these virtues, he was convinced he had learned them more thoroughly than most graduate students. The forest enfolding him now like a warm green cloak had been such an exacting teacher. After weeks of waiting for permits in Jakarta and the towns of the East Borneo coast, he had searched out a study site: two solid months of following brown rivers that snaked endlessly into the jungle, of trudging through hundreds of acres of forest to examine terrain and census primates. Finally he settled on a tract of lowland rain forest where the Mentoko Stream fed the Sangatta River. Naming the spot for its major stream, he and his hired men hacked out a clearing for the base camp and built a crude house of ironwood poles and nipa-palm thatch, then plotted and cleared and marked trails, at last selecting a troop of *berangat* monkeys to study. That was a milestone, finding his berangat. But to get the research going he still had to habituate them to his presence, learn their ways, systematize his data collection, and train Burhan and Nurdin, who spoke no English and had never ventured more than a half mile into the forest from the kampong (and then only to cut ironwood shingles and collect resins for caulking prahus).

The very first week, the river flooded not once but twice, forcing them to lug all the supplies and equipment through waist-deep water to the nearest ridge crest. A month later, Nurdin missed three weeks of work because of a cobra bite; not long afterward, Burhan stepped on a scorpion hidden in the roof thatch piled at the edge of the clearing—two weeks lost on the house, during which the unused thatch all rotted out and had to be replaced. Once, running at top speed after his berangat as they leapt and bounded through the canopy like the devil's own acrobats, Freeman tripped cresting a steep ridge and tumbled fifty feet into the gorge below, spraining an ankle so severely that he had to sit out a whole month in camp.

He remembered the day, too, just three months into his preparatory work, that Pak Idris, the rotund district head, had stepped from his prahu and waddled up the sandy beach toward Freeman's house, waving a piece of paper. "*Ada surat!* Mister Richard *harus langsung keluar!*" Official instructions from Jakarta: he'd have to leave immediately.

With the national elections still two months away, all foreign researchers were to interrupt their work and report to the nearest major city, remaining there for three months! When he asked Idris why, the little man replied, "Protection." There were excitable people around who might run amok at election time and hurt Mister Richard; better he should go to Samarinda, the provincial capital, where the police could keep an eye on him.

The young American had looked at Idris with wide-eyed exasperation. "Pak," he asked in his still-crude Indonesian, "how could anyone hurt me out here in the forest, thirty kilometers from the kampong?"

Idris grinned. "Jakarta must think Mister lives in Sangatta. Those Javanese townies believe only Dayak tribes live in the forest. It's unthinkable for civilized people to live here, you know." The old man shook his head, waving a stubby hand at Freeman's stilted house with its thatched roof and half walls. "*I* know where Mister lives because I see it with my own eyes!"

When they had reached the kampong, where Freeman stood glumly in the rain, clutching his mud-spattered suitcase as the thick reddish clay corkscrewed its way farther up and around his shoes every time he moved, Idris patted the letter in his shirt pocket and fixed him with a knowing look. "I have accompanied Mister out of his research site," he announced. "I have no further responsibilities concerning this matter. Have a good trip to Samarinda, Mister Richard. Selamat jalan."

The moment Idris began his officious retreat up the oozing road, Nurdin motioned Freeman back into the prahu and took him upstream to camp. Months later, in Jakarta, he learned from an Australian businessman the real reason for the order: around election time the regime's strong-arm tactics, best shielded from prying foreign eyes, were more visible in the countryside than in the cities.

Freeman took a swig from his canteen and handed it over his shoulder to Burhan, laughing softly to himself as he pictured the district head doing his best not to wink while wishing him a good trip to the city. Idris's smile had had a certain ambiguity, with the corners of the mouth held almost straight while the eyes twinkled. He seemed to be relishing the little play he was staging.

Freeman had seen several versions of that smile in Indonesia, probably the most memorable of them on the lined face of old Pak Sukino when Freeman had tried to explain his research on berangat. Sukino was the kampong's most respected *dukun*—dispenser of home remedies, breaker of spells and curses, expert in prophecy and divination. From Freeman's berangat talk, the old man inferred an astonishing lack of interest in the monkeys' useful magical properties. He started to lecture the young bearded Mister about monkey magic and its ancient role in the harmony of the world, but he stopped as soon as he realized the Mister was listening only out of politeness. "Anyway," he said, adjusting his sarong, "I hope you find what you are looking for. And I hope it will contribute to the harmony of the world." And he smiled that funny half smile, eyes twinkling.

It had been Freeman's sole conversation with the dukun. Later, pondering that smile, he decided it signaled a rough acceptance of him and the strange Western "magic" he was working in the forest. Ever since then he had felt a certain affection for the old man.

As the prahu headed upstream into the green stillness, Freeman's thoughts turned to the berangat. Compared with them, all the other obstacles had been minor. *Presbytis hosei:* Hose's Leaf Monkey—sleek, slender, mysterious leapers of the subfamily Colobinae, unstudied until now because they were so hard to keep up with in the high forest and accustom to human observers. When he arrived in Borneo, he had not yet actually seen one, not even a photo of a live one—only a grainy black-and-white snapshot of a rather squashed juvenile specimen in Lord Medway's *Mammals of Borneo*. As soon has he laid eyes on them in the forest, though, he fell hopelessly in love with them. They were charcoal-gray above and cream below, with hands and feet smartly gloved and booted in black, and with black face masks extending just below the nose. They were a magical troop of sky bandits that swept like the wind out of nowhere to stalk or chase, then steal or race away among the tall trees. They were breathtaking.

The first time he encountered them, the big male was on the ground eating fallen *kelinsai* fruits. Freeman was walking the main riverside trail in silence, and as the kelinsai tree sat in a deep gully, he was shielded from the monkeys' view until he crested the adjacent bluff. There he froze, not ten yards from the male, and the monkeys in turn froze. Then, all at once, the whole forest was in motion. At the border of his vision he saw the others rattle and splash the canopy as the male vaulted a tall meranti in three prodigious bounds to leap off after his troop. It was as if the law of gravity had been suspended. Within seconds the forest was perfectly still, as though the berangat had never been there. At that moment, staring blankly into the chaos of vegetation around him, it hit Freeman with new revelatory power what a feat of endurance it would be to study these monkeys. At the same time, he was irresistibly drawn to them, as though the wake of their flight exerted a tangible pull. He realized then that until he uncovered their secrets, there was simply no other creature on earth that he would be content to study.

Over the next six months he trudged through the forest for days at a time without a sighting. Whenever he was lucky enough to find them, they would bolt a hundred yards through the canopy and scale an emergent, where they'd sit motionless for hours, invisible. And then there was the wind. Though windy days were rare, they drove him to tears in those early months. Rain was easy by comparison: in a downpour the berangat huddled miserably against branches and one another, refusing to budge until the rain let up. But when the wind arose, whipping the canopy for many seconds at a stretch, it not only masked their movements but forced them to travel cryptically to keep from falling; they seemed to melt away into the jostling, twisting canopy, fragmenting the day's hard-earned data and thereby rendering it useless. It took him months of agony to develop that sixth sense of where they would go in the wind, so he could catch up with them and save the day's work.

The motor died behind him. Burhan rose.

"Have to take a piss, Boss."

Freeman rose to do the same, steadying himself at the side of the prahu as it drifted back downstream. "Nurdin with the berangat today?" he asked Burhan.

The Indonesian had droopy eyes and a jet-black mustache that glistened in the sun. He did not answer right away. Freeman repeated the question.

"No, Boss," Burhan said after a moment, zipping his fly. "Nurdin's in the kampong. Went down yesterday. One of his kids is sick."

"Too bad. Is it serious?"

"I hope not, Boss."

"When will Nurdin come upstream?"

"Maybe besok."

Freeman smiled at the redundant phrase. Over a year ago the men had begun adding the qualifier *maybe* to *tomorrow,* to avoid further misunderstandings. Burhan returned the smile guardedly and leaned on the handle of the motor to lift the long propeller shaft clear of the river bottom.

It was a typical situation. Nurdin had wanted an unscheduled visit with his family near the kampong, so he had invented a sick child. Next week, Burhan would accidentally-on-purpose run out of cigarettes and need to make another run down to the kampong. A year ago, Freeman would have been irritated by such nonsense. It happened partly because they were afraid that a white man would be incapable of understanding their personal needs apart from illnesses, cigarettes, and Muslim holidays. During their first year together, Freeman and his men had evolved a tacit compromise that allowed bogus sick children and unexpected cigarette shortages so long as they occurred only during the intervals between blocks of monkey follows. These were loyal, hardworking men, but if Freeman had not learned to understand them, there were a hundred ways his doctoral dissertation might have blown up in his face. One of Ray Brock's favorite stories was about the graduate student gathering data in Sumatra who had made his men work normal hours through the holy month of Ramadan, forcing them to break the daily fast or become dangerously dehydrated. This student had lectured the Koran to them, arguing that the Prophet had excepted men in unusual circumstances from the standard restrictions. Openly contradicting their boss or expressing resentment would have caused him to lose face, so instead these men had sabotaged his research by falsifying six months' worth of data.

Freeman glanced at his watch. Two hours gone. Two more would see them back at Mentoko, where they would haul the supplies up the riverbank to the house. After a bath in the cool river, he would take a leisurely stroll in the forest to survey the inevitable changes that had occurred during his two-week absence: tree-falls, landslips, new fruits and flowers on the trails. As soon as Nurdin came back upstream, they would locate the berangat and start the month's follows.

With the smooth gliding motion of the prahu beginning to lull him to sleep, Freeman realized he was smiling again. He had first arrived at Mentoko with just enough grant money for two years' work, needing at least a full year of data on berangat to produce a respectable dissertation and ultimately take his place among the ranks of tenured zoologists. It had taken him an entire year just to learn his way around the forest, habituate the monkeys, train himself and his men to collect data properly. Now, with six months of solid data under his belt, it would be just six more months until he broke camp and carried home that precious year's worth of data. Glowing with satisfaction, he thought of the secure routine that he had so painstakingly fashioned from the chaos of those early months.

It had been a remarkable year and a half. He was finally at ease in this country, this forest. He had conquered them by adapting, bending. Had he been unable or unwilling to bend, a host of adversaries could have broken him: hungry land leeches, poisonous centipedes, fire ants, bureaucratic red tape, his men, his monkeys, the loneliness. But he had licked them all. Now nothing could throw him off stride.

The next morning found Freeman clearing trails in the forest, savoring the *thwack* of his parang blade against bamboo. There had to have been a windy day or two while he had been away, for a flood was the only other thing that could have forced so much bamboo down across the riverside trail, and there was no evidence of flooding. He would have preferred to cut a man-sized tunnel through the mess, but then layers of bamboo would keep coming down and eventually it would all have to be cleared anyway.

It felt good to wield a parang again, but he wished one of the men was there to help. With the expected nicotine fit coming a week ahead of "schedule," Burhan had gone downstream early that morning. For once, Freeman had indulged himself in a mild show of irritation at his man's need to return to the kampong so soon. Nurdin still had the second prahu, and Burhan was well aware of his boss's distaste for being stranded at Mentoko without a prahu. The brief exchange had been all too predictable: Why hadn't Burhan bought cigarettes the day before? He'd forgotten. Burhan knew, of course, that Freeman knew the men were useless without their smokes. Fortunately, the outcome had proved satisfactory: Burhan's unsolicited promise to return the following day was a sure sign of guilt. Punctuality for a carton of cigarettes was a fair trade anywhere in Indonesia.

It took him all of an hour to clear the bamboo. Then he headed west on the trail, a dark brown slit that knifed its way through a sea of green, mounting steep ridges and plummeting into deeply cut streambeds. Though to Freeman they were like highways, the Mentoko trails were actually little wider than the occasional cobras that slithered across them or the lianas that ran alongside them like pipelines for fifty yards or more before lifting back into the canopy. He was standing with a boot resting on one of those foot-thick lianas when he heard a rustling in the canopy to the south. Sudden gooseflesh broke out on his shoulders and back. As with so many forest things, it took a long layoff to remind him of the magic of that sound. In an instant his mind had run through its list of arboreal creatures, eliminating all species of birds and squirrels right off. Even the giant squirrels, though loud when spooked, had a certain lightness to them. A more substantial sound was always a primate:

gibbons traveling arm over arm, with a regular cadence like pebbles skimming a lake surface; *kra,* the common macaque monkeys, making their nondescript mélange of rustles, rattles, and splashes; or the berangat, who might have been named for the distinctive loud thumps they made bounding through the canopy, ricocheting off the sturdier boughs. What was coming toward him now, however, was bigger than any of those, so heavy that he could hear the creak of smaller trees bending under its weight.

The orangutan came swimming through the foliage like an enormous orange octopus, arms and legs twisting about its distended belly. Nurdin had been the first to see her, over a year before, and Freeman remembered him returning to camp still spellbound from watching her. Proudly Nurdin announced that he had named the orangutan Sindora for the first tree species whose fruit he had seen her eat; then, grinning from ear to ear, he dubbed her juvenile son Unyil, in homage to a popular Indonesian cartoon character. It was one of the first times that Nurdin's rich enthusiasm for the forest and its creatures had shone through.

When Sindora had crossed the trail, Freeman heard Unyil coming, hurrying to catch up. It was late morning now, hours since the gibbons had abandoned their slide-whistle songs and hours more until the cicadas would strike up their ratchety drone. Save for the two apes swishing along to a fruiting tree somewhere, the forest was silent. Freeman listened until their sound was lost in the perpetual mutter of a stream beyond the next ridge. Ears open for canopy noise, he resumed his deliberate pace along the trail. Sindora and Unyil had whetted his appetite: now he longed for the rushing *splash-rattle* of berangat, for the big male's gruff chugging call that heralded the start of each long move. Orangutan, gibbon, even kra, were beautiful to watch, but for sheer excitement none of them could hold a candle to

berangat. And, of course, none of them were *his* the way
the berangat were. He had staked his claim to the berangat,
captured them with ingenuity, hard work, perseverance.

Freeman recalled how that sense of ownership had bud-
ded at the very moment they had finally accepted him. After
the long months of their fleeing, acceptance had bestowed
on him a feeling almost of blessedness. There was something
truly astonishing about being accepted not as an unshakable
adversary or tolerable annoyance but as a natural part of
their world, like a wild pig or civet cat. Still, that heady
sense of having captured them and made them his own had
fully blossomed only after months of follows. Studying
them day after day required such intense, sustained concentration that he had almost become one of them in the
process. Indeed, there were times, as he crept after them
through the canebrake labyrinths on the riverbank or ran
beneath them along the floor of the high forest, when he
felt the boundary between him and them begin to blur.
Near the end of particularly grueling dawn-to-dusk follows
that left him alternately giggling and weeping from the
strain, he would peer through binoculars upraised for the
thousandth time that day, and suddenly the spasms in his
back and shoulders would relax, the ache from the leeches
in his boots would go numb, the sweat soaking his heavy
fatigues would evaporate—his entire body and mind would
fall miraculously away—and his unfettered soul would
float up among the branches and expand until there was no
Richard Freeman anymore, but only trees, flecks of sky,
berangat. At night, he sometimes dreamed to the beat of
their subtlest rhythms: the way they groomed each other
raptly, husked *kernanga* fruit with their teeth to scrape the
oily turquoise arils from the seeds, daintily sucked the nec-
taries of the little white *kayu bunga* flowers, dusting him
with a steady snowfall of blossoms. In his dream, the blooms

would settle onto his open notebook below, and he would feel himself smiling in his sleep, knowing he had captured something of the berangat's magic.

After wolfing down a peanut-butter-and-jelly sandwich around noon, Freeman spent several hours alternating silent walking with more trail clearing. Near the southern boundary of the study site, an uprooted *tengkawang* was further evidence of recent wind. The mammoth tree had angled across a trail, dragging with it a hill-sized tangle of lianas, vines, and smaller trees. He hacked at the jumble until there was enough room to climb over the fallen giant to the trail, then turned back toward camp, making a mental note to have the men cut notches in the tengkawang with their parangs to ease the climb.

Since his sighting of Sindora and Unyil, there had been little wildlife. A garnet pitta had hopped along a trail in front of him for a while, and later he had caught a glimpse of the slender form of a racket-tailed drongo flitting by in the subcanopy gloom. The late-afternoon sun slanted into the forest, bathing it from canopy to understory in buttery gold. Soon he should hear the comforting *keting-ting-ting* of Burhan's prahu downstream. As usual, he would wait to resume data collection until Nurdin arrived with the other prahu. In a way, it was Nurdin's affinity for berangat and the forest that had been the glue holding the work together. As he walked, Freeman visualized his best man's long, weathered face with its intelligent eyes and prominent cheekbones. He smiled. It was always good to see Nurdin again after a layoff.

He had just levered himself over a rotting tree-fall on a ridge trail and was descending the slope when he saw movement in the canopy to the south. Branches dipped and foliage shimmered at an unhurried pace that suggested kra on their customary journey back to the river to sleep in the overhanging trees. As the motion approached, however, he saw that it was not kra but his berangat. For some reason, they were moving like cats on the prowl, creeping along branches, stretching to grasp connecting vines instead of leaping to farther footholds. He watched, motionless, stunned that he had mistaken them for kra—something he had not done in more than a year—but at the same time realizing he was not to blame, for the monkeys were indeed traveling more like cautious kra than bold berangat.

The troop slipped by overhead, failing to notice Freeman, whose olive drabs blended into the understory. His eyes followed them toward the *maligara* tree that he knew was in bloom two ridges to the west. They moved cohesively—all twelve, he guessed, including the infants. Cowlick, the old matriarch named for the protruding tuft of hair on her crown, was in the lead, as she often was. Oddly, though, along her belly clung her juvenile daughter, Pout, who had not been carried like that before dark for some months now.

With the troop barely out of sight over the ridge, Freeman reached down to flick a leech from his boot rim and eased himself over the first ridge and up the next. He was not ready to let the berangat see him yet. Sighting them unnoticed was a ritual he enjoyed after these layoffs: it always brought back the delicious thrill he had felt in those early months whenever he found the magical creatures that his career depended on. And now he could savor that thrill without the old accompanying pang of fear that he might ultimately fail.

The low, spreading maligara rose from a gorge, so that as he crested the ridge he could peer straight into its crown through a clump of spiny rattan vines. It was full of berangat greedily stuffing their mouths with fleshy yellow petals.

They all seemed to be there: Cowlick, Pout, Whitey, No-nose, Red, Scruffy with her infant, the juveniles. . . .

Wait a minute, thought Freeman.

He craned his neck for a clearer view. Where was Grinner? The big male, so named because of the old fight scar that twisted his upper lip into a permanent sneer, was missing. Probably off foraging alone, Freeman guessed. That might explain their style of travel: he had observed something similar once before when Grinner had wandered off to forage alone for a few hours. Still, in the eight or nine months since their acceptance of him, Freeman had never seen them so subdued.

Crouching on the ridge crest, shrouded in rattan, he watched the monkeys feed, their elegant pelts almost black in the dying day. From far off to the northwest came a faint rumble: rain approaching. He started to reach for his poncho but stopped, realizing he would have to endure the rain for less than an hour because the berangat would soon select their sleeping tree. He had already decided to follow them to it and go out again to them before dawn. It would be interesting to see how long it took Grinner to rejoin them this time.

Parting the rattan, Freeman rose and took a step down the slope toward the base of the maligara. Just then the tree was rocked by violent shudders as the monkeys bolted from it en masse. Instinctively, he took a step in the direction of their flight, but caught himself and stood watching them vanish to the south. It was pointless to run after them in this terrain; in order to stick with them, he would have to see which tree they chose for a hideout, and they were so fast they had probably already done it, quietly tucked themselves into some dense crown a hundred yards away and fifty yards up.

He loitered there on the ridge crest, trying to get his bearings, again aware of the approaching roar of the downpour. His nostalgic ritual was not supposed to have included a sickening reminder of the way he had been taunted by the sight of fleeing berangat rumps back in the early days. There had to be an explanation. A coincidence—their sighting a python or eagle at the very moment he had revealed himself—was extremely unlikely. The obvious alternative was that his long absence had weakened their acceptance of him. His previous absences had made them only a little wary, but this time they had been without Grinner on first contact: maybe that had been enough to do it. In any case, he thought, it shouldn't take them long to settle down again—a day or two at the most.

As the low rumble of the storm overtook him, Freeman heard for an instant the individual raindrops along its leading edge. Then a tidal wave of sound washed over him. Peering up into the gathering darkness, he could still see flecks of light in the forest's great domed shell off to the northeast. It occurred to him, as always, how strange it was to be in a tropical downpour and stay completely dry for the first few minutes. The forest canopy was so dense and deep that there were always two rainfalls: a roaring deluge that cascaded onto the canopy like an ephemeral waterfall, followed beneath the canopy by a hard drizzle that persisted long after the downpour had spent itself.

Gingerly fingering a stem between its fishhook barbs, Freeman parted the rattan again and slipped through to the trail. A crude stairway of alternating slopes and plateaus, it ran for a half mile along the ridge down to the river. He associated this homeward hike in late afternoon with the drone of cicadas, but now all he could hear was the storm's vast roar enveloping him like the echo of white water hurtling through a canyon.

It took five minutes for stem-flow and leaf-drip to find the understory, and by the time Freeman reached camp, it had been raining under the canopy for nearly half an hour. Drenched, he stepped out of the rain and into the clearing.

It wasn't until noon the following day that Freeman finally heard the prahu. He scowled at the noise. He was in a rotten mood. Rising before dawn, he had gulped a cup of instant coffee and entered the forest just as the river was beginning to show through the dimness. In the thick fog that drifted like smoke off the river, he followed his flashlight beam from one traditional sleeping tree to the next without a sighting. It was almost ten o'clock when he found the berangat far to the southwest of camp, feeding on the unripe seeds of *nyatoh* fruit. Grinner was still conspicuously absent, and the troop fled like demons the moment they saw Freeman. An hour later, they fled with equal zeal when he relocated them three hundred yards to the east. He had sat dejected on a clammy log ever since, watching the liver-brown leeches inchworm their way to his boots from the understory, flicking off the ones that got above the thick muslin knee socks that served as leech guards.

In all three of the encounters since his return, there had been a desperate quality to the monkeys' flight that belied a transitory skittishness. This terrified Freeman. He had calculated it over and over—the amount of data needed, the remaining funds, the date by which he had to be home to claim his teaching assistantship—and each way he figured it, the bottom line was that he would simply not be able to complete his work unless these wretched animals calmed down very soon. And now, on top of everything else, Burhan was nearly a day late.

He took the trails at top speed and reached camp before

the prahu. Grasping one of the house frame's ironwood poles, he hoisted himself onto the verandah without benefit of the front step, hung binoculars and pack on their customary nails, leapt from the verandah, and marched down the crude footholds in the riverbank to the strip of sandy beach. Greeting Burhan there instead of at the house would signal his displeasure with sufficient force that he could forgo raising his voice. Listening to the motor's stutter downstream, he planted his boots in the sand and collected himself.

The prahu came around a bend in the river and angled toward camp, nosing into the wet sand right in front of Freeman. Burhan always dressed in full field gear to and from the kampong, where anything resembling a uniform conferred status. His holstered canteen clattered as he swung himself over the side of the prahu, a sheepish grin on his face.

"Sorry, Tuan," he said quickly without looking up. He was already lifting plastic bags of fruits and vegetables from the prahu. Freeman knew Burhan would use the informal *Boss* again only when his guilt had begun to ease.

"So, what happened?" Freeman said softly.

Burhan reached a creased note toward him. It was signed by Pak Sahar. Burhan said, "The motor broke down on the way up yesterday. I couldn't fix it, so I rowed back to the kampong. It was already late."

"Pak Sahar fix it properly?"

"I think so, Tuan. Feels okay now."

Freeman squinted into the painful glare and nodded at the house. "The sun is hot," he said, taking one of the bags of groceries from Burhan. They sought the shade of the verandah, where Freeman poured them tall glasses of water from a plastic container. After drinking in silence, he made tea on his little kerosene stove in the house and carried the pot and cups out to the verandah. They sat in rattan chairs, facing each other across a low table with legs of thick rattan stems bound with rattan strips.

Burhan dumped four heaping spoonfuls of sugar into his tea and stirred it. "There is one trouble, Tuan," he said, indicating the note in Freeman's hand. "Pak Sahar asks twenty-five thousand rupiah, but I can pay him only five."

"All right," Freeman replied, frowning at the scrawled note. "Burhan will take the rest down to him when Nurdin returns with the other prahu."

Burhan sat awkwardly, shoulders hunched. "But there is another trouble, Tuan." He took out a cigarette and lit it with a match. The clove-scented smoke twisted lazily into the roof thatch. "Pak Sahar . . . he needs the money tomorrow. His eldest son, Haris, must ride the big boat to Samarinda the day after tomorrow. One of Sahar's nephews died of cholera; Sahar cannot go himself, so he sends Haris."

"So, it is like that. How is Nurdin's son?"

"Very sick, Tuan. Cholera. Maybe he will die."

Freeman clasped his hands behind his head and tilted his chair back a little, eyes on Burhan's glistening face. He reminded himself that his men knew how he felt about being in camp without a prahu and starting late on a month's follows. What Burhan had said might all be true— all, that is, except for the cost of the repairs. Undoubtedly, Sahar required no more than twenty thousand but had billed him twenty-five at Burhan's urging, the extra five thousand serving as Burhan's "commission."

"Cholera," said Freeman, "is a very bad disease. I hope Nurdin's son will get well and have a long life."

Burhan nodded. "Yes, Tuan. Very bad disease. The mother may boil water in the kitchen, but the child will still sneak a drink from the river by the outhouse."

Freeman rested his palms on his knees and leaned forward. "Burhan, there is trouble with the berangat. It is like this: whenever they see me they run away, already three times in two days. And I have not yet sighted Grinner." He looked straight into Burhan's eyes. "When did Burhan or Nurdin last follow them?"

For just an instant, the Indonesian's pupils narrowed. "Five days ago, Tuan."

"Did they run away?"

"No, Tuan."

"Grinner was there?"

"Yes, Tuan."

Burhan looked away briefly, then back at Freeman. The American saw nothing in particular in those droopy eyes, but there was a worrisome tightness in the jaw muscles. Lifting the metal lid from his cup, Freeman sipped his tea. "I'm concerned that something may have happened to Grinner," he said, letting his eyebrows arch as though it were a question. "I don't think he slept with the others last night."

Burhan stared back, impassive. "Perhaps python, krait, leopard. Who knows? Maybe he got tired of the females. . . ." He flashed a disarming smile, but again Freeman noticed an involuntary flexing of the jaw muscles. It made him decide to pay Nurdin a visit.

Leaning back in his chair, he said blandly, "It is like this, Burhan. Pak Sahar needs his money, so tomorrow morning at six Burhan will go down to the kampong. I will go with Burhan because I've been meaning to speak with Pak Idris." He stood up and placed a booted foot on the seat of his chair. "So, until tomorrow."

Burhan rose with a deferential nod.

"Until tomorrow, Boss."

At ten forty-five the next morning, Freeman and Burhan stepped from the prahu onto the landing at Sangatta, where they bantered for a few minutes with the half dozen or so barefoot men who always seemed to be waiting there for something that never came. During the ride downstream, the American had worked out a contingency plan for taking his next cautious step into a delicate situation. If one of Nurdin's children was indeed sick, he would simply express his concern over tea, offer Nurdin a hefty advance on his wages, and on leaving, mention the problem with the berangat to see if Nurdin had any information to volunteer. Probably Nurdin knew nothing, but it was possible he was staying in the kampong to avoid having to report some sort of bad news.

Freeman instructed Burhan to take the twenty thousand rupiah to Sahar immediately, then ambled up the hill toward the district head's office. When he sensed that Burhan was out of sight, he stopped abruptly, snapping his fingers as though he had forgotten something in case anyone was watching, and backtracked to the dirt road that led west along the river to Nurdin's house, beyond the kampong. It was brutally hot, palms and papaya trees affording scanty shade. The previous day's mud had dried to a spongy clay. The sky was clear, and the glare off the yellow-brown river kept forcing Freeman's gaze to the other side of the road, where little shacks and two-room board houses were perched on stilts in front of meager rice plots. A gnarled old man in a traditional black Indonesian cap gave him a wide berth but nodded at his respectful greeting. A group of children playing in the scrap wood from a sawmill grew quiet as he passed, then broke into spasms of giggling. He was still a minute's walk from the house when he spied Nurdin's twelve-year-old son, Muin, standing in his underpants on the outhouse boardwalk, sluicing himself with river water from a dipper tied by a string to one of the planks. The boy must have seen Freeman coming just then, for suddenly he dropped the dipper and dashed across the road to the house.

As Freeman stepped up onto the verandah and slipped off his sandals, Nurdin's wife, Déwi, appeared at the screen door. She wore an uneasy smile.

"What is the news, Mister Richard?"

"The news is fine, Déwi."

"Please come in and sit down. Mister wants to drink coffee or tea?"

"Just tea, thank you."

Freeman sat on the threadbare sofa, feeling awkward and large in the cramped sitting room, while Déwi put the kettle on in the kitchen. The room was rather upscale for Sangatta, with a Formica coffee table and a battered old curio case standing against one of the three walls to which Nurdin had tacked cheap plywood paneling. The fourth, still its original plaited bamboo for ventilation, was the only one that was not all warped. Smudged picture calendars from Samarinda businesses decorated the paneled walls. Freeman watched pale green geckos dart across the ceiling. Out of the corner of his eye, he noticed Muin's brown face peeking around the kitchen doorjamb. There came a staccato whisper from Déwi, and the face vanished.

When Déwi finally reappeared carrying a tarnished metal tray, she was wearing a fresh sarong patterned with brightly colored flowers. The glossy raven hair that had hung nearly to her waist was now pulled neatly back into a bun fastened with lacquered barrettes. Bending gracefully at the knees, she set the tray on the coffee table in front of her guest and held out a circular cookie tin. Freeman selected a cookie; he took a bite of it and a sip of the sickly sweet tea.

"Delicious," he said.

Déwi smiled more openly this time, exposing crooked teeth. "Thank you, Mister Richard. I'm sorry they're not fresh. Nurdin forgot to buy more the last time he went to Samarinda."

"No, no," said Freeman. "Delicious, truly." He knew that Nurdin had not been to Samarinda in more than a year, that the expensive store-bought cookies were stale because they were brought out only for important guests. To be served stale Samarinda cookies in Sangatta was a distinct honor.

After a while he asked, "Is Nurdin in the kampong?"

The young woman sat stiffly in a rattan chair, hands folded in her lap. "Yes, Mister. Nurdin took the sick one in the prahu to the dukun."

"Oh? Which dukun?"

"Pak Sukino."

"Ah. Pak Sukino is a very wise man." He took another bite of cookie and a sip of tea. Then he said, "It's so quiet—where are the other children?"

"Oh, they're playing behind the house."

He had noticed earlier that the prahu was indeed gone, which fit Déwi's story, but now he realized that there were no shouts or shrieks of laughter coming from the backyard. Freeman and Déwi chatted about the weather, the children, the teacher who had developed a goiter, the local muezzin, whose laryngitis had for two days now foisted on believers a hapless substitute prayer-caller. Freeman tried to think of a tactful way of getting a glimpse of the backyard. If he waited to look from the road after leaving, the children—if they were indeed there now—might be long gone to a neighbor's or the kampong. He couldn't invite himself into the kitchen for a look from the back window without offending his hostess, and if he asked for a banana from the backyard, either Déwi would claim that none was ripe or he would have to violate the code of hospitality by insisting on fetching it himself. Though the house was sweltering in the rising temperature, it would be the height of rudeness to go out for air uninvited. Even if he were excused for such rudeness as a naturally uncouth Westerner, Déwi would watch from the house to see if he went snooping in the backyard.

Suddenly Freeman heard something that made him forget tact. It came from behind the house: a sharp cough that punched through the flimsy walls like a gunshot. Then muffled giggling. Without a word, he leapt through the front door and off the verandah, stunned by this sound that belonged to the high forest. In the backyard, he found Nurdin's children—Muin, the three daughters, and the younger son—squatting all in a row with their backs to him in front of a small bamboo cage that had been lashed together with rattan strips. His mind grasped at scraps of detail as the whole picture emerged: the younger boy reaching toward the cage, the pale underside of the *markeladi* leaf in his outstretched hand, the dark-green bite marks in the lighter green of the bamboo shafts, the curved scar on the face behind the bars.

When Grinner's jaw jabbed at Freeman from the force of another bark-cough, four of the children's heads snapped around as if on springs. Finding the American's bearded face, eight eyes widened. The younger boy, who alone had failed to notice Freeman, snatched the leaf back to his chest at Grinner's bark and laughed hilariously, bouncing on his haunches. Muin reached over and gave him a shove.

Freeman walked slowly toward the cage, staring into it. Grinner groomed a forearm with feigned nonchalance.

Freeman turned to Muin. "What's going on here?"

The boy stood motionless, spindly arms pressed to his

sides. His voice was barely audible. "We guard the wind monkey . . . until Papa returns."

Freeman realized he was trembling. "Muin," he said, trying desperately to contain his growing panic, "what do you mean by *wind monkey?*"

Muin's brow knotted as he struggled to understand the question's intent. He gestured at the cage. "This, Tuan," he said. "Berangat."

Freeman looked from Muin to Grinner and back. "Go find your father," he ordered.

The boy took off around the house and headed down the road to the kampong at a run. Freeman walked numbly back to the verandah and entered the sitting room, where he paced back and forth like a caged bear. Déwi was no-where to be seen. Probably hiding in the kitchen, he thought. Kutai people had a tendency to disappear when disaster hit a friend or acquaintance, unable to bear the look on the victim's face.

And this *was* a disaster, the finality of which was only now beginning to sink in. The trapping of Grinner would make the troop skittish for months, whether or not the male was returned to them. Freeman's research was ruined. Pure and simple. Time to pack up and go home. Forget the dissertation, the Ph.D.—forget zoology altogether. Grant money was too scarce for him ever to get more now: this failure would taint him beyond reprieve. Oh, he could write up his six months' worth of data for a master's degree, but that would only put him in the running for a job teaching bonehead biology at some junior college, not a decent university position. It was a funny thing, though: even as these thoughts raked him, he felt no anger. He was holding on to the anger deep down, as if there were still a chance that Nurdin's explanation would make everything all right again. As if he could repeat it to the berangat and they would stop running away.

He was still pacing half an hour later when he heard the steady *keting-ting-ting* approach and cut off with a snap. From the window he saw Muin, Nurdin, and Pak Sukino climb out of the prahu in bright sunlight. Along with white T-shirts and rubber sandals, Nurdin wore loose-fitting khaki shorts and Sukino a checked sarong. Burhan was with them, but he stayed in the prahu, his face turned toward the river. Nurdin's and Sukino's expressions were grave as they mounted the verandah and entered the room. Both said, *"Selamat siang,"* and nodded, but only Sukino made eye contact with Freeman, who forced himself to return the greeting.

When Sukino had lowered his squat body and Nurdin his slim sinewy one into rattan chairs, Déwi brought them all sweetened tea in glass cups with metal lids. For a minute they chatted about the weather and one another's health. Then, clasping his thick hands, the dukun cleared his throat and fixed Freeman with an authoritative look that left no doubt that his family had resided in the village for many generations.

"Muin says Mister Richard has seen the male berangat," he said.

Freeman nodded. He waited for the old man to continue. Sukino took out a cloved cigarette and lit it with a safety match. Thin streams of smoke ran from his nostrils.

"The berangat is very valuable, Mister Richard. I believe it is a wind monkey."

Freeman said, "I'm not yet familiar with wind monkeys, Pak. Does Bapak wish to explain?"

Sukino drew on the cigarette, exhaling smoke as he began to speak. "The story of the wind monkey comes originally from Sumatra," he said solemnly. "It was told to me a long time ago by a Buginese sailor. Of course, everyone knows that monkeys—indeed, all animals—have magic. But the magic of the wind monkey is especially strong. What a man first notices about the creature—the thing that gives it away—is that it has the interesting habit of vanishing whenever the wind touches it. But that is only a small part of what it can do. If a man succeeds in catching one, he can learn to use its magic for doing good—for his family and village."

"But all monkeys are hard to see in the wind," Freeman said. "And there are no berangat in Sumatra."

Sukino shrugged. "So Sumatran wind monkeys are different. This is a Kutai wind monkey." He paused to sip his tea, making a loud *zooping* sound with his lips. Then he said, "As for ordinary monkeys in the wind—well, they may be hard to see, but I think they cannot disappear."

Freeman was still thinking about the difficulties he and his men had had trying to follow berangat on windy days. He looked at Nurdin, and Nurdin looked away. "So," he said matter-of-factly, "Nurdin was planning all along to capture a berangat."

Nurdin's body went rigid, his eyes widening as he turned to his boss. "No, Mister Richard, no!" he cried. "The first time I watched berangat, I knew from the way they looked and moved that they had great magic. You saw it, too—I could tell from the way you talked about them. Soon after that, I saw them vanish in the wind. But I did not yet know of the wind monkey! Pak Sukino told me only a month ago!" He looked imploringly at the dukun, who nodded. "Then I was thinking about berangat and wind monkeys every day. And in the week after Mister Richard's departure, one day a big wind came up and the berangat vanished once more, and then I was *certain* they were wind monkeys!"

Sukino leaned forward with a conspiratorial air, resting his forearms against his thighs. "When Nurdin told me of the Mentoko wind monkeys, I advised him to capture one. Only one, I said, for it isn't good to be greedy. I told him Mister Richard would not miss one monkey. We discussed how much the monkey could mean to our village: for two years running now the hot season is too dry—bad for *ladang*—and we must buy rice from Samarinda; the old muezzin of the mosque, a very holy man, keeps getting sick, and it takes me longer each time to cure him. What's more, there are rumors that the Pertamina oil company will abandon the drilling sites to the south and everyone will go back to Samarinda and Balikpapan, to Java and Bali and Sulawesi. I ask you: what will happen to our shops and eating places?"

The old man sat back with a cold smile.

"So I rode the big boat to Samarinda and hired a Dayak tribesman from up the Mahakam River to trap us a wind monkey." Pride broadened his smile. "Nurdin followed the berangat to their sleeping place, and before dawn the Dayak spread a net on the ground under the tree, covered it with leaves, and placed a lot of ripe rambutan fruit on it. We hid. As the sun rose, the male came down to snatch the fruit, the Dayak pulled the cord—ha! We had him!" Sukino's eyes flashed as he relived the triumph. "The Dayak, he had such trouble getting the animal into his sack—later he demanded we pay twenty thousand extra because he'd been bitten! I told him, 'No deal.' A good thing the stupid savage had never heard of wind monkeys or he would have charged us ten times as much to begin with!"

Sukino slapped his thigh and laughed. Nurdin chuckled softly.

"Just five days ago we got him," added the dukun, lighting another cigarette. Nurdin lit up, too, and within seconds the odor of cloves permeated the room. It was a sweet, cloying smell that in a small enclosed space could bring a nonsmoker to the verge of swooning.

Freeman turned to look out of the window at the skinny figure in the prahu. So that was why Burhan had been so eager to go downstream again right away: they'd just caught Grinner and he couldn't stand to be away from the action. Turning back to the two men sipping their tea and puffing their cigarettes, Freeman felt the rage finally beginning to build inside him. It was over now. The explanation was over, the work was over, his career was over before it had begun. He looked from Sukino's smug face to Nurdin's pained one.

"So now what?" he asked, no longer trying to blunt the edge on his voice. Though he had intended it as a rhetorical question, he knew there would be some rehearsed answer. He kept looking at Nurdin, but it was Sukino who spoke.

"Mister understands, I trust, that we have no intention of disrupting his work. Nurdin has contracted with me to watch over the wind monkey in his absence, so that Mister can resume his work right away. And so, everything is pleasantly resolved and there is really nothing more to bother about . . . except for one inconsequential matter that I now take it upon myself to mention to Mister, with all due respect: that is, under no foreseeable circumstances can the wind monkey be returned to the forest."

Freeman trembled. Should he bother trying to explain it to Sukino, or should he just get up and walk out? He was so furious with Nurdin that he thought the latter course might be the wiser. But he stayed. He felt too alone to go just yet.

"It wouldn't matter," he said.

The dukun's eyebrows arched, but Nurdin's expression did not change. He understood.

"It wouldn't matter," Freeman repeated, "if Pak released Grinner back to his troop. The capture has made them fearful; now they run away whenever I meet them. And they will keep running for three months or four or six— who knows how many? And I don't have even a single month to wait for them to lose their fear. I have enough money left for only six months of work, and each of those months must yield useful information like the previous six to make a full year's knowledge of berangat ways. Anything less will not make a Ph.D. dissertation." He could hear the fury rising in his voice. "Without a Ph.D. degree, I cannot become a professor of zoology. *Do you understand?*"

The American looked into Sukino's face. He saw there a profound perplexity. In spite of himself, he knew exactly what the old man was thinking: how strange this Westerner was; how odd it was that he had been paid a fortune to travel halfway around the world to live like a savage in the jungle and scribble in a notebook while he watched monkeys piss and shit and jump around in the trees day after day; how he would be paid an even larger fortune to write many pages about the monkeys and teach students about them; how his anger flashed like fire and disturbed the harmony of the world over trivialities, such as the capture of a single monkey, and how he believed that his prestige and livelihood were somehow jeopardized by such trivialities. What could it matter to this young American if he stopped watching monkeys and went home to America, where everyone was rich, and made a lot of money doing something more sensible?

Freeman rose. "I'm going back to Mentoko," he announced. When Nurdin started to get up, Freeman motioned him to sit.

"There is no longer any work at Mentoko," he told

Nurdin. "Tell that to Burhan. Nurdin and Burhan may keep the prahus until further word from me."

Nurdin nodded, both hurt and relieved that Freeman did not want his company on the ride upstream. He was also pleased to have the use of a prahu, though he knew Freeman had loaned it not out of the goodness of his heart but because it would be impossible for him to hire a kampong man to take him upstream without also hiring the man's prahu.

"Selamat tinggal," Freeman said.

"Selamat jalan, Mister," answered Sukino, and Nurdin more softly.

From the prahu, Burhan waved when he saw Freeman emerge from the house. His boss did not appear to notice. Burhan watched the tall white man walk slowly down the dirt road in the sun toward the kampong.

In the kampong nothing was heard of the American scientist for close to three weeks. Pak Sahar, on his return from Mentoko, reported with amazement that when he had named an outrageously high opening price for the trip, Freeman had not bothered to haggle over a single rupiah, nor had he given Sahar a date for coming back upstream to fetch him. Nurdin was concerned when he heard this, but since there seemed to be nothing he could do about it, he went off into the forest north of the kampong to cut iron-wood shingles with his brother Sudirman.

At first, Burhan assumed that Freeman's threat to provide no more wages at Mentoko was an idle one. After all, there was still six months' worth of project money left. On second thought, however, he wasn't so sure. It occurred to him that it might all be a scheme of Freeman's to steal the remaining project money, but Sukino pointed out that if that were the case, then why hadn't Freeman been stealing the money from the beginning without bothering to pay any wages or follow monkeys? To this, Burhan could only agree and shake his head over his boss's inscrutability.

Burhan and Sukino debated the question of whether or not Freeman would fake the remaining six months of data he claimed he needed. They concurred finally that while a rational man with no other course open to him would surely fake the data, Mister Richard was not entirely rational and might, because of his strange attachment to the berangat, wait at Mentoko until the monkeys calmed down and then start work again.

Since Burhan had no idea how long it would take his boss to send for him, he hitchhiked the thirteen kilometers up to the Pertamina main office to see if they were hiring dock guards or stevedores or men to unload the boxy sky vans that landed daily on an airstrip in the jungle. The official he spoke to, a haughty Javanese fellow with long curved nails on his pinky fingers, told him to inquire again next month about a dock guard position that might be open. This excited Burhan tremendously; he had always envied the dock guards their smart uniforms and their work, which consisted mainly of sitting around playing dominoes in a little office by the river. Glad to have something to look forward to for a whole month, he hitched a ride on a muddy flatbed truck back to the kampong and walked out to Nurdin's house, where he avoided his own wife and children by sitting in Déwi's kitchen, slurping cup after cup of sweet tea. From there he could watch Pak Sukino propitiate the wind monkey by arranging *mardarah* branches in various configurations before the cage in the backyard and chanting in Old Kutai dialect and the smattering of Arabic he knew.

The hot season had arrived roughly on schedule, and the monotony of the days increased as showers and downpours came less frequently. The brown river fell at least fifteen feet and grew sluggish, occasionally lacking enough force to keep the sea from pushing its way upstream with a load of debris from the sawmills on the delta. The kampong roads were rarely muddy, and the swallows sailed and swooped along the riverbanks in greater numbers to harvest the crops of insects flushed from the vegetation by the less frequent rains. The wife of Yatna, seller of salted fish at the morning market, gave birth to another daughter on her fifth attempt at a son, but the infant died after two days. A band of male kra raided Pak Soetrisno's garden at the eastern edge of the kampong, cleaning him out of yams and cucumbers. Pak Tangké, the old muezzin, recovered his voice long enough to wail prayers over the little mosque's crackling loud-speaker for a few days, then lapsed into illness again.

It had been exactly two weeks and five days since Free-man's departure, when Pak Sukino, squatting at the whet-stone on his verandah to sharpen his parang, looked up and spied his nine-year-old grandson, Yan, racing barefoot up the road toward him. Yan liked to hang around the dock in the kampong, and by the time the boy stood panting at the edge of the verandah, his grandfather had guessed he had run all the way from there.

"What's the news, boy?"

"Pak, the white man is in the kampong; he left a suitcase with Darsono the dock guard and is coming to see Pak."

Sukino handed Yan the glass of water he had been drink-ing from. "And how did Mister get downstream?"

The boy downed the water in one draught and swiped at his dripping chin. "He came down with Hari and Yunis, who were hand-logging above Mentoko. He hailed them on their way down; they thought he would yell at them for logging too close to Mentoko, but he only wanted a ride."

Frowning, Sukino stood up and sheathed his parang. "Did Mister tell Yan he was coming here?"

"Oh, no, Pak. Darsono told me."

Sukino's frown relaxed as he took a drag on the cigarette stuck to his lower lip. For Freeman to have sent ahead word of his visit would have been very rude, implying that he considered himself an extremely important guest who warranted elaborate preparation by his host.

"Well," Sukino said, "I'd better go tell Yan's grandmother to put the kettle on."

"He's not coming until after lunch, Pak. First he goes to Nurdin and Burhan."

"Ah, it is like that." Drawing his parang, the dukun examined its blade with a callused thumb and squatted again at the whetstone. "Yan said Mister brought a suitcase with him?"

"Yes, Pak."

"I want Yan to go tell the district head and the village headman about Mister, just in case Darsono forgot to. And be sure to tell them I sent you."

"Yes, Pak. Thank you, Pak."

The boy took off down the road at full speed as his grandfather ran the parang blade along the whetstone with short, expert strokes.

Around noon, when his wife, Ita, brought him his lunch of noodles and eggs, Sukino told her that the sky did not want to rain until evening. She replied that she hoped the American tuan would come and go in time for her to walk down to the afternoon market to buy tomatoes and *kankung* for the evening meal. Resting a hand on his shoulder as he began to eat, she waited for a response. She had noticed that he had chain-smoked ever since informing her of the tuan's visit; now she mentioned the evening meal in the same sentence with the tuan so that her husband would have something else to respond to if he did not want to talk about the tuan. Eventually, between mouthfuls of noodles, Sukino told her that rice with a little onion would be fine if she couldn't get tomatoes or kankung. She watched him eat for a while to make sure he had nothing to add, then went back into the kitchen to eat her own lunch.

The American's tall figure appeared on the road in midafternoon. Calling to Ita, Sukino went out onto the verandah. By the time Freeman had reached the twisted *binuang* tree in front of the house of Mursan the puppet-maker, it was evident that he was walking at a relaxed pace with his customary long strides, swinging his arms absentmindedly. Sukino thought it a good sign. Perhaps the harmony of the world would not be too badly disturbed today, after all.

The two men greeted each other with broad smiles and a firm handshake. Freeman took out a handkerchief to wipe the sweat from his beard. When they were seated inside, Ita appeared in a fresh sarong to serve sweetened tea. Sukino lit a cigarette.

He said, "The sky does not want to rain until evening."

"That's good for the afternoon market, Pak," Freeman replied.

"Yes, that's so. But I'm afraid this hot season is going to be too dry again."

"I hope not, Pak. I hope there will be sufficient rain."

The dukun nodded gravely. "Yes, so do I." He started to bring his cup to his lips, but paused to remove a gnat that had landed in it. Wiping his fingers on his sarong, he looked up at Freeman. "Mister has already seen Nurdin and Burhan?"

"Yes, Pak."

"How are they?"

"Fine. Nurdin and Sudirman have already sold many ironwood shingles. Burhan seems in good spirits."

Sukino nodded. He smoked for a while, deep in thought. When he finally spoke again, his tone of voice was poised midway between curiosity and indifference.

"Is Mister still angry with them?"

It had not occurred to Sukino to mention himself in this regard, as that would have placed his guest in an uncomfortable position.

"No, Pak," Freeman answered. "Not anymore."

Sukino's eyebrows arched and his lips parted. "Then Mister will take them back to Mentoko?"

"No, Pak. There is no work at Mentoko."

"No work? Then what has Mister been doing up there these past weeks?"

"Just thinking," said Freeman. "Having a last chat with the forest."

Sukino's brow furrowed as he lifted his cup to his lips again. The suitcase, then, meant what it had appeared to mean.

"So Mister is leaving Mentoko for good?"

"Yes, Pak. Darsono the dock guard is waiting in the kampong to drive me up to Kilo Thirteen. I'm booked on the sky van to Balikpapan later this afternoon."

The dukun smoked in silence for a while.

He said, "But you are no longer angry with the men?"

"Not anymore, Pak." Leaning back in his chair, Freeman folded his arms across his chest. "Does Bapak have any news about the wind monkey?"

Sukino's face fell, but then quickly recovered its stoic calm. "The wind monkey is a fake," he said.

"A fake?"

"It is like this, Mister Richard. The berangat were all

possessed by forest *hantu*—spirits. These hantu made the berangat hide when the wind blew, tricking Nurdin and Burhan into believing that the monkeys were genuine wind monkeys. As soon as we captured the male, his hantu departed; now he has only ordinary monkey magic."

The dukun stubbed out his cigarette in the ashtray. Looking into Freeman's eyes, he smiled gently and said, "Mister does not believe in hantu."

Freeman held the eye contact for a moment, then looked away at a gecko racing across the wall. It was a question disguised as a statement—not so concealed that the American had missed it, but just enough to have softened its naïveté.

"Actually," said Freeman, "we Westerners also have hantu. I've been thinking about them lately. They live inside our hearts. Sometimes, when we see the great magic of the world, they make our hearts ache with longing for it, so that we feel we must capture it and own it, perhaps find a way to use it to our own advantage. Some of these hantu have good consequences for a person, others bad. It depends on the hantu and the person."

Intense concentration had frozen Sukino's smile. "We too are sometimes entered by hantu—some good, some bad," he said. "Has Mister ever come across an Indonesian hantu?"

"Not yet, Pak. It may not be possible for me to have contact with them the way Bapak does. But from what I've learned of them, they don't seem so different from our Western hantu."

The dukun's mouth lost most of its smile, but his eyes twinkled. He nodded. "What Mister says is good, in my opinion. I will think it over." He continued to nod with satisfaction. It both surprised and pleased him to hear the expert of Western scientific magic say that he believed in hantu. Once, a Pertamina official from Jakarta had told him that many white people and even some educated Indonesians thought hantu did not exist, a notion he found preposterous.

"So things are all right again between Mister and his men?"

"Yes, Pak. Everything is settled. I gave Nurdin one prahu and Burhan the other. There were a lot of things at Mentoko I couldn't take with me, so the men will go upstream tomorrow to fetch them and then divide them among their families and friends. I also gave the men letters of recommendation in Indonesian and English."

"Excellent," said Sukino, rising along with his guest. "Mister Richard is very generous."

They went out onto the verandah and looked off past Mursan's house and the binuang tree toward the river. Heat rose along the road and fields, making everything shimmer. It was an appropriate moment for Freeman to offer the dukun a small parting gift, but he had not bothered to bring any gifts this time. He had already given Sukino and the men Grinner, who would fetch a good price as a pet from some well-off Pertamina official.

Sukino asked him, "Will Mister become a professor now?"

Freeman shook his head. "It will be very difficult, Pak. Perhaps I will do something else. I need to think it over for a while."

The dukun nodded. He could not imagine why it would be hard for an American to become a professor if that was what he wanted, but figured the young man must have his reasons for saying so. "The future is unpredictable," was all he said to Freeman. But to himself he said, May Mister someday find a way to capture the magic of the world.

Grasping the hand that Sukino extended, Freeman said, "Selamat tinggal, Pak."

"Selamat jalan, Mister Richard. Until we meet again."

Before going into the house for another cup of tea and a cigarette, Sukino watched Freeman stride down the road toward the kampong until the image of the young man's body was distorted by the heat.

# LAST STAND

Wartono Romli sat as still as the batiked herons on his Javanese dress shirt, his small dark eyes shifting from one diner to another. The Bertrams and Levins were already eating, but he could not bring himself to do so without verbal permission from his host.

Douglas Bertram looked up from his veal parmigiana and realized he had forgotten the Indonesian custom. "Oh, I'm sorry, Wartono—please eat."

Wartono smiled, revealing teeth yellowed by a lifetime of cloved cigarettes. "Thank you, Mister Doug." Holding his veal steady with his fork as though it were a dagger, he cut off a small piece and pushed it with the fork onto his spoon in the Asian manner.

Clarice Bertram stared at their guest for a long moment. She took a sip of wine and said brightly, "Doug tells me it's been quite a while since the last time you were overseas."

Wartono nodded. "Almost fifty years ago. I was in Java taking my botany degree at Bogor—it was called Buitenzorg in those days—and the Rijksherbarium at Leiden brought me there to identify botanical specimens from Borneo. I did not want to go, but I was a Dutch subject then."

"And your work has been mostly in Borneo?" Bob Levin asked between forkfuls of salad.

"Yes. East Borneo—Kalimantan Timur Province."

"And you teach in Jakarta?"

"For a time I taught there. When the government made Mulawarman University at Samarinda, the capital of Kalimantan Timur, they let me go there to be closer to my forest."

Harriet Levin, a colleague of Doug Bertram's at the university, took the stem of her wineglass between thumb and forefinger and gently rotated it, watching the swirl of its contents. "What's your interest in our California flora that you've come all this way now?" she asked.

"Sequoia," said Wartono. "The big trees. Mister Doug told me he will study them. In Jakarta."

Harriet glanced at their host.

"I was in Jakarta last month for a conservation conference," Bertram explained. "When I met Wartono, I told him I'd spent a year's postdoc in East Kalimantan studying dipterocarps but that ever since then I'd been working on conifers here. I mentioned the new project on sequoias and Wartono said he'd like to see them, so I invited him to visit us."

Harriet looked again at Bertram. She knew how much

he had left unsaid just then. Though their eyes met for only an instant, there passed between them a full acknowledgment of the irony of Wartono's visit.

Bertram resumed eating, careful not to look at Clarice. In a way, Clarice had created that irony, for it was she who had brought about the change in his plans to build his career on the Borneo research: had he not relented on the issue, she never would have married him. He could hardly blame her for not wanting to spend a good part of her life either separated from him or living in the remote rain forest, but his understanding had not made the decision any easier. Once he had finally come to that decision, the transition it entailed had been at least as difficult. The university had hired him as a tropical botanist, and so the switch to domestic research had been a precarious one for professional as well as emotional reasons. *Thank God for Harriet Levin* was a frequent thought of Bertram's nowadays. Not only had she helped him develop a new research project close to home but she had also smoothed things over with the rest of the botany department.

Looking at the little man sitting across the table, Bertram felt a twinge of regret. He envied Wartono's spending his life in the forests of the big trees—the very smell of them seemed to have worked its way into his skin over the years. The things that man must know! Only toward the end of his postdoc had Bertram begun to get a sense of the true richness and complexity of those great trees, of the distinct "personalities" they had acquired in the course of millions of years of evolution. Now he had to start again from scratch with the sequoias.

Harriet asked Wartono about his interest in sequoias, and the old man sat back in his chair, searching for the right words. Finally he said, "Very big, very old trees are special.

They have been most important in my life. One even saved my life."

Interested queries came simultaneously from the four Americans. Wartono was pensive. He sipped his soft drink.

"Well," he said. "It was during Second World War. I was in the forest with Laduh, my Dayak man, on River Mahakam near Tenggarong, upstream of Samarinda. One day we heard very loud noise, like bombs. I sent Laduh to Tenggarong; he returned with news of Japanese in Samarinda. I thought what must we do. I knew a place far upstream with big *tebu hitam* tree. So we paddled to where our prahu could not go anymore, and we hid the prahu in bamboo and walked into the forest to look for the tebu hitam. We walked a whole day and still we were not there yet: I was forgetting where the tebu hitam was. But that night, with the forest very quiet, we heard it—it was saying to us, 'this way, this way.' And next morning we found it. We put our tent under it and stayed there almost three years. No one found us. We lived off the forest; Laduh climbed trees to get the fruit and there were edible vines near the river. We dug roots; we shot many wild pigs."

"What kind of weapon?" asked Bob Levin.

"Bow and arrows. Poisoned arrows. Laduh knew how to make the poison and was a good shot. I was not so good." The old man gave a self-effacing grin. "We went back to Tenggarong after there was more bombing. The Japanese were gone; there were English and Australians. Later the Dutch came back and we went to war against them."

For a time no one looked up; silverware clanked softly against plates, napkins moved between laps and mouths. Bertram was both amused and disappointed by Wartono's story. It amused him that Wartono, in his isolation and desperate need, had been fooled by the same rain forest sounds that Bertram himself had so often mistaken for voices: the grumbling of unseen streams, breezes and animals rustling the canopy, the rooting of wild pigs, the chatter of monkeys. He was disappointed, on the other hand, to find that Wartono did not have the discipline to eschew the inevitable anthropomorphic fancies that scientists were heir to. Indeed, it appeared that Wartono was not really a scientist at all, but an animist with a science degree.

Later, Bertram walked the Levins to their car. It was an August evening in the Sacramento Valley and the temperature was still over a hundred degrees. Bob ducked into the car to start the air conditioner.

"Not much for shoptalk, is he?" Harriet said to Bertram. "How did he handle himself at the conference?"

"He wasn't at the conference," said Bertram. "I'd missed lunch and ducked out of the conference to get a bite at a little restaurant down the street, where I met him; he was in Jakarta visiting relatives and noticed my name tag from the conference. In Indonesia, it's common courtesy to exchange addresses with new acquaintances and invite them to visit you. I never expected him to show up."

Harriet started to reach for the car door handle, then paused. "Doug, am I crazy or did Wartono say that a tree spoke to him?"

Bertram chuckled. "I had a few hallucinations of my own in the rain forest, but I never gave in to them. I've met a few other scientists like Wartono over there: a thin veneer of knowledge on top of a basically prescientific outlook. In Wartono's case, I'm not surprised."

"Why's that?"

"Family background. His mother was a Javanese peasant and his father was a Dayak who worked as a guide for the Royal Dutch Shell surveyors. The Dayaks are hunter-gatherers in the Bornean interior. Interesting combination of parental influences: traditional Javanese mysticism and Dayak animism."

Harriet slid into the passenger's seat and lowered her window as Bertram leaned down toward her to catch the blast of cool air. "I don't envy you having to show him around," she said. "Pretty dull, I imagine."

Bertram sighed. "I ought to be more forgiving, but this sort of burns me. I expect a little stimulating discussion when I host a colleague."

"Maybe he'll still come up with something worthwhile."

"I was more hopeful before the talking tree story." Bertram straightened up into the hot air and took a step back from the car. "I'm up to my keester in work right now, anyway. I'll show him the study site tomorrow and hope he finds whatever it is he came for. If I get any useful insights out of him, I'll consider it a bonus."

Harriet gave Bertram a sympathetic smile as Bob engaged the clutch and eased the car out of the driveway.

Having made the long drive down to Redwood Canyon twice before, Bertram was ready for the monotony of the flatlands between Sacramento and Fresno. What he hadn't expected was a steady stream of radio music uninterrupted by conversation. Three hours into the trip, Wartono had still not said a word to him. Much of the time the man's eyes were closed. Bertram spoke to him several times without getting a response; Wartono seemed lost in some sort of meditation.

When they had passed through Fresno and traversed the miles of orchards to where the Sierra foothills swung into view around a bend, Wartono suddenly opened his eyes and looked around him. Bertram gazed ahead to the tawny hills baking in the August sun. Straw-colored grass and summer-browned wild oats cloaked their sloping shoulders; dark patches of rock outcroppings mimicked the chaparral vegetation that would soon appear. Some miles farther on, the dark patches turned from gray to dark green and brown and rust where the rock was replaced by live oaks and manzanita, first in clumps, then scattered uniformly over the undulating terrain.

Wartono maintained his silence through the little plateau villages and valley hamlets, but he seemed to grow more and more alert as they climbed into the wild country. At two thousand feet they passed the first ponderosa pines towering over the scrub. Soon frequent breaks in the wall of roadside vegetation revealed broad vistas of valley and surrounding mountains blanketed with pine and fir. As the car slowed into the rangers' checkpoint at the entrance to Sequoia and Kings Canyon National Parks, the Indonesian spoke.

"This sequoia, yes?"

Bertram nodded. Broken off low on the ruddy bole, the old tree's height was negligible but its immense girth made it craterlike.

"Wider than an Indonesian house, Mister Doug!"

"You'll see undamaged ones soon," said Bertram. "Watch the forest for patches of red."

Wartono's sharp eyes spotted the enormous trunks looming in the forest understory like rusty behemoths, their upper boles and narrow tubular crowns obscured by the foreground of smaller trees. Bertram had to watch for the inconspicuous turnoff to Redwood Canyon. Where a paved road branched off to Hume Lake on the left, he turned right onto a dirt apron resembling a turnout and coasted to a narrow unpaved road whose entrance was hidden from the main road by dense firs. A small sign stated: REDWOOD

CANYON—SNOW REMOVAL DISCONTINUED BEYOND THIS POINT—PASS AT OWN RISK.

"We're heading down to the study site now," Bertram told Wartono. "In a minute you'll see a burned-out area to your left."

The road wound sharply along a slope, with steep rocky terrain on the right. Soon they were looking down an embankment into a most peculiar stretch of forest. It was a large stand of Douglas fir, singed and defoliated by a vigorous ground fire. The trees were so dense that they formed a continuous network of interlocking branches; the late-morning sun was still low enough to shine obliquely through the latticework, producing a diffuse, back-lit glow around each silhouetted bough. The effect was magical, ghostly.

"Not much burning like this in the rain forest," Wartono commented as the burn slipped from view.

"Yes, but it's quite common in these dry forests. I'll tell you more about it while we hike through the canyon."

The road leveled off onto the floor of the canyon and curved past a chalet-style ranger station. Beyond this was a large patch of cleared ground that might once have been a gravel parking lot, where they stopped and got out. Bertram sat on the car's rear bumper to lace up his hiking boots. Wartono removed his rubber sandals and waited. As they started down the trail, Bertram saw on the soles of his companion's feet the massive calluses that protected him from the sharpest stones and brambles.

Bertram watched as Wartono squatted to examine the pale purple flowers of mountain lupine and the fuzzy horsemint leaves, which felt like flannel to the touch. Did he really speak to the horsemint plants as he stroked them? Crossing the first stream, Wartono stopped to listen to its delicate eddies in the intense silence of the canyon. He watched a chipmunk dart among the fallen trees and rock outcroppings along the bank, then turned back to regard something in the stream. Bertram noticed a sudden uneasiness in his bearing.

"What is it, Wartono?"

"There. You see? Very strange. . . ."

He was pointing at a dense stand of bracken fern and horsetails. Bertram knew instantly it was the latter that had caught his eye. They were indeed an odd sight: shiny, asparaguslike plants of repeating segments, projecting from the streambed in a swath of evil-looking spikes. They lanced upward, impaling tiny conifer seedlings.

"I think these know sequoias," Wartono said, staring. "Perhaps they are here to be near the sequoias."

Bertram shifted his weight. "Well," he ventured, "those horsetails are primitive plants; they're probably the only existing species that was here back when the sequoias covered the western slopes of the Sierras. Of course, they grow in other places, too."

Wartono smiled. "Perhaps all seek sequoias, but only some find."

They were surrounded by dizzying slopes. Scanning the forest along the ridge to the north, Bertram saw a familiar gap where the intensely azure sky seemed nearer than the trees. His guest was about to get his first full view of a sequoia. Wartono turned to where the trail cut sharply around a bluff that hid the forest beyond. "There," he said firmly. "The big trees." He walked toward them.

My God, thought Bertram as they rounded the curve, how could he have known? For coming into view was a great wall of dried mud and tangled roots—the base of a fallen sequoia—and thirty yards beyond stood one of its colossal brothers, dwarfing the lofty sugar pine that was its nearest neighbor. Bertram paused at the uprooted base to point out the shallowness of the root system, but Wartono had already drifted down the trail toward the living tree. Bertram followed and together they stood gazing in silence along the gargantuan bole. From an incurved base resembling the foot of an enormous elephant, the deeply fissured trunk rose one hundred and fifty feet into the sky before sprouting its oddly tubular crown. The only sounds were the screeches of jays and the chattering of a lone squirrel, whose acrobatics in the sugar pine set a high bough to rocking. One of the tree's big pendulous cones fell to the earth with a thud, but Wartono did not notice. He was transfixed by the sight of the sequoia.

He said, "This one very old, yes?"

"Maybe several thousand years," Bertram answered. "The big ones are all very old. Except for bristlecone pines, whose growth is severely habitat-limited, they're the oldest living things on the planet."

"And the largest, perhaps?"

Bertram nodded. "The coast redwoods and some rain forest trees get taller, and there are a couple of species with greater girths, but for sheer massiveness *Sequoiadendron giganteum* is the largest. Magnificent trees." He took a deep breath and raised a hand to his brow. "Let's keep walking; I feel a little dizzy standing still."

Wartono looked at him. "You too?"

"I've felt this way each time I've been down here. Probably from the variations in altitude."

They headed into the canyon proper, the true preserve of the sequoias. With their columnar crowns permitting close proximity, some of the trees stood in pairs, even small clumps of three or four. Most stood solitary, like monstrous sentinels. Scattered throughout the canyon, in the huge shadows of their parents, were middle-aged trees hundreds of years old, as well as poles, saplings, and thousands of seedlings. Here and there lay uprooted sequoias with root systems like tank-sized collages of driftwood. The incurved bases of the standing trees made them appear rootless, as though they had been set down and balanced there by some titanic hand.

Again Bertram complained of light-headedness, and the two men sat down on the trunk of a fallen fir. The American rubbed his eyes with the heels of his hands.

Wartono asked, "What will you work on here?"

"I'm going to study how the spatial distribution and age-grading of the sequoias are affected by fire-induced germination of seeds."

"*Fire-induced*—what is this?"

"In dry coniferous forests, a number of tree species have adapted to periodic ground fires. Sequoia seedlings need sunlight and contact with bare mineral soil to grow; fires provide both by eliminating competing trees and clearing away the underbrush."

Wartono was perplexed. "These sequoias do not fear fire?"

"No, they love it. You see, the trees don't shed their cones until there's a fire. They accumulate cones in huge numbers over time, and when a ground fire sweeps through, the heat dries out the cones and opens them up. A week or two later the cones drop and their seeds germinate in the topsoil, which has been cleared and enriched by the fire. A lot of seedlings are sacrificed in a fire, but the reseeding more than makes up for that."

Looking off into the forest of giants, Wartono took a cigarette lighter and a clove-scented cigarette from his shirt pocket. He cupped a hand around the flame as he lit the cigarette. "Are many other creatures also killed by these fires?"

"Quite a few. The adult sequoias almost always survive, though. Their outer bark is so thick that they usually get off with just a singed trunk. Even when an injury allows fire to get into the wood, they rarely die." Bertram's eyes searched the forest. He pointed at a sequoia fifty yards from the trail. "There's a good example. The base has been completely hollowed out by fire, but it'll probably live and bear cones for centuries."

After some moments, Wartono said, "What *do* sequoias fear, Mister Doug?"

"Not much anymore. A gradual warming of the climate killed most of them and drastically restricted their range. Then we logged them pretty aggressively in the late nineteenth century, destroyed about a third of the population. When the lumber company scouts discovered them, their eyes must have lit up at the number of board feet each tree could yield. But it would take a week for a team of four lumberjacks with axes and crosscut saws to fell a big one, and when they'd finally get it down, as likely as not the bole would shatter into worthless debris. The heartwood turned out to be weak and brittle—not very useful commercially—and the intact logs were just too big to be handled efficiently. By World War One the logging was over."

"Long time ago," Wartono murmured. He flicked his lighter, watching it snap into flame. "But maybe for such old trees, not so long. . . ." He closed his eyes and put a hand to his brow. When he opened his eyes again, he gazed up into the open canopy of this forest that was so different from the forests he knew. "So," he said, "not many sequoias left, yes?"

"A mere remnant of the former population," Bertram replied. "That's the main thing endangering them now: their small numbers." The American stretched his legs out in front of him and crossed his ankles. The palms of his

hands rested on the log. "Most of them are here in Redwood Canyon—I like to think they've made their last stand
here. That's why the Park Service doesn't publicize the
place. We haven't seen a soul in over an hour, but some of
the smaller groves just a few miles away are overrun with
tourists right now. Tourists are rough on sequoias: they
tromp on seedlings and take cones home as souvenirs. That's
one of the reasons the Park Service keeps quiet about the
canyon."

"And the other reasons?" Wartono asked.

Bertram did not speak for a moment. "Interesting story,"
he said. "When I came up with the idea for the study, I went
to the Park Service people and they showed me a few of
the smaller groves inundated with tourists. They must have
known I couldn't work there; on the other hand, Redwood
Canyon is ideal, but they never mentioned it. I found it on
the map by chance, got curious, and went looking. I drove
past it a few times—you saw how poorly marked the
entrance is—and when I finally got down here, I was
stunned. I went back to the park superintendent and asked
him why he hadn't told me. He hemmed and hawed and
said it slipped his mind. Then he tried to scare me away
from it. By the way, Wartono, make sure that cigarette is
out when you're done with it."

Wartono looked at Bertram through slitted eyes. He
dropped the cigarette and crushed it against the ground with
a callused foot.

Suddenly Bertram rose and started walking. Wartono
followed. They went south at a right angle to the trail, out
among the big trees, through the endless patchwork created
by the sun on the forest floor.

"Mister Doug," Wartono said as they walked, "how did
this man try to frighten you?"

Bertram appeared to be listening to something above

them in one of the big trees. Straining to hear, Wartono noticed a faint rumbling. He distinctly felt the vibrations, but he could not tell where they were coming from.

Bertram answered, "He told me about some scientists who died here in the canyon. One was a Park Service man in the 1930s. Then, about twenty years ago, there was a team of three from UCLA."

"How did they die?"

"In ground fires."

They strolled through a sunlit patch and back into shadow. A gentle breeze had come up suddenly, rustling the long boughs of the sugar pines.

"At first I thought he was lying," Bertram continued. "But I checked the old newspapers and found it was the truth. There was evidence that these people had set the fires themselves: in both cases, there was no one else in the canyon at the time and the days were sunny summer days— no lightning, little or no wind through the morning. It was reported that strong winds picked up suddenly and spread the fires. I think the superintendent believes that these scientists illegally set controlled burns for their research and weren't prepared for shifting winds. I'd told him that my project involved fire-induced germination, so he might have been suspicious I'd try the same thing." Frowning, Bertram shook his head. "Hard to believe, though. How could those researchers have been so careless?"

They had stopped before a cluster of old sequoias bunched so closely together that the sun was blotted out over a stretch of forest the size of a small lake. There were five trees, their bases charred all round and the lower trunks scarred with black pockmarks where fire had eaten into their thick hides. The largest stood a bit forward and to the west, like the leader of a phalanx of ancient forest gods. Fire had hollowed out its base, leaving the black mouth of a cave.

Before it and elsewhere among the trees lay a clutter of dead branches accumulated since the last fire.

Peering upward, Wartono breathed through clenched teeth. Sequoia foliage shimmered in the afternoon breeze. The sight reminded him of wind playing across the surface of a lake, teasing forth little eddies and ripples. As this notion floated through his mind, a delicious calm settled over him. High above, vast clouds were approaching in a sky that had been empty moments before. The shade cast by the sequoias deepened, enveloping him.

Bertram took his arm and guided him toward the hollow tree trunk. "Let's go inside," the American whispered. "It's really weird in there—I looked into one of the smaller ones last time."

They were at the entrance to the great tree. At once Wartono realized that his feeling of peace was fast turning into one of emptiness, as though his mind and will were being sucked out of him. With a chill, he recognized the sensation. He had experienced it once before while standing in a partially logged Bornean forest beneath the great remaining *merantis, kapurs, tengkawangs*—the old proud giants that had seen their kin brought down and mutilated. But the sensation was much stronger now. He felt powerless.

"Mister Doug," he mumbled, tongue thick like a drunken man's, "we must go . . . the trees do not want us. . . ."

"Wartono!" Bertram hissed into his ear. "It *wants* us to come inside! Can't you hear it?"

Wartono saw that his companion's eyes were glazed over. The young American was looking stupidly into the darkness of the great hollow, his expression blank as a cow's. The rumbling came again; Wartono felt it course through his body. Then, in one awful moment, the sensation became sound. A great voice, deep and beguiling, beckoned.

*This way, this way. . . .*

Wartono raised a gnarled hand and slapped his own face. He reached for where Bertram's arm should have been, but it was too late; the American had vanished, swallowed up in the blackness. Swooning, Wartono thrust out his arms and clutched at the rough bark of the hollow's rim to keep from being drawn in. With a grunt, he pushed off from the tree and stumbled backward. A rock sent him sprawling into the pile of fallen branches; jagged wood tore his arms, twigs lashed his eyes. He looked back at the tree and saw a tiny flame flickering in its maw. All of a sudden he remembered placing his lighter on the fallen fir and Bertram sitting there with his hand resting beside it.

The flame drifted out of view. Then the hollow began to glow a lovely soft red in the shade from clouds that were moving fast overhead. The glow flickered and brightened until the hollow's outline sharpened from the illumination within. Wartono felt the rumbling cease. His mind was clear again.

Someone screamed.

The huge tree's mouth spat fire. Bertram, his flannel shirt aflame, shot from the hollow and tumbled in a burning heap onto the matting of dried foliage between the tree and the spot where Wartono lay. Bertram struggled to his feet, but the flames had already ignited his beard and hair. Shrieking, he staggered back and forth in front of the sequoia. Wartono thought of using his own shirt to douse the fire, but suddenly the flaming mass headed straight at him. He clawed frantically at the surrounding tangle, throwing himself clear of the branches just as Bertram came crashing into them. He scrambled to his feet, hearing the dry wood rapidly catch fire, and stumbled away in what he prayed was the direction of the trail. He looked back once over his shoulder to see the heap of debris crackling and whooshing like a bonfire, already sending tentacles of flame along the ground. Its heat draft wavered crazily in the wind.

Wartono found the trail and ran. He felt a sudden pang of guilt about the naïve American's fate, but realized that he could not fault himself for failing to comprehend the sequoias' rage in time. It had taken him many years in his own forest to know the spirits of the old giants—the gentle, the sly, the proud and angry. No one could fathom the most powerful forest spirit on earth in a few hours' time; he had not even known of the trees' past mistreatment until he had already begun to fall under their spell.

Flying along the winding trail, with the wind whipping at the trees around him and the mounting roar of the fire behind, Wartono remembered the ranger station at the mouth of the canyon. He would have to hitch a ride out with the rangers, then find some way of making the long trip north to tell poor Mrs. Bertram the horrible news and get his things. Then home. He had been away too long already.

# LASMI

According to an ancient Indonesian prophecy, a race of white-skinned giants from the West will rule the land for centuries, only to be driven out by little yellow men from the North whose reign will last no longer than a crop of corn. Though the Dutch did rule Java for nearly two hundred years, it was only by comparison that the reign of their Japanese conquerors lasted no longer than a crop of corn. For Lasmi, however, the prophecy of her ancestors came true, for she was born in the West Javan highland town of Ciwidey just two months before the Japanese surrendered to the Allies and the bloody revolution against the resurgent Dutch began. Thus, even as a baby, Lasmi gave Papa reason to believe that his firstborn was a child of destiny. Mama kept silent on the subject of destiny. To her, *destiny* was just a dreamer's word for fate.

Mama's family were *priyayi* elite, descendants of the old Pajajaran royalty who had converted to Islam centuries ago and come to form the class of civil servants under the Dutch. Mama possessed the famous priyayi attributes that were her birthright: fair skin and a narrow, regal face with a long nose; slim shoulders and ample hips from which a sarong or *kain batik* flowed gracefully; a refined knowledge of classical Sundanese arts; a *halus* manner of sophistication and self-restraint. A trick of fate had denied her a priyayi husband, however. Her mother, who would have made sure she got a priyayi husband, died giving birth to her, and her father, unable to care for his infant daughter, gave the girl into the care of her aunt, the wife of a village headman in the town of Padalarang on the outskirts of Bandung. Mama's father, a pretender to Islam whose parents had married him into a devout Muslim family for its inherited wealth, then fell in love with the beautiful but despised former mistress of a Dutch soldier and took the woman back to his hometown of Ciwidey as his wife. His first wife's family never forgave him this indiscretion, and for years Mama was permitted only occasional brief visits with him. Meanwhile, her uncle treated her poorly, making her a servant in his home despite her wealth. Because Mama greatly feared her uncle, it was not until she was fifteen years old that she broke down and told her father how miserable she was. Her father was stricken with guilt and took her away to Ciwidey. Disillusioned with his own class, he selected a young merchant as her husband. A week before their wedding, a courier arrived from Padalarang with a note of congratulations and a small sum of money from the aunt and uncle who had raised Mama. Mama assumed the money was a wedding gift. Months later she discovered that

her uncle had forged her signature to documents that transferred all her property to him for a sum of money equaling
that which he had given her before the wedding. Though
Papa told her over and over that her uncle was nothing but
a priyayi weasel who maintained his high position by swin-
dling others, Mama always felt that she had been rightfully
punished for the disgrace she had brought upon her ancestors and descendants by marrying an ordinary merchant.

It was not only in occupation that Papa was the opposite
of a priyayi man. He was also passionate, impatient, with
a brash self-assertiveness that often served him well in the
coarse ways of business. His appearance fit his personality:
he was short and stocky, with a large round head, and his
leathery skin was darker than a coconut husk. His eyes were
almond-shaped, the consequence of a great-grandfather's
marriage to a Chinese woman. People sometimes joked that
that was why he was successful in business.

The irony was that Papa, like Mama, had royal Pajajaran
ancestors. But they were the *other* Pajajaran, the black-sheep
nobles who had refused to submit to the Muslim conquerors
from the north coast and fled into the wild mountains of
the Priangan to live simple ascetic lives as keepers of the old
beliefs. Eventually they had emerged from the forests to
take up residence in mountain towns and hamlets and
become merchants and farmers. Papa, who had taken over
his father's batik trade, was unusual in that he was only
second-generation merchant stock. His father's father was
one of the last of the true Sundanese *orang sakti,* a traditional
mystic who lived alone on the top of a wooded hill south
of Ciwidey. When Lasmi was a baby, it was said that her
great-grandfather still possessed the power to change himself into a white tiger, the royal emblem of the Pajajaran
dynasty. Indeed, not long before his death, hunters sighted
a white tiger prowling the forests around Ciwidey. This

was at a time when the local people believed there had been no tigers in the vicinity for more than thirty years.

As an adult, Lasmi could still recall a trip in Papa's Ford pickup truck into the mountains to see Great-Grandfather. She was then four years old. His was a tiny bamboo hut badly in need of new roof thatch, crowded by mango, guava, and banana trees. In the lotus position on the bare earth before the hut he sat, an old man clad only in a loincloth. He had flowing white hair and an ugly beard that sprouted from several moles on his face. He smiled at Lasmi and took her small hands in his rough, bony ones. Several months later, just before he died, Great-Grandfather visited her. He came down into town for the first time in thirty years, traversing the ten miles of hills and valleys barefoot, wearing a threadbare sarong and leaning on a walking stick. Lasmi was napping in her room before supper. When she awoke, he was already gone. Papa sat cross-legged on the floor in the corner, beaming at her. She said, "What is it, Papa?" and he answered, "Great-Grandfather was here; he sat right beside your bed and spoke to you." "Why?" she asked, her mind still clouded with sleep. "Because you're special," Papa said.

When Lasmi was old enough to understand, Papa told her what Great-Grandfather had said to her as she slept. She had inherited the spiritual *kesaktian* of her royal ancestors, a power that would enable her to hear Great-Grandfather speak to her from the spirit world beyond the grave. If she was ever in trouble she was to call on him for aid and guidance. If she did so faithfully, something extraordinary and wonderful would happen someday. Papa was an adept in Sundanese mysticism (although he had inherited only a small amount of Great-Grandfather's kesaktian). Soon he began giving Lasmi lessons in meditation three or four times a week to prepare her for making contact with Great-

Grandfather's spirit. The training lasted four years, during which she was often sleepy in the daytime, for Papa believed that night was the best time for beginners to learn, and he would keep her practicing until dawn. No matter how hard she concentrated, however, Lasmi never really succeeded in making contact with Great-Grandfather. Sometimes, deep in meditation, she sensed his spirit hovering just beyond the borders of her awareness, and she would think of the time years ago when Great-Grandfather had sat by her bed and spoken to her but she had not heard. She began to believe that most of the kesaktian meant for her had settled instead in her brother Nino.

Nino was the youngest of the five children and had never seen Great-Grandfather, but he was the one most open to the influence of the old man's spirit. While still a boy of six and seven, he would run home from his favorite play spot in the big bamboo grove behind the train station and, in a state of great excitement, whisper into Lasmi's ear, "I heard the roar of a white tiger in the forest: it was *Great-Grandfather!*" Lasmi assumed the tiger's roar was the train growling in the distance on its way up from Bandung, but she began to have second thoughts as Nino's susceptibility grew with the years. Once, when he developed a crush on a neighbor's daughter but was too shy to ask her to a *wayang* puppet show in the town square, he went off into the southern hills—to the very hill, Lasmi suspected, where Great-Grandfather had lived—and returned a day later. He went straight to the girl's parents and asked their permission to take her to the wayang. Another time, hiking alone in the forest around Lake Patenggang, he lost his way. After praying to Great-Grandfather for help, he was startled to hear the roar of a tiger nearby. Terrified, he headed in the direction opposite the roar and soon came upon familiar surroundings and found his way home by nightfall.

If Papa failed to develop in Lasmi the kesaktian Great-Grandfather had promised her, he succeeded handsomely in giving her the soul of a merchant. When she wasn't in school, Lasmi could usually be found in Papa's stall at the *pasar,* unrolling bolts of cloth and weighing parcels of tea for customers. (Aside from his batik trade, Papa was a local agent for the state-owned tea plantation near Lake Patenggang.) Occasionally Papa took her to the big pasars in Bandung and Jakarta. Bandung was both exciting and comfortable: nearly everyone was Sundanese like she, and the weather, though warmer and muggier than the mountain crispness of Ciwidey, was not unbearable. Jakarta, on the other hand, was frightening and repulsive, a sprawling, steamy expanse of mosquitoes and fetid canals. It was populated with big fearsome Bataks and loud Minangkabaus from Sumatra, knife-carrying Buginese from Sulawesi, black Ambonese, and a steady stream of poor Javanese migrants from the countryside of central and east Java. Until adolescence, Lasmi assumed she would marry a Ciwidey merchant like Papa and lead a contented life, traveling now and then to Bandung and seldom, if ever, to Jakarta. Marrying a farmer was unthinkable. She did enjoy riding with Papa into the western hills to the little hamlet of Cibodas, where the rice paddies made emerald stairways of the slopes and turned the flooded valleys into cracked mirrors. But when she was old enough to understand misery, her heart would sink at the sight of the farmers trudging knee-deep in mud behind wooden plows, and of their wives, bent low from the waist, harvesting the paddy with their flimsy, finger-length knives so as not to disturb the rice goddess who resided in the grains.

In spite of her regrets, Mama was the perfect merchant's wife. She accompanied Papa to the pasar each day, rising before dawn to cook the day's meals that she would carry along. In the evening, she kept Papa's complicated accounts. She never complained. Like a proper Sundanese couple, Papa made the decisions and Mama abided by them. In certain cases, though, Mama let her wishes be known in no uncertain terms, like the time just before Lasmi's graduation from grade school. In those days Ciwidey had no middle school, and Papa conveniently assumed that grade school would be the extent of Lasmi's education, after which she would be free to help him full-time with his batik and tea businesses. Mama had always assumed that Lasmi would be boarded at her wealthy younger brother's priyayi household in Bandung, where she would attend middle school. Mama had, in fact, already arranged it with him.

"Mun!" Papa barked, using Mama's nickname and slapping the kitchen table for emphasis. "What can Lasmi possibly need with middle school!"

Mama became fierce. "Do you want the poor girl to be an ignorant dolt like—" She caught herself, realizing that Lasmi could hear them from the sitting room.

Papa flushed and stalked off with a contemptuous snort. The argument was over. Papa, so full of bluster and sharp commands, dreamer of lordly Pajajaran dreams, was a paper tiger when Mama stood up to him.

At Pak Massina's fine house on Jalan Pandawa in Bandung, Lasmi quickly became enamored of priyayi life. The setting itself was hardly new, for in those days Jalan Pandawa was practically in the countryside, with rice fields lining one side of the street, along which barefoot farmers led their muddy buffaloes. But in her uncle's house were fine material things, modern conveniences, halus sensibilities. She was allowed to share a bedroom with only one person instead of four. The backyard was smaller than the one in Ciwidey, but it wasn't cluttered with ugly storage sheds reeking of tea and moldy fabric. Bu Massina had twice as many servants as Mama. Each day they placed fresh orchids on the dining table and polished the fine mahogany furniture. In place of the traditional rice room, dark and quiet and into which only Mama and the servant who helped prepare meals were allowed to go, so as not to disturb the sleeping rice goddess, there was a remarkable metal contraption, kept right out in the open in the kitchen, that could be set to disgorge through a spout the precise amount of rice needed for a meal. There was an upright piano in the sitting room and other musical instruments and a professional music teacher who came to the house. Lasmi learned to play the Sundanese harp. Bu Massina never rose before dawn or did any strenuous work, but if she did get tired or sore she called her personal masseuse.

Pak Massina ran the Office of Civilian Records downtown. Each morning at ten, except Sunday, his chauffeur drove him to work in his white Mercedes, and he returned promptly at three, except on Friday, when he came home before lunch to attend the mosque. He was an extremely attractive man—tall, fair-skinned, dignified in bearing— the opposite of Papa. Lasmi idolized him. He didn't smack his lips when he ate, and he dined with European utensils instead of his fingers. Papa always ridiculed people who ate with spoons and forks, but Pak Massina was so expert at it that he made it look perfectly natural.

Lasmi matured into an attractive young woman, with her dark skin, round face, and almond-shaped eyes. Her small mouth gave her a pouting, sensual look and her slanted eyes were sleepy and alluring. She was voluptuous, with the muscular but shapely legs and feet that Sundanese men prized. She saved up her allowance for the Bandung shops, where she bought modern outfits like the ones in the magazines that were always lying around the house. The priyayi boys flocked to her. Papa kept as close tabs on her as he could, periodically interrogating her about the boys she knew. He insisted she spend every weekend in Ciwidey and would drive his battered pickup truck into Bandung on Friday afternoons to fetch her. Before moving to Bandung, Lasmi had never thought to question Papa's social status, but on those Friday afternoons, when she would come out of her room and see him sitting awkwardly in an expensive wing chair and looking uncomfortable in one of his best batik shirts, her heart would sink. She soon realized that she no longer wanted a merchant like Papa for a husband, but a civil servant like her uncle. At the time, she had no inkling that Pak Massina had inherited all his wealth and that his family could never have lived so elegantly on his meager civil servant's salary.

In her last year of middle school Lasmi had a boyfriend. His name was Hari and he was from a priyayi family in Tasikmalaya. Like Lasmi, he was staying with Bandung relations in order to attend school. Though he was only Lasmi's age—fifteen—he looked at least nineteen and had smooth fair skin and a long beautiful nose. Lasmi and Hari often walked together along Jalan Pandawa and bought snacks from the pushcart vendors. Hari was very gentle and halus, and Lasmi was in love with him. The sound of his voice made her heart flutter, and whenever she looked into his dark eyes she forgot everything else in the world. She dreamed of marrying him, but he was still too young to marry. She knew, as well, that Papa would never approve of her marrying a priyayi man. She didn't even have the courage to tell him about Hari; she knew he would rant and rave and make her feel as if she had mortally wounded him. But her thoughts were completely wrapped up in Hari. That, at least, was one way to avoid thinking about her fat old suitor in Ciwidey.

Pak Gedé had had his eye on Lasmi for several years, and

during the summer before her last year at middle school he began paying weekly visits to the house. He was a heavyset middle-aged widower, a beef trader who had become one of the richest men in Ciwidey by buying steers, paying local farmers to fatten them, butchering them, and taking the beef to market in Bandung, Cimahi, and Sukabumi. Whenever he came to visit, Papa would bow and scrape while Mama bustled off into the bedroom to put on a fresh sarong before rushing to the kitchen to brew tea. Mama served him store-bought biscuits. He always brought a present for Lasmi: a gold bracelet, a bright ribbon or rhinestoned barrette for her hair, a sarong of high-quality fabric. Papa would call Lasmi into the sitting room, where Pak Gedé was parked on the sofa with teacup and *kretek* cigarette in hand, his belly spilling onto his lap. After she said, *"Selamat soré,* Pak," and curtsied, Pak Gedé would smile a broad paternal smile and draw from behind his back the gift he had brought. Placing it in Lasmi's hands, he would reach up and give her hair a few strokes. "There you are, my pretty girl," he'd say. She would hold her breath because his hands smelled of steers' blood. As he stroked her hair she would stand stiff, wishing she could close her eyes so she wouldn't have to look into his crude smiling face. Then she would mumble, *"Terima kasih,* Pak," and run into her room with the present and place it in a corner with the others.

These visits went on for months, carrying over into Lasmi's last year of middle school. Every weekend, when she came home from Bandung, Pak Gedé brought her another gift. Though the pile of gifts eventually took up most of her share of the bedroom's space, she never wore or used any of them. It was her way of refusing Pak Gedé's imminent proposal. She sensed that Papa regarded her marriage to the trader as a way of reclaiming her from the priyayi milieu that had stolen her from him. She realized also that

Mama, in the absence of a legitimate priyayi suitor, was powerless to stop it. Lasmi knew, however, that she could never bring herself to marry a crude, old, illiterate beef trader who smelled of steers' blood. The very thought of his touch sent her into paroxysms of revulsion. So she kept adding gifts to the pile in the corner of her room, trying to work up the courage to give them all back (knowing that Pak Gedé would never marry a girl who had humiliated him). But the courage wouldn't come. She didn't want to disgrace her parents. She told herself that if she never wore any of the gifts, Pak Gedé would eventually take the hint and leave her alone.

One Saturday evening Lasmi came home with her sister and brothers from the pasar and found the house full of guests. They were crammed into the sitting room on borrowed chairs, sipping tea and talking in polite, formal voices. The air was hazy with the clove-scented smoke of kreteks. Peering in from the hallway, Lasmi noticed Pak Gedé sitting smugly in the place of honor next to Papa. The atmosphere was solemn and expectant. Lasmi realized that the guests were all relatives of Pak Gedé: he had come to ask for her hand in marriage. She thought of the pile of gifts in her room and cursed herself for not having had the nerve to return them. She thought of Hari and felt her heart breaking apart inside her chest. Everyone in the sitting room turned to look at her. When Pak Gedé's dull eyes met hers, she broke away and ran into the kitchen. Papa's voice called after her, "Don't be long, dear—we need you in here. . . ."

Clutching the edge of a cupboard shelf, Lasmi started to cry. She could hear them buzzing in the sitting room; soon Papa would come to see what was keeping her. She slipped quietly out the kitchen door and ran around the family fish pond, between two rows of young beans in the garden, and up into the hills behind the yard. It was a chilly November night. As she ran she could see her breath pluming in bursts in the moonlight. The grass was cold underfoot as she kicked off her sandals to run faster. She thought of hiding in the vast green sea of the tea plantation, but it was much too far. She ran instead to a large communal fish pond back in the hills not far from the house. She didn't break stride when she reached it but jumped right in and worked her feet along the mucky bottom until she got to the center. Up to her chin in freezing water, she stood as still as she could, flinching at the nibbles of curious goldfish and carp. Within minutes she was shivering violently. Above her the huge night sky was dusted with stars. It had never looked so beautiful. It was far, far away—where she wanted to be. Ten minutes or so passed before she heard Papa and her brothers calling. She saw the wandering beams of flashlights and frosty breath rising in the night air. Circles of light played over the fish pond and coalesced on her. Papa's voice trembled with fear and anger: "For God's sake, Lasmi, come out of there! They've all gone—I told them you were ill!"

Papa said nothing more that evening, leaving Lasmi to Mama, who wrapped her in blankets and whimpered. Lasmi couldn't tell whether the whimpering was from worry about her or from humiliation. Papa sulked in his room until the next morning. When he finally summoned her Lasmi could tell from his sagging face that his pride had been deeply wounded. Sitting cross-legged on the bed in a faded house sarong, he explained with controlled anger that Lasmi must marry Pak Gedé in two weeks and that there were to be no more embarrassing displays of contrariness.

Lasmi took a deep breath and said, "No."

Papa said, "All right, then, how long? Three weeks? A month? We'll stall for time."

She looked Papa in the eye. "You can stall as long as you like, but it won't do any good. I won't marry the old goat!"

Tears spilled down Lasmi's cheeks.

Papa's eyes widened and his mouth fell open. His lips worked, trying to form words. Finally he said, "Go to your room, girl. You'll stay there until you change your mind."

Lasmi spent the next three weeks alone in her room. (Papa made her brothers and sister sleep in the sitting room.) At mealtime, Mama would silently open the door and with downcast, suffering eyes lay a plate of fried rice or noodles and eggs on the floor. Lasmi ate nothing the first three days but gradually realized she needed to keep up her strength for what might be a long ordeal. She was determined not to marry Pak Gedé, no matter how intense her parents' humiliation. Every few days, Papa would report to her on his progress in stalling Pak Gedé. He would knock on her bedroom door, clear his throat to get her attention, and say gravely, "He's given us another week," or "Two more weeks." Lasmi ignored these reports. Remembering Great-Grandfather's instructions, she spent long hours praying to his spirit for help. The old man's spirit did not speak to her directly, but one night Nino slipped a message under her door: "I've been to the hill—Great-Grandfather will send help." The next day, Lasmi's uncle Yofan began sneaking school lessons to her through the bedroom window. In her third week of captivity, Lasmi asked him to take all the gifts back to Pak Gedé. Uncle Yofan refused at first and began avoiding her gaze when handing the lessons through the window, but he finally gave in. One night Lasmi passed all the gifts out to him and he took them in a handcart to Pak Gedé. The next evening, Pak Gedé withdrew his request for Lasmi's hand in marriage. From the bedroom she heard his hoarse muttering and Papa's contrite moans. No one said a word to Lasmi for several days. On the fourth morning, Mama and Papa came into her room and told her that they had decided she must marry her second cousin Zainal.

Lasmi had met Zainal once when he visited the Massina house in Bandung. He was not as good-looking as Hari but, coming as he did from Mama's side of the family, he was priyayi and educated. In fact, he had only one more year left of college, after which, Lasmi assumed, he would take a lucrative government position. If she couldn't have Hari, she could at least live in Bandung and have the kind of life she dreamed of. Besides, she didn't feel she had much of a choice after having humiliated Mama and Papa with the Pak Gedé fiasco.

Lasmi was fifteen when she married Zainal and moved into his parents' small home in Bandung. She didn't understand why the house was in such a poor neighborhood. It wasn't until Zainal got a job in the Department of Education and Culture and they moved into another small house in a poor neighborhood of Karawang that Lasmi understood the priyayi facts of life: wealth came from inheritance and graft, not salaries. Her in-laws' small inheritances had been used up long ago, and what was more, her father-in-law had an unfortunate streak of honesty that had kept him from exploiting his government position the way his colleagues had exploited theirs. Soon after Lasmi and Zainal moved into their new house with their baby son, Yendra, Zainal's parents sold the Bandung house and moved in with them. The money from the sale was no help to Lasmi, because all of it went for Zainal's younger brother's education. Lasmi's life was not turning out as she had expected. She started praying to Great-Grandfather again, but nothing happened.

Karawang was on the outskirts of Jakarta, and Lasmi hated it there. Jakarta was hot and muggy, overpopulated, infested with mosquitoes. Its filthy canals stank. The water

Lasmi used was polluted with human waste, and though she tried to boil all of it, she occasionally ran out of kerosene for the stove before Zainal's payday. The children would get sick—their second son, Yusuf, had been born by then—and the kerosene money, when she finally got it, would go to the clinic instead. Whenever Papa visited from Ciwidey he would fume over the way Lasmi lived, then rush out and bring back armloads of groceries from the pasar. Lasmi's in-laws never lifted a finger to help her. They expected to be waited on like royalty. Papa would lose his temper and scream at them and Zainal. Lasmi sensed he was angry mainly with himself for having let Mama talk him into making the match in the first place.

It was not only Zainal's poverty that tortured Papa—it was his religion as well. Papa had raised Lasmi in the old Sundanese religion, teaching her to meditate and pray to Lord Shiva, to Vishnu and Buddha, and to her ancestors and the Mahakuasa, the Great Power that moved all things. She remembered how, when the muezzin's call to prayer rang out in sinuous Arabic from the little Ciwidey mosque, Papa would turn to Mama and say, "Mun—if this Allah is so powerful, why can't it speak to us in Sundanese?" That had made a deep impression on Lasmi. She considered Islam a foreign religion. Married to Zainal, she was forced to practice Islam nonetheless.

Allah turned out to be a hard God. He was a God who demanded total submission to his commands: bathing and praying five times a day, reciting from the Koran, fasting during Ramadan, and taking great care not to touch one's husband when one was menstruating. This last command was the only one Lasmi didn't mind. Eventually she pretended to have her period three weeks out of each month. Zainal knew she was lying most of the time, but he didn't want to risk contamination by investigating personally and was too embarrassed to order their female servant to find out the truth for him. After ten years of this charade, Zainal began having affairs, then punished Lasmi for driving him to these sinful acts. He flew into rages and slapped her, even struck her with his fists. Soon he was striking her not only for making him sin but for failing to perform her household chores the way he wanted them performed.

Lasmi was saddled with chores. She had a servant to help with the children—four now—but she had to do all the cooking and cleaning herself, not only for her own family but for her in-laws and for Zainal's other relatives, who visited often and stayed for weeks at a time. On top of that, she took in sewing on consignment from a nearby factory to supplement Zainal's meager income. (He refused to take bribes and other extra monies to provide a decent living for his family, saying it was against the will of Allah.) Every night from suppertime until the predawn call to prayer, Lasmi worked at her antique Singer sewing machine. Then she had to get up at the crack of dawn to cook rice, because Zainal liked a big breakfast of rice with chicken or goat meat or broiled fish. If breakfast wasn't ready at seven sharp, he would fly into a rage and hit her. These blows grew more ferocious after he was transferred to the Padalarang office, because there Lasmi and Zainal were shielded from the prying eyes of his parents, who had remained in the Karawang house. (From her earnings Lasmi had provided her in-laws with a cook and a maid in order to keep them from moving to Padalarang.) Though Lasmi worked even harder as a seamstress in Padalarang than she had in Karawang, all of the extra income went to support the Karawang servants, and she was almost happy when the head of the Karawang office died suddenly and Zainal was transferred back to take his place. The consequent decrease in the frequency and severity of beatings not only improved her health but also made it far less embarrassing to carry out her duties in the civil servants' Women's Auxiliary. In Bandung and Padalarang, Zainal had gotten so carried away that he had often struck her in places where her clothing couldn't conceal the bruises.

It wasn't Zainal's violent rages that weighed most heavily on Lasmi's heart, however: it was his zeal in overseeing her obedience to Allah. She could begin to understand his fury at his breakfast not being ready or his shirts not being ironed on time, for she knew he had been terribly spoiled as a child. But nothing in her experience had prepared her for his rigid approach to religion. Papa's mysticism was personal, private, unconcerned with rules of conduct or strict rituals. What difference, she wondered, could it make to Zainal— so long as she kept up appearances in public—if now and then in the privacy of her own home she didn't bother to answer the call to prayer? Yet he screamed at her for this, called her an infidel who would burn in Neraka and take their children with her.

When, after more than twenty years of marriage, it was finally clear that Zainal would never rise higher than the Karawang office, he became completely absorbed in religion. He forced Lasmi to take lessons in Arabic so she could read the Koran daily instead of just memorizing passages for recitation. Every night she was reduced to tears while studying. One night she got up from her books, walked to the bus depot, and bought a ticket to Ciwidey. There she wept in Mama's arms while Papa sat with his head in his hands, cursing Zainal under his breath. She wanted to separate from Zainal and move back to the Padalarang house, which had been left with Uncle Yofan's family. Papa was sympathetic but could no longer help her financially, having lost his batik business years ago during the economic chaos of the mid-1960s. Now he was just a poor old tea peddler who didn't understand bank credit and complained incessantly about all the Chinese who were getting rich despite having to go like ordinary beggars to the banks for capital. Mama, in spite of her guilt over having exploited the Pak Gedé fiasco to make amends with her side of the family, was unsympathetic. She told Lasmi that a proper Sundanese woman didn't complain but accepted whatever fate brought her. Besides, she said, leaving Zainal would damage the children beyond repair, especially Yogi and Yofi, who were just ten and eleven. Nino, on vacation from his job as a hospital orderly in Jakarta, sat on the verandah listening to all this in anguished silence.

One evening, about a week after Lasmi had returned to Karawang, Nino showed up unexpectedly at her house while the family was having supper. When she opened the door and saw the wild look on his face, she was too startled to speak. His hair was disheveled and his chin covered with a frizzy growth of beard. In an unnaturally deep voice he said, "Lasmi, I've come to save you." He looked different, not like her brother.

Lasmi said, "Nino?" but he didn't seem to recognize his name. His eyes were strange and distant, but he wasn't amok: his manner was very controlled. Lasmi shrank from him as he pushed past her into the sitting room. Again he said, "I've come to save you."

In the dining room, Zainal looked up from his plate, his mouth full of food. "What did he say? Why is he speaking Indonesian instead of Sundanese? He's crazy!"

At that, Nino's face twisted into a snarl, his fingers into claws. He let out a low growl. Zainal jumped up from the table and cowered behind his chair. The children gaped.

"I'm *what*?" Nino roared at Zainal.

"He thinks he's a tiger!" Zainal jabbered, crouching lower. "He's possessed by the Devil!"

It was obvious to Lasmi that Nino had turned *sakti.* Great-Grandfather was speaking through him. Nino growled again. From behind his chair Zainal cried, "In the name of Allah, get him out of here!"

"Come on, Nino," Lasmi said, trembling. "Let's go for a walk."

"So, you don't believe me!" he snarled at her. "But I will return. You'll see. And then you'll believe."

Nino turned and left.

Lasmi was stunned that Great-Grandfather had sent her a sign. It had been such a long time since Nino had gone to the hill when Mama and Papa were pressuring Lasmi to marry Pak Gedé. Over the years, fatigue and fear of Zainal had made her neglect her meditation, and things had gotten so bad that she thought Great-Grandfather had deserted her. Now she was filled with anticipation. It really seemed as if the extraordinary and wonderful thing prophesied by Great-Grandfather was about to come true. Day after day she cooked rice and boiled water, did her sewing and studied Arabic, tended the flower garden and inhaled the reek of copra and moist earth, and waited for her savior. She waited a year, praying five times a day, chairing meetings of the Women's Auxiliary, lighting the mosquito coils in the evenings. Secretly, before dawn, when everyone was asleep, she would sit in the lotus position on the dank bathroom floorboards and pray to Great-Grandfather and the Mahakuasa.

One day, her brother Yudi came with news that Nino had left his wife and children and his job at the hospital and wandered off into the southern mountains to meditate and seek Lord Shiva, Lord Buddha, and the Mahakuasa. Lasmi thought Nino half crazy and realized he might have been mistaken about the sign. Besides, she was tired of waiting. She took Yendra, Yogi, and Yofi and moved back to the Padalarang house. Yusuf didn't want to change high schools and stayed in Karawang with his father. Zainal cried tears of humiliation and pleaded with Lasmi to stay, saying he would never again strike her or have an affair. But her mind was made up.

The Padalarang house was in disrepair because the growth of Uncle Yofan's scrap metal business had failed to keep pace with that of his family. His sons, who now ran the business, were barely able to support him and Aunt Ratna. So Lasmi opened a stall at the pasar, from which she sold clothing that she made from factory remnants, and within a year she had saved enough money to retile the roof. Though the work was hard and unremitting, freedom from Zainal's rages and oppressive religion made it quite bearable. She was happy to be back in the Bandung area. The house was on one of the steepest streets in Padalarang and the view from the verandah reminded Lasmi of Ciwidey. Across the street, terraced paddies climbed to the very crest of a ridge that rose from a stream where saronged women scrubbed their laundry on the rocks and spread bright colors along the bank to dry in the sun. Among the palms atop the ridge was a solitary flame tree, the scarlet blossoms of which warmed Lasmi's heart. Now she heard only pure Priangan Sundanese spoken all around, a welcome change from Jakartanese, which was an ugly patchwork of Javanese, Sundanese, and Indonesian. And now that she could ignore the call to prayer, she felt lighthearted whenever it rang out from the local mosque's loudspeakers. Sometimes, remembering Papa's habitual remark of long ago, she would laugh gaily at the chant and pretend to address the Mahakuasa: "Why can't You teach Allah to speak Sundanese?" That would start Uncle Yofan laughing, his malformed sinuses making him quack like a duck, and Yendra, Yogi, Yofi, and Aunt Ratna would all laugh, too. Zainal had considered laughter during the call to prayer disrespectful to Allah;

now, thinking how their laughter *intended* disrespect, Lasmi would laugh harder still. She wondered if she had been foolish to wait a year for a savior. Perhaps breaking free of Zainal was itself the extraordinary and wonderful occurrence Great-Grandfather had promised so long ago.

Despite her newfound freedom and gaiety, however, Lasmi remained troubled. She was now an unmarried woman. The moment Zainal had realized she was never coming back, he had gone straight to the Religious Court of Bandung, where their marriage had been recorded twenty-six years before, and divorced her. He remarried. Now Lasmi was a woman over forty without a husband. There was no shame in having been divorced, but not having a husband at her age was a disgrace. Sometimes she felt lonely too. She wasn't desperate enough to marry a poor man, but men with decent incomes or inherited wealth were interested in a woman of her years only as a second or third wife or as a concubine. Lasmi swore she would never stoop to such an arrangement. Still, she worried that time would eventually weaken her resolve.

Yendra was the second problem. He suffered terribly from the divorce. He had been enrolled in the Hotel and Restaurant Academy in Jakarta but dropped out to look after Lasmi in Padalarang. Zainal despised him for that. Though Yendra dutifully took Yogi and Yofi on the bus to Karawang every Sunday to visit their father, Zainal wouldn't speak to him. Yendra broke up with his Karawang sweetheart, claiming he never wanted to marry, and started hanging out in bars and discotheques in Bandung. To raise money for beer, cigarettes, and the lottery, he bought and sold used cars. When he bought a stolen car from a con man with phony papers, he was arrested by the policeman who was in cahoots with the con man. A court date was set and Yendra was released so he could scrounge money for a bribe. Lasmi put nearly all the money she had into a plain white envelope and, concealing it in a manila folder, carried it to the police station. Nervously she approached the arresting officer at his desk, introduced herself, and placed the folder on the desk. The policeman, a wiry little man with prominent veins on his smooth forearms, waited until the other officers were looking away before he opened the folder and the envelope. After counting the money, he looked up at Lasmi, amused. He handed back the folder, keeping the envelope. He wanted more.

Lasmi hurried home and spent the rest of the day brooding over how she could get her hands on enough money to extricate Yendra from his pending court appearance. The obvious thing to do was to appeal to her relatives for help. But Mama's family hated Lasmi for disgracing Zainal by leaving him, and Papa's family and her brothers and sister were so poor that even small contributions would be too difficult. Lasmi didn't want to burden anyone. She felt that by leaving Zainal she alone had caused Yendra's predicament and hence she alone must raise the money. The situation seemed impossible. The policeman apparently wanted a lot more than she had offered him, and she had only one month to get it.

As Lasmi stared at the sun setting behind her beautiful flame tree on the ridge crest across the street, she recalled the way the policeman had looked her up and down before he'd smiled and returned the folder, as though calculating how much money she might earn in a month. The solution was clear: prostitution. It was because she was attractive, she realized, that the officer had been amused at the paltry sum; had she been ugly, he might have accepted it. She had unwittingly weakened her position by dressing up and wearing makeup as a sign of respect for the officer. All evening she cursed herself for having been so stupid. She went to bed in a state of numbness, doubting for the first time the wisdom of leaving Zainal.

Lasmi awoke in the middle of the night with a brilliant idea. She had dreamed about the wife of the head of Zainal's Padalarang office, who had become a successful business-woman by obtaining government contracts through the department. It had been common knowledge in the Women's Auxiliary that she had acquired contracts through illegal access to the secret government bid ceilings and that she had obtained bank loans in exchange for sexual favors from her secretary. It was the latter fact that Lasmi now latched on to. If she was forced to sell herself, she thought, wouldn't it be better to do it once for a small business loan rather than repeatedly for petty cash? From unspeakable degradation might actually come a better life. And there was already a business opportunity waiting to be seized. Yendra had told her about a friend of his named Waya, who had a big chunk of ready cash and a family link to a potentially lucrative tobacco deal in Mojokerto, East Java. Waya needed a partner to put up half the capital. Lasmi could sign a contract with him contingent on her getting a bank loan, and they and Yendra could go off to Mojokerto by bus to purchase the tobacco and have it shipped back to one of the cigarette factories near Bandung. On the way to Mojokerto they could stop in central Java to get the bank loan: this would ensure that the bank director would be Javanese (she had often heard that Javanese men craved Sundanese women) and would shield the ignoble origin of the business venture from Bandung gossip. After the final sale, she'd pay off the loan and still have enough money to buy a local clothing shop in addition to paying Yendra's bribe.

The idea of compromising herself with a banker was horrifying, but the thought of Yendra going to prison was far worse. The next morning, Lasmi rode the bus into Bandung and bought a pair of tight-fitting blue corduroy designer jeans and a pair of carved-wood high-heeled sandals. On a piece of spiral notebook paper she wrote out a contract, which she signed and took to Waya to sign. Late that afternoon, with Waya and Yendra, she boarded the cheap night bus bound for Jogjakarta, deep in central Java.

Lasmi had never been outside her own province of West Java, the traditional home of the Sundanese people. As the bus hurtled down the two-lane highway in the fading light, along the great central Javan plateau between phalanxes of blue-ridged mountains and lavender volcanoes, it was as if she were riding back into time, back to her childhood in Ciwidey. The Javanese heartland was as poor as the Priangan of thirty years ago. Cars and motorbikes were replaced more and more by bicycles, electric lights gave way to pressure lamps. The bus rolled through mud-choked villages and towns with crumbling walls and pavements. Houses were of plaited bamboo; the roadside was populated with scrawny chickens and ducks. The old people looked weary, beaten down. Stooped men in sarongs and women carrying loads of vegetables shuffled along beside stagnant drainage ditches.

Despite these distractions, Lasmi was unable to rid her mind of what awaited her in Jogjakarta. She stared out at the dim towns and fields being sucked backward into the night and wondered what the bank director would look like. She shuddered when she visualized an ugly little Javanese man she once knew; making him more handsome didn't help. Would it be better or worse that he wasn't Sundanese and couldn't whisper sexual intimacies in her language— would she then feel more violated or less? Would she be able to block it out? Would time help her forget? And what about poor Yendra? Surely he had guessed what she intended to do but was too terrified of prison to stop her. Would he be able to forget, or would guilt consume him?

The outskirts of Jogjakarta were sun-bleached and battered, but downtown there were modern stores, expensive hotels, and European tourists who had come to see the ancient temples and the Sultan's palace. Lasmi had never seen so many Europeans. She gawked at their hulking bodies as they stood bargaining with the souvenir peddlers in the arcade along Jalan Malioboro. She checked into the old Mutiara Hotel, taking one room for herself and another for Yendra and Waya. The hotel was very expensive, with hot water and air-conditioning and television sets, but she needed a nice place in case the bank director insisted on having their liaison in her room. She reminded herself that she was a businesswoman now. The expensive rooms were an investment. She would include their cost in the loan application and pay the bill as soon as the loan came through.

The next afternoon Lasmi headed for the bank, dressed in the blue corduroy jeans, a lacy jacket with padded shoulders, and high-heeled sandals. As she strolled through the Mutiara lobby, she noticed a tall bearded European sitting alone in the hotel restaurant. He was at a corner table under one of the lazy ceiling fans, a newspaper spread out on the white linen tablecloth before him. He seemed wilted from the heat, and slightly forlorn. He looked up as she passed. Their eyes met. Lasmi turned away, but only after a long moment. She had taken in his strong features and lonely expression, but was quickly distracted as she steeled herself for the task at hand.

He was still there when she returned from the bank an hour later. Before, there had been a few lunch diners, but now, except for the European and the waiters in their slim white jackets, the restaurant was empty. Lasmi wanted the

European to look at her as he had earlier that afternoon. She strolled past his table to the bar and asked the bartender for the time. When she turned back to look at the European, he was staring at her. She smiled. He returned the smile and said, *"Selamat siang."* He speaks Indonesian, she thought as she walked down the first-floor corridor to her room. She realized how silly it was to suppose that someone speaks Indonesian because he can say *selamat siang,* but she felt somehow that she could talk to this European.

In her room, Lasmi undressed and lay on the bed, day-dreaming. The liaison with the bank director had been set for tomorrow afternoon. She had expected to feel anguish and dread, but for the moment she felt only relief that the loan had been promised. Her thoughts drifted to the banker's oblong face and fine features, his delicate hands and slim safari-suited body and monotonous Javanese-accented Indonesian. He had been powerfully attracted to her, and she knew he wanted her as a mistress, not just a one-night stand. She thought of him now without disgust, only as a logistical obstacle. Could he make trouble for her when she refused to be his mistress? She might have to sleep with him more than once to string him along until the loan came through. In any case, her degradation would be briefer than it would have been had she chosen the red-light district of Bandung as her source of bribe money.

Suddenly she thought of the European in the restaurant. She had only two memories of Europeans, both from early childhood. The first was of the day during the revolution when the Dutch soldiers had come to take Papa away for giving aid and comfort to the rebels. Papa was eating his breakfast when there was the thud of boots on the verandah. The soldiers walked right through the open front door, grabbed Papa by the arms, and dragged him out into the front yard. Lasmi dashed out onto the verandah. A servant chased her and clapped a hand over her eyes, but Lasmi bit the woman on the wrist in time to see the soldiers hit Papa with their rifle butts and push him off down the road to the Chinese storekeeper's house that served as a prison. This chilling memory forced itself rudely into her daydream but was soon replaced by a second, more pleasant recollection. A Dutch colonel had occupied the house next door in Ciwidey and Lasmi remembered how his cook would call her by name. He was a giant of a man, nearly six feet tall, in an apron and wooden shoes, smelling of exotic foods. He gave Lasmi little treats—delicious pastries and candies—and whenever he called she would run to him and he would lift her high in the air and laugh. Now, lying on the bed in her hotel room, remembering this for the first time in many years, Lasmi smiled and fell asleep.

That evening she saw the European sitting by himself in a rattan chair on the patio. Lasmi was drawn to him. She had awakened with the bank director in her mind and a knot in her stomach, nauseated with fear and shame at what was in store for her tomorrow. Yendra was off somewhere with Waya, not wanting to know what she was doing or with whom she was doing it. She wanted desperately to talk to someone.

Trembling slightly, Lasmi walked over to the European and greeted him in Indonesian. He invited her to sit with him and ordered two coffees. They chatted and she began to relax. The evening was hot and muggy, saturated with the fragrances of jasmine and frangipani. There were well-dressed Indonesians, Europeans, and Japanese on the patio, and Lasmi felt wonderfully cosmopolitan sitting among them, conversing with a European for the first time in her life. His name was Curt and he was an American engineer who had spent three years in East Kalimantan working for a company called Bechtel that was building an oil refinery for the government. He was vacationing on his way back to the States. He had supervised Indonesian workers, and his Indonesian was quite good. He told her a little about himself: he was forty-four, divorced for seven years, and had an eleven-year-old son in America. Mostly, though, he listened. As Lasmi spoke of herself, Curt's profound interest kept her talking. They smiled often at each other. She liked his smile: it was genuine and confiding. She looked into his eyes and realized that he wasn't a playboy like the American men in the movies. He was, she thought, a gentle, *halus*, lonely man.

She told Curt the story of her life, from her girlhood in Ciwidey to Yendra's arrest—things she wouldn't have imagined telling a stranger. At this last piece of information Curt stopped smiling and averted his eyes. Lasmi shivered, as if the hearth fire had gone out on a chilly Ciwidey morning. Then she realized that Curt thought she was going to ask for money. She mentioned the loan and the tobacco deal. Relief passed across Curt's face; his smile returned and the sparkle came back into his eyes.

Yendra joined them. Lasmi was startled; she hadn't expected to see him for another day or so. To her further surprise, he grew immediately friendly with Curt. After half an hour of conversation, Yendra whispered to Lasmi that he needed to talk to her privately. They excused themselves and walked to the corridor. Lasmi saw that her son's eyes were as wide as saucers. "What is it?" she said.

Yendra checked to make sure they were alone in the corridor and in a loud whisper said, "Bu, that's *him*—your savior!"

"What?"

"The one who possessed Nino and came to you and said he would return!"

"A European?" She thought his guilt was making him grasp at straws.

Leaning closer, Yendra took hold of her arm. "Don't you remember that night, Bu? Nino was a tiger—a *white* tiger—and he spoke Indonesian instead of Sundanese. Curt is a white man who speaks Indonesian but not Sundanese! He's divorced and your age, and I'll bet he's rich, working for a big American company like that!" Lasmi didn't respond. Yendra prodded, "When was the last time a European man approached you, Bu?"

"But *I* approached *him,*" she said.

Yendra gasped. "That proves it! Bu, have you ever thought of approaching a European?"

Lasmi shook her head. Yendra was right: ordinarily, she wouldn't consider approaching a European. Something must have moved her.

Yendra pushed her toward the lobby. "Go back to him, Bu! Quickly! Talk to him, charm him, make him fall in love with you!"

Poor Yendra, she thought, he's crazy with guilt. And yet she knew he was right. Curt must be rich: he was American and employed by a big company, and he vacationed at expensive hotels. Perhaps this was the destiny of which Great-Grandfather had spoken. Marrying a rich American might be wonderful, and there was no doubt that it would be extraordinary. She imagined that he would take her away to America, where she would finally have a big beautiful house like Pak Massina's, with lots of servants, and she would send money to her children and brothers and sister at home and make their lives easier than her own had been.

She went back to the patio and sat with Curt. She charmed him, smiling and complimenting his Indonesian, laughing at every joke he made. When he drew a pocket dictionary from the back pocket of his slacks to look up a word Lasmi had used, she took it from him and wrote her Padalarang address on the flyleaf, signing it *Salam manis,* Lasmi—*Sweet greetings.* Curt blushed at this, but recovered and looked deep into her eyes. She thought of Hari, her boyfriend from middle school, who had looked into her eyes in the same way, making her heart flutter and ache. Curt invited her to the lounge, where they sat in rattan chairs at a little glass-top table. He ordered a glass of wine and asked Lasmi what she wanted to drink. She told him that she had once tasted beer but found it far too bitter. He ordered her a strawberry daiquiri. It was pink and sweet and delicious—not at all like beer—and she drank two of them quickly through a short narrow straw. Curt leaned over and kissed her on the cheek and asked her to come to his room. Her head was swimming, and the Javanese bank director seemed part of another life.

In the air-conditioned room, Curt's warm fingers felt wonderful against her skin as he undressed her. He kissed her breasts. Lasmi lay stiff as a board in shocked delight. Zainal had never kissed her body. She clung to Curt as he made love to her, marveling at the hairiness of his body. Afterward she fell asleep with his arm around her, her head nestled against his chest.

She awoke before dawn, hearing the call to prayer from a distance. Lasmi had never slept anywhere so sheltered from that ubiquitous sound. In the dimness, she saw Curt's face turned to her, his cheek pressed into the pillow. He looked boyish in spite of the beard and mustache. Lasmi was overcome with tenderness for him and started to cry. She thought of Hari and wondered if this was *jatu cinta*—falling in love. If it was, she would never again doubt the power of Great-Grandfather's spirit.

Lasmi suddenly remembered the bank director, and her

heart turned over. She felt only loathing for the little man now. Sleeping with Curt was one thing—she had been destined to become his lover—but when the banker came to her room today she would become a common whore. She had less than twelve hours to be saved. Papa had always told her never to take destiny for granted but to help it along even when she knew where it would lead. She climbed out of bed, went to the closet, and found an extra sheet. Wrapping herself in the sheet, she sat in the lotus position on the carpet between the bed and the wardrobe and prayed to Great-Grandfather and the Mahakuasa. As she prayed, she sensed their benevolent auras fill the room.

Dawn was breaking when she became aware of Curt watching her from the bed. She hid her tear-stained face in her hands.

Curt sat up. "What is it, Lasmi? What's wrong?" Naked, he hurried to her and took her in his arms. "What kind of trouble are you in, *Sayang?*"

She was so thrilled to hear him call her *Sayang* that she burst into tears again. She told him everything, even about the bank director.

Curt said, "All right, Sayang, stop crying. I'll lend you the money myself. Without interest. You can stop here on the way back from Mojokerto and pay me back."

Why does he trust me? she wondered. Is it Great-Grandfather's influence? Through tears she told him that Yendra and Waya would go and she would stay with him as insurance until they got back. The truth was, she didn't want to leave him.

That morning Curt cashed a thousand dollars in traveler's checks and gave the money to Yendra, who with Waya boarded the bus for Malang in the East Javan highlands, where they would catch a bus for Mojokerto. At noon Curt and Lasmi checked out of the Mutiara. Curt paid Lasmi's bill and they took a room together at the Peti Mas Guest House, a pleasant place half a block from Malioboro on a narrow side street called Jalan Dagen. Relaxing in a café later that afternoon, Lasmi glowed as she pictured the bank director rapping impatiently on the door of her empty room at the Mutiara.

The week passed like a dream. They strolled arm in arm along Malioboro, shopped for souvenirs, dined in restaurants, attended wayang shows, talked, made love. Curt was charming, gentle, considerate, doting. By the end of the week, however, Lasmi had learned enough about him to doubt that he had been sent by Great-Grandfather. In the years since his divorce he had fallen in love with several women, all of whom had ultimately rejected him, and he was now desperate to settle down. He wasn't rich, either. She first realized this when he began talking one evening about the cost of living in America. She was stunned to hear the things that Americans were forced to buy—things that she had never even heard of, such as insurance for homes and cars and belongings. In a year an American paid more for each of these than a low-level Indonesian civil servant received in salary. Americans had to heat their homes, as well, and spend fortunes on gasoline because places were all so far apart that they had to drive everywhere. And taxes—devastating sums were paid as taxes, not just on property but on *income*! Lasmi added these expenses to the staggering cost of housing and compared the total with Curt's salary. Her heart sank. Then he admitted that he didn't even own a house. He owned something called a *condominium*. The way he described this, it sounded as if he lived in an apartment building. Even more shocking, he didn't have a single servant. No house and no servants, and he didn't seem ashamed of it! Once again things were not working out as Lasmi had expected.

Yet she'd fallen in love with this man! She couldn't rid her mind of his face, his voice, his body. She had never imagined that a woman could crave a man's body like this. She felt possessed. She had hardly thought of her children in Padalarang and Karawang. Perhaps Great-Grandfather *was* working some sort of magic after all. But what could his plan be? To save her from a loveless life and leave her poor in the bargain? To steal her away from family and homeland without giving her the means to make a better life for her children? Lasmi began to feel as if a dense fog had settled around her. Each night she rose from Curt's side and prayed to Great-Grandfather to tell her what her true destiny was. He neither spoke to her nor sent a sign, but she kept praying.

Several more days passed. Finally Yendra phoned from the central telephone office in Mojokerto with terrible news. A truck driver and Waya's cousin, with whom they had contracted to do business, had disappeared with the tobacco and all of the money. It was useless to go to the police. They would demand a hefty bribe for investigating the matter, and even in the unlikely event that they managed to track down the stolen tobacco, the thieves would have disappeared long ago among Java's millions. With only pocket change, Yendra would have to hitchhike back to Jogjakarta. Lasmi nearly choked with humiliation. When she told Curt, he only shook his head and said he had known it might happen. He could have just given Lasmi the money to pay Yendra's bribe to begin with, he continued, but he hadn't known then what he knew now: that he loved her and wanted to marry her and take her to America. Even as Lasmi wept with relief, she made a feeble attempt to extract concessions: what about Yogi and Yofi in Padalarang? They couldn't go with her, Curt answered, but she could visit them, perhaps for several months each year, and send them money whenever he could afford it. Besides, soon Yogi and Yofi would be grown and able to provide for themselves. She told Curt that she would marry him and that the children would stay in Padalarang with Yendra and Uncle Yofan and Aunt Ratna.

Two days later Yendra arrived. He was depressed and exhausted from his trip, but his spirits lifted when Lasmi told him what had happened in his absence. For dinner that evening, Curt took them to an open-air restaurant that served Western food. He ordered steaks for everyone. As they feasted on the thick, juicy slabs of meat, Yendra proudly told Curt about his great-great-grandfather and his Uncle Nino's possession by Curt's spirit.

"What do you think?" Yendra asked him. "Do you believe it?"

Curt ran a hand through his hair. "I don't know," he said. "How can you be sure Nino was really possessed?"

"Oh," said Yendra, "if you had seen his eyes, you'd be sure, too."

"But how do you know it was I and not someone else?"

Around a mouthful of steak Yendra replied, "Mama's falling in love with you proves that, doesn't it?"

Curt turned to watch the pedicabs gliding up and down Malioboro. He shrugged. "Maybe Lasmi fell in love with me because she believed the prophecy, even though it wasn't really true."

Yendra and Lasmi exchanged glances. Now Curt was talking some sort of European nonsense. Yendra dropped the subject. Analyzing things wasn't what the situation called for, anyway, he thought. It was better to just enjoy the fact that he wouldn't have to go to prison and that Mama had finally found love.

Curt had less than a week of vacation left, so they made plans to return together to West Java to pay Yendra's bribe and tell Lasmi's family the news that she and Curt would be married in America. Yendra was ecstatic about getting to ride back in a hired sedan instead of the night bus. Curt called his company's Jakarta office and instructed its staff to begin making arrangements for Lasmi's visa. On their final day in Jogjakarta, they scheduled a late-morning trip to the airline office to reserve a seat for Lasmi on Curt's flight to America. But first they hired a hotel taxi to take them out to Borobudur, the famous Buddhist monument in the countryside northwest of the city.

Borobudur was a gigantic ziggurat of square galleries and circular terraces with no accessible inner chamber. Viewed from the path below, it loomed like a frozen tidal wave of stone, festooned with hundreds of niched Buddha figures and bell-shaped stupas, and crowned by a great central stupa. One did not enter Borobudur: one scaled it like a mountain. At first, walking for the better part of an hour round and round the balustraded galleries, they saw nothing but blue sky, fluffy white clouds, and endless friezes of the lives of the Buddhas. When at last they reached the open terraces, the monument seemed to fall away beneath them to spread its stone mantle over the plain.

Lasmi gazed off across miles of pale earth and palm groves, her hair ruffled by a cool morning breeze. In the early sunlight, rustling palm fronds gleamed like eddies on a green sea. The level plain was rimmed with craggy mountains, tan and blue and lavender, some capped with snow.

"Look," Yendra said beside her. "There's something inside these bells."

Curt nodded. "Buddhas. If you can reach through a hole in the stone latticework and touch his face, you might have a request granted. But you have to find one whose head hasn't been knocked off by Muslims."

"Idolatry," Lasmi murmured, picturing Zainal bashing those beautiful heads.

With Curt's camera, the two men took pictures of each other straining at one of the stupas to touch the Buddha inside. On the other side of the terrace, Lasmi stood looking down at the stream of tourists flowing up the path to the monument. A thousand years ago, she mused, they would have been pilgrims in saffron robes. She recalled what Curt had told her in the car: it had taken four generations of slaves a hundred years to build Borobudur. Thousands had died of cholera and exposure, and thousands more of starvation when the granaries of the Sailendra kings ran low and rations were halved, then quartered. How apt, she thought, that it had been in the service of the teaching that all earthly existence is suffering.

Moving around the terrace to a more secluded spot, Lasmi stood directly behind a man-sized Buddha image whose enclosing bell of stone had been removed to display the fine workmanship. It sat frozen in eternal reflection, looking off across the plain toward snowcapped Mount Merapi, where the ancient gods of Java were said to dwell. The serene figure brought to mind Great-Grandfather sitting before his hut on the hill. It struck her that Great-Grandfather had been born into a time vastly different from her own and not so different from that ancient time when rivers of pilgrims had flowed daily to this place, when all of Java—the lavender mountains, the glittering palms, the cracked-mirror paddies, the very stones of the temples and shrines—must have bristled and shimmered with kesaktian.

Just then Lasmi was infused with a sudden vision of what had happened to her homeland. For centuries the old kesaktian had been departing from the sacred places, draining away like the rice goddess's life-giving water from so many holes in the paddy dikes. Islam had burst the first holes, then the Europeans and the Japanese had opened more, and now it was the fast-food restaurants and movie theaters and discotheques. In Great-Grandfather's day there had still been enough kesaktian to affect the course of events from time to time. Now the spiritual power of her ancestors was all but exhausted. That was why Great-Grandfather hadn't been able to keep his promise, she thought. His sakti spirit was weak and dying, perhaps already dead. All the benevolent spirits that watched over people were dying. Maybe she would not even leave a spirit to watch over her own children when she died.

Mama was right, after all. It was only blind fate that shaped people's lives nowadays. Indeed, her own life had been shaped by blind, uncaring forces. Long ago she had been saved from Pak Gedé only to be delivered into the hands of Zainal. Now she had been saved from Zainal and an old age of loneliness and disgrace only to fall in love like a giggling schoolgirl with a lonely foreigner who needed a wife and who would now tear her away from her homeland and children not yet grown. Lasmi burned with shame as she turned it over in her mind. To leave children not yet grown for *the love of a man.* How could it be that she, who had raised four children and endured twenty-six years of Zainal, did not have the strength to live without this European? What would happen next year and the next—five, ten years from now? Would Curt grow tired of his aging Indonesian wife? Would she go crazy with guilt and longing and run from him as she had from Zainal?

Gazing up into the blue immensity of the Javan sky, Lasmi felt as if she were fifteen again, neck-deep in the fish pond, staring at the icy, distant stars.

"Hey!"

She looked down. Curt was waving from one of the terraces below. He flashed a bearded grin and aimed the zoom lens of his camera at her. Her heart flooded with passion and tenderness, and her eyes filled with tears. Yendra appeared at Curt's side.

"Come on, Sayang!" Curt called. "We need to get to the airline office!"

The sun was getting hot. Down on the plain, palm groves reflected the light in sheets of white and silver. Moving toward the steps, Lasmi paused at a bell stupa and peered in through the latticework of diamond-shaped holes. The Buddha figure inside had been spared by the vandals. Its face, in shadow, was tilted slightly downward, the expression cool and tranquil.

Lasmi thought, If there is any real kesaktian left in Java, it must be here. She might never see this place again. What should she pray for? She tried to imagine what she needed more than anything, something she could carry with her wherever she went. She knew. She had always thought her supply of it inexhaustible, but now, dizzy with love and sick with foreseen longing, she felt it draining away like so much water from the paddy fields.

Lasmi thrust her hand and forearm into a hole in the lattice, her cheek pressed against stone still cool from the night. Her fingers touched stone. She traced a noble eyebrow, the bridge of a nose.

She closed her eyes tight against the sun and prayed for strength.

# MIRACLE
# OF THE
# MALIGARAS

Dusk had settled on the forest. Bats streamed from the black mouths of trails and wheeled about the clearing. From where Willem Van Groot stood toweling his midriff on the verandah of his house, the river appeared motionless. Eleven months of low rainfall had reduced long stretches of the Sangatta to a trickle linking stagnant pools. At times Van Groot felt as if he lived in a desert oasis: the deep channel that flowed past his house remained an abundant source of water for drinking and bathing, even as the forest wilted and smoke from the fires near the kampong drifted through camp.

He hung his towel on the line under the verandah thatch, slipped into a pair of khaki shorts, and lowered himself into a rattan chair. He gazed out at the forest and sky. The clicking of tall bamboo at the edge of the clearing made him imagine the forest lush and full again. This fantasy was enhanced by the way the river curved sharply southward on either side of the house, concealing the clutter of exposed logs and boulders around each bend. Dusk blurred the great drooping leaves of staghorn ferns and blended the bare crowns of parched canopy trees into the background of hardier neighbors that had not yet begun to die of thirst.

After savoring the illusion for a time, Van Groot retrieved his kerosene lantern from the house and knelt on the verandah to light it. Kerosene from the jerry can, lighter fluid, the striking of a match, the mantle glowing to the rhythmic hiss of the hand pump: it was a ritual he missed when he was away from camp. He carried the lantern into the house and raised it to its customary nail high on the center pole. The house was a single room seven by four meters on a frame of ironwood poles, with a board floor raised a meter off the ground. The walls and roof were of nipa-palm thatch. All but the rear wall were half walls, affording easy entrance and exit to breezes, snakes, and scorpions. Mosquito netting suspended from the ceiling in one corner protected a kapok mattress on a board bedframe. The table Van Groot used for dining and writing stood opposite the bed, in front of the kitchen. The kitchen was another table, upon which sat a Chinese-made kerosene stove shielded from breezes by a piece of cardboard that had been bent into an arc and propped up around it.

He lit the stove to cook dinner. Tonight's was simple fare, even for a tropical botanist in the field: a package of rice noodles and a few fried slices of Indonesian corned beef. The drought had long since strangled his supply of fresh fruit and vegetables from the kampong, and he was still too tired from his recent trip to bother washing and cooking rice. Three days ago he had completed the two-day journey from Balikpapan with supplies. The first day, his Pertamina sky van had departed eight hours behind schedule because of the heavy smoke from slash-and-burn fires spreading out of control all over eastern Borneo. The second day had treated him to the grueling prahu ride from the kampong to Mentoko Camp. The long drought had turned the ride into a push-and-drag ordeal. His Indonesian men were built low to the ground, but Van Groot stood a backbreaking six-two, and every muscle in his body still ached. Since his return, three days of censusing vegetation plots had drained him of energy. Tomorrow would be a day of relaxation. He would sleep late, catch up on data transcription, maybe read a spy novel from his trunkful of moldy paperbacks.

He finished eating and scraped the leftover corned beef from his plate into Mitzi's dish. The tabby came running from her sleeping place on the verandah. He went back to the table and switched on the shortwave radio. The voice of the BBC announcer reminded him that it was springtime in Europe. Here it was eternal summer. Even now, after nightfall, his body was coated with sweat. There was no breeze. Despite the heat, he was glad the sea breeze died down in the evening, diminishing the flow of smoke from the coast.

Van Groot regarded the smoke more as a nuisance than a warning. It had been drifting upstream for so long that he had begun to think of the fires as distant and benign. Perhaps they would never reach Mentoko, he mused. If they did, they would most likely spread through the bordering logged forest and die when they ran out of old logging slash for fuel at the boundaries of the study site. Still, there was the deep layer of dry leaf litter carpeting the forest floor, a form of fuel that wouldn't respect boundaries. With conscious effort he banished the fires from his thoughts and turned to his evening's paperwork.

The prospect of losing Mentoko was too painful to bear. Van Groot could imagine the loss of individual plants, even species, but not his entire study site. Mentoko had been his savior twelve years earlier when the job he coveted was awarded to another man. At the time, he had spent more than twenty years as a research associate at the Leiden Rijksherbarium in Holland and considered himself first in line for the curatorship of tropical plants. When the position went instead to a systematist from the University of Utrecht, he was crushed. He was still indignant about it. A *systematist,* no less—a man who had spent his entire life in sterile laboratories dissecting flower specimens. Systematists fulfilled a necessary function, of course, but to have one steal the job that was rightfully his—especially after he had worked so hard to build the Southeast Asian collection— had been more than he could handle.

Now it seemed almost amusing how well things had worked out. What was at first a bitter disappointment made him realize that his career was heading in the wrong direction, anyway. The curatorship would have cut his annual field time from six months to three, and it became clear that what he really needed was more time *away* from the Rijksherbarium. He was weary of petty feuds, professional jealousies, scientific turf wars. He realized, too, that it was not just more field time that he needed but a new field site where he could start afresh and alone. The Ketambe site in Sumatra had become the worst of both worlds. Perennial nuisances—humidity, leeches, snakes, tigers—had been compounded in recent years by marauding park officials, cranky tourists, and a half-dozen scientists with their retinues of graduate students and local assistants. They were destroying his sense of intimacy with the forest. When, one day in Jakarta, a young American primatologist offered him a newly vacant study site in Borneo, Van Groot jumped at the chance. He traveled back to Leiden, where he went straight to the director of the Rijksherbarium to demand that his annual field time be increased to nine months and that he be given exclusive access to the new study site. While he knew that the unseemly haste with which the director yielded had been taken by some of his colleagues as an indication that he was no longer wanted at Ketambe, Van Groot preferred to see in it a veiled apology for his having been treated so shabbily in the matter of the curatorship.

In contrast, the last twelve years had passed quite peacefully. He spent three months each autumn in Leiden, analyzing data and writing up publications, and nine months in his beautiful forest away from everyone. It was an ideal life. The isolation didn't bother him; on the contrary, he welcomed it. After all, it was his love of plants, not people, that had guided him into botany in the first place. At Mentoko he was literally surrounded by plants. His Indonesian men even had their own camp a half kilometer downstream and across the river so that his privacy was not disturbed.

Willem Van Groot was fifty-six years old. He had been divorced in his twenties and never remarried. He had no children. Over the years, he had worked closely with a number of colleagues but would have been hard-pressed to name a single friend among them. On occasion he would catch a glimpse of himself in the little mirror he kept on one of the wall poles (and which he no longer used for shaving) and would see a balding, graying man with a jowly face—a faded, indistinct version of his younger self. Years ago those eyes had seemed more engaging, more interested in others. But he had always been shy and uncomfortable with people, and he suspected that those traits had played a role in his failing to get the curatorship. He imagined his colleagues laughing at him for even applying. Since then, his relations with them had worsened; it seemed they treated him more distantly every time he returned to Leiden. Perhaps they thought all the time he spent alone at Mentoko made him a bit strange. Let them, he told himself. They weren't worth caring about.

He worked for an hour transcribing raw data into his permanent notebooks. The dozens of cheap Indonesian school notebooks were filled with immaculate phenological records, forming a twelve-year chronicle of the fruiting and flowering activity of more than five hundred species of trees and lianas in rectangular plots scattered over three square kilometers of forest. He felt a much stronger attachment to these notebooks than to his journal articles. The latter were written in what he regarded as cold, impersonal jargon and printed on glossy, antiseptic paper. He had always seethed at the way they were mangled by copy editors and style editors (not to mention peer reviewers—as if anyone could *possibly* be his peer in understanding Mentoko!). His notebooks were different: spotted with mold, their pages smelled of the forest; species were named in the graceful Kutai dialect instead of ugly Latin binomials; data were not bland statistical summaries but wonderful idiosyncratic stories. In place of jargon was a richly descriptive code that had blossomed from his unique knowledge of Mentoko and its ways. Van Groot often said that he didn't impose theories on Mentoko's flora; rather, he waited patiently for the plants to express themselves, to reveal their secrets to him in their own good time. He was content to make a faithful record of their lives and leave the abstractions to his colleagues.

He had just closed his current notebook and placed it atop the others when a sheet of paper protruding from the stack caught his eye. He felt a twinge in his chest. He started to reach for the sheet of paper but drew his hand back. The lantern was fading; it needed pumping. He attended to it, then went to urinate from the end of the verandah. He made another cup of instant coffee and returned to the table. With a deep breath, he drew the letter from among the notebooks and read it for the first time in more than a month. It was dated 22 December 1982. To it was paper-clipped a carbon copy of his response of 4 March 1983 (it was now April 21).

*Dear Dr. Van Groot,*
*A while back I had occasion to read your very*
*interesting article, "Miracle of the Maligaras," in*
Natural History. *The "miracle" you described therein*
*struck me as one well worth explaining. Lately I've*
*been mulling over an idea or two about maligaras, and*
*I now judge these ideas sufficiently developed to warrant*
*the scrutiny of the Maligara Man himself.*

Van Groot winced at the sobriquet. When it had been coined by a fellow fieldworker at a conference in Zurich, he'd swelled with pride, for he dearly loved maligara trees and was gratified to be identified with them. Hearing it from the likes of David Cairns-Smith was altogether different, however. Not for a moment was he taken in by the Englishman's flattery.

Van Groot had first become aware of the famous Cambridge theoretician's true opinion of him fifteen years earlier. It happened at an international conference at the Rijksherbarium. At the time, Cairns-Smith was still a hotshot graduate student new to the field (with a lower degree in mathematics). Van Groot was on his way to the bar when he happened to pass Cairns-Smith chatting with some young American and British colleagues. "You know," he overhead him say, "none of these herbarium hacks, like Sorel in Paris or Van Groot here in Leiden, could recognize a real idea if it fell on them from one of their precious specimens. And to think they wield such power over the rest of us—" Cairns-Smith stopped in midsentence as though he had noticed the eavesdropper. Van Groot had paused, pretending to search for someone across the crowded ballroom; with eyes averted, he continued to the bar, flushing crimson with embarrassment as the words seared themselves into his memory. The next day he attended a symposium on reproduction in tropical plants, unaware that it was to include a slide lecture by the young Cambridge phenom. The lecture was little more than a list of mathematical formulae that supposedly proved something about the evolution of apiform pistils in orchids. Van Groot was tempted to walk out. At one point he thought the speaker looked straight at him.

Now, clutching the letter, he felt a sudden rush of anger. He had never been able to erase the image of that condescending smile teasing the corners of that weak mouth, flickering across those pale, deceptively gentle eyes. He was sure Cairns-Smith had been mocking him. The arrogant little bastard must have suspected he'd overheard the insult. Van Groot reread the first paragraph of the letter, marveling that the man could mock him like this again after fifteen years of silence. *The Maligara Man.* Lofty theorists like Cairns-Smith, he thought, disdained such nicknames as fit only for data gatherers, the lowly "plodders" who had been left behind by the grand debates of the discipline and sought refuge in exotic species with extraordinary attributes. And there was the hypocrisy of that deferential, almost obsequious remark about ideas being "sufficiently developed" to "warrant" Van Groot's "scrutiny." But the most galling line of all was the one about the "miracle" of the maligaras being "well worth explaining." Van Groot reread the sentence with a cold smile. How innocuous it might look to the naïve, he thought. Again its razor edge cut him, the implication that what he had described he could not explain, that he might not even *want* his remarkable findings explained. The tone of ridicule was unmistakable.

He took a deep breath and forced himself to resume reading. Cairns-Smith mentioned that he had already contacted the Rijksherbarium's director, "an old friend," about his interest in the maligaras. He went on to summarize his new theory of the evolution of unpredictable phenological activity in rain forest plants. (Van Groot skipped this part; he hadn't understood it before and wouldn't bother trying now.) Evidently the maligara was the first real-life example Cairns-Smith had come across that seemed to fit the theory perfectly. He wanted to visit Mentoko for a few weeks in the winter for the purpose of taking samples and detailed observations that might confirm the apparent fit between fact and theory.

As Van Groot read, a wild pig rooting for tubers near the house let out a deep snort, expressing with uncanny precision the botanist's own feelings. A "visit"—hah! An *invasion.* It was just like a theorist to notice something in the literature as he relaxed in his proverbial armchair—something that appeared to fit one of his precious equations—and swoop down on the poor unsuspecting "hack" who had published it, enlisting his aid under professional duress disguised as "scientific cooperation" and garnering a junket to some exotic field site in the bargain. It was pure exploitation! The Great Man would traipse into Mentoko and, after spending a few easy weeks there, rush back to his fancy computer, leaving Van Groot to endure heat and mud, torrential rains, leeches, fire ants, and possibly malaria and dysentery and dengue fever.

He glared down at the letter on the table before him. Tears came to his eyes. After causing him fifteen years of festering resentment, his tormentor was now asking a favor.

And the horrible irony was that Van Groot could not refuse.

A decade ago it would have been easy: a brief letter of rejection with some nebulous excuse about logistical problems or poor timing would have done the trick. But the years had inverted the two men's relative standings in the profession. Now the Englishman's stature was so imposing that no ordinary scientist like Van Groot could ever hope to get away with saying no to him. A refusal would only delay the inevitable. Cairns-Smith would fire off a letter to his friend, the director of the Rijksherbarium, who would then write to Van Groot demanding a change of heart. If he valued his job, Van Groot would have no choice but to relent. He was trapped.

The pig had drifted nearer in the clearing. Van Groot scowled at the darkness beyond the glimmer of the lantern. Invaders must not be permitted. He rose from his chair and moved swiftly across the floorboards toward the noise. He grabbed one of the smooth, golf ball–sized stones that he routinely retrieved from streambeds to place along the ironwood rims of the half walls. Peering into the night, he identified the pig's dim shape and with a fierce grunt hurled the stone. There was a *thwack,* followed by a startled squeal and the crash of the pig fleeing through the brittle underbrush. "Run, you son of a bitch!" Van Groot shouted.

He returned to the table and again looked down at the letter. The violence of the throw and the sound of the stone hitting the pig's side had been satisfying. His anger subsided. In its wake, however, arose a feeling of powerlessness. He read his response clipped to the letter. Stalling for time had been his only recourse. He had informed Cairns-Smith of the fires spreading through Kutai and expressed his regret that his travels around the game reserve to monitor them had kept him from giving the request his full attention. It was a bald-faced lie: his reconnaissance had consisted of nothing more than watching the smoke drift through Mentoko day after day. But it was a plausible lie, and Cairns-Smith would not have suspected that it contained anything less sincere than a scientist's genuine concern for the safety of his study site. Unfortunately, he couldn't afford to put the Englishman off any longer. His procrastination must have already brought him dangerously close to offending the Great Man. Nothing short of fire sweeping through Mentoko and killing all the maligaras could keep Cairns-Smith away.

*The fire,* thought Van Groot suddenly. That was it: he could tell an even bigger lie! He could claim that the maligaras had all been *destroyed by the fire.*

He broke out laughing. He was grasping at straws. It would be only a matter of time before the lie was uncovered. Field botanists showed up at Mentoko unannounced from time to time; eventually one of them would see the living trees. On account of the article in *Natural History,* complete with photographs of the maligaras' vegetative and reproductive structures, any botanist would recognize them. Word would get back to Cairns-Smith, news of whose interest in maligaras would have spread like wildfire through the scientific community, as did news of all his interests. There would be a scandal. Van Groot would be fired, blackballed, his career and reputation destroyed. No, it was impossible. As much as he hated to do it, he had no choice but to write the man and pledge his full cooperation.

He struck the table with his fist, startling Mitzi, who leapt from her chair and darted off to the verandah. What a fool he had been to publish "Miracle of the Maligaras"! Even the title—his ingenuous attempt at expressing his affection for the enigmatic trees—would ultimately prove an embarrassment. He closed his eyes and vizualized Cairns-Smith's mocking rejoinder in the title of a future *Natural*

*History* cover story: "MIRACLE" OF THE MALIGARAS DEMYSTIFIED.

Suddenly the picture was disrupted by a sound like that of a low-flying airplane. A huge cicada shot into the house and glanced off the lantern. It hit the wall thatch on either side of the room before finding its way back out into the night. Van Groot was again conscious of the voice of the BBC commentator; he reached across the table and switched off the radio. The first wave of silence washed over him. The second would come when he snuffed out the lantern, extinguishing its cozy hiss. He yawned. Time for bed. He brushed his teeth with boiled water and urinated from the verandah again, then switched on his flashlight and turned the pressure knob on the lantern. The hissing stopped; the light from the glowing mantle faded and went out. Save for his flashlight beam, the camp was engulfed in darkness. He slipped under the mosquito netting, switched off the flashlight, and stretched out face up on the lumpy kapok mattress. The night was hot and still, but he knew he would sleep soundly. He was too exhausted to dwell on his troubles.

In his growing drowsiness Van Groot's thoughts slipped into a maligara reverie. He pictured them: the supple crowns that barely reached the lowest boughs of the tallest subcanopy trees; the big fleshy yellow flowers that the primates loved to eat; the extraordinary chalky floriform fruits that unfolded like blossoms to reveal a dozen tiny seeds with brilliant scarlet arils. Originally he had thought that the habits of trees with such a distinctive appearance would have a definite pattern. But the trees occurred with equal frequency singly and in groves, on ridge crests and at the edges of streams, in well-drained and poorly drained soils, in light and shade. Some flowered and fruited thrice in a year and waited five years to become active again, others flowered and fruited annually for years at a time, still others flowered without fruiting. They never did anything in synchrony: the collective activity of the several dozen individuals Van Groot monitored seemed to change kaleidoscopically over months, even weeks. The maligaras were the free spirits of the forest—outlaws, outwitting even the clever monkeys and apes that came in search of food. And yet they were also humble and industrious. For millennia they had thrived under the towering canopy—in the vast shadows of great *tengkawangs, merantis, kapurs, kerwings*—leafing, flowering, and fruiting in their inimitable manner. They seemed to embody the aloofness of the ancient rain forest. Van Groot appreciated the privacy with which they went about their primeval tasks of germination, growth, reproduction, death, and decay. In the maligaras, he thought, perhaps the nosy English theorist would finally meet his match.

As he drifted toward sleep a big canopy tree went down off to the southeast. It was close enough for him to hear the deep, ominous creaking before the avalanche of sound, like a mountain collapsing into dust. Moments later came the indignant bellow of an orangutan, its sleep disturbed.

Such a puny protest, thought Van Groot.

He had a most unusual awakening the next morning. He had just dreamed he was waking up in Balikpapan at a friend's house, from which he could hear the constant rumble of the great gas flare at the Pertamina installation a mile away. Realizing he was truly awake, he opened his eyes and peered up into the blackness. It was the familiar predawn blackness of Mentoko Camp. Yet he could not shake the sensation of being in Balikpapan. His gaze fell on the luminous dial of his field clock. It was five in the morning. Why had he awakened before dawn? Dozing, he had another fantasy: that Pertamina, after thirteen years of operation downstream at Sangatta, had built a refinery overnight in the forest across the river from Mentoko. Then, in one heart-stopping instant, the truth hit him.

He grabbed his flashlight, slid out of bed, and made his way upstream along the riverside trail toward the sound. Already certain the fire was not in the study site but across the river, he felt no immediate danger; still, his heart pounded. He nearly blundered into a thick column of fire ants streaming across the narrow trail. He ran to a little bend in the river two hundred meters from camp. What he saw left him breathless: across the river, another two hundred meters upstream and no more than a hundred back from the water's edge, an enormous meranti was engulfed in flames. None of the trees crowding around it were on fire; the victim stood alone like a great slender torch in the darkness. Beneath it, where the dense mat of dried leaves was burning, the understory glowed as though floodlit by the flaming crown. Van Groot's eyes followed a ribbon of dull orange through the understory to a distant ridge. Just as he looked back at the meranti, a huge bird's-nest fern high on the bole, near to bursting from its load of dry leaf litter, caught fire with a *whoosh,* unfurling a thick tongue of flame into the air.

Van Groot walked back toward camp, trying to assess the situation. For months the fire must have been traveling upstream, not in a broad front but like a meandering river system with main channels, tributaries, and oxbows in an anastamosing web of fire that crisscrossed, joined, parted, curved back on itself. It seemed likely that large tracts of the logged forest across the river were already burning and that last night a finger of fire had used a parched streambed to poke its way through the high ridge paralleling the river.

Now it would spread along the river in either direction on the near side of the ridge. Where and when it would jump the river was impossible to say.

He had almost reached camp when he heard the motor of a prahu downstream. A pang of guilt stabbed him. His men's camp lay on the side of the river where the fire was, but he hadn't thought of the danger to them until the instant he heard the prahu. The motor signaled distress: to save gasoline, he had ordered the men to use only their paddles for trips between camps. Van Groot hurried into camp and down the sandy beach to the water's edge. He trained his flashlight on Nurdin's stocky figure as the prahu came to rest in the sand.

"*Selamat pagi,* Tuan." Nurdin climbed from the prahu.

"*Pagi,* Nurdin. Where's Johan? Is he all right?"

"Yes, Tuan. He's in camp watching the fire. It's close behind us: no sleep all night. But it hasn't moved up into the bamboo yet."

Though the only light came from the pair of flashlights pointing at the sand, Van Groot could see that Nurdin's face was haggard. "Is it too dangerous in the camp?" he asked. "Do Nurdin and Johan want to go downstream?"

Nurdin licked his lips. "I don't think so, Tuan. It's not so dangerous yet."

"Does Nurdin want to go down?" Van Groot pressed him.

"That depends on what Tuan wants."

Van Groot said that he wanted to stay, that Mentoko would be safe as long as the wind didn't shift. Without hesitation Nurdin replied, "Then Johan and I want to stay."

Van Groot felt a surge of affection for Nurdin. He tried to see through the darkness into the man's eyes. "Is Nurdin afraid? Don't be ashamed to say so."

"No, Tuan."

He told Nurdin to come with Johan to his own camp the moment theirs was no longer safe. They would continue gathering data as usual, with Nurdin replacing him in the forest at noon. Van Groot and Johan would monitor the fire's progress in the afternoon. The sky was already a deep blue when Nurdin took the prahu back downstream. Van Groot returned to the bend in the river to watch the fire as dawn broke. The monotonous greens, browns, and grays of the forest were broken by the flames. Smoke turned the brightening air magenta, mauve, lavender. Soon, as if nothing extraordinary was happening, the dawn chorusing of gibbons rang out over the forest.

The work went quickly that day, for only the little *pelawan* trees were still fruiting and nothing at all was flowering anymore. The bright scarlet husks of the pelawan fruit made for easy density estimates. As the morning wore on and the shock of the fire's arrival softened somewhat, Van Groot found himself feeling guardedly optimistic. Where he worked in the primary forest, more than a kilometer from the river, the rumble of flames to the north seemed only a faint memory of what he had heard earlier. Even if the wind shifted, he thought, the fire might not jump the river. Mentoko might make it through the crisis. Despite the prolonged drought, his study site was still reasonably intact. The thin-skinned lianas had been hit especially hard by water stress, and perhaps a third of the big merantis and kerwings—particularly on the bone-dry ridge crests—were dead. But a majority of the latter and virtually all of the hardier tengkawangs, *ipils,* and ironwoods, and the better protected riverine species, were still alive. Most important to Van Groot, the humble subcanopy trees that thrived in the deep shade of the giants and in splashes of sunlight along streams seemed fine. The *kelinsais* and *kernangas* and *nyatohs* had flowered and fruited well into the drought, the maligaras right up until a few weeks ago, and the pelawans were fruiting even now. He felt certain that Mentoko would not abandon him. At one point he gazed up into the chalky smoke clouding the crowns of emergents and imagined it was only morning fog drifting off the river.

Before returning to camp for lunch, Van Groot trudged up and down the riverside trail to check the forest along the opposite bank. The fire looked less menacing in broad daylight. It had spread along the river from its entry point, as he had anticipated, but it had traveled only a hundred meters in either direction. In some places it appeared to have wandered back over the ridge. In only one spot had it reached the riverbank. There it had found its way into an old hollow *binuang* tree truncated at midbole. With flames visible through a gaping hole in the trunk, the binuang resembled a fireplace belching smoke from a damaged chimney. Sparks flew straight up in the heat draft and fell harmlessly into the river.

By evening the fire had reached the ridge slope directly across the river from camp. Van Groot carefully wrapped his notebooks, correspondence, passport, and permits in heavy plastic, put them in his pack, and stuffed some clothes around them. He set the pack in the center of the table and lay his sheathed parang across it. There was no sleep that night. He sat on the verandah drinking cup after cup of strong coffee as Mitzi prowled the forest around camp, her eyes reflecting the firelight.

By three in the morning, the fire had run all the way up the slope and climbed several large trees. The steady roar was almost soothing now. Van Groot sat transfixed by the terrible beauty of the scene: the slope awash in flames, the immense trees burning for hours. Some fell with thunderous crashes; others came apart piecemeal and cascaded down the slope, crackling and popping like enormous firecrackers.

Two hours later the fire showed signs of having run its course. High on the ridge a great ipil still burned like a beacon, but the slope itself seemed to be smoldering rather than burning. Van Groot sat staring at the fire until dawn, wishing it away, willing it back downstream and over the ridge. It was crucial that it not move up into the large bamboo grove on the opposite bank. The grove was barely thirty meters from camp, and he knew what happened when dry bamboo caught fire. It wouldn't matter which way the wind was blowing then: the bamboo would go up all at once like a great bonfire, creating its own violent winds that would shower the camp with glowing cinders. With any luck, he thought, the bamboo would be bypassed; surely it would have caught by now.

The men were due in camp at six. At five-thirty Van Groot pulled on his boots and hiked upstream to check on things. In a day's time the fire had traveled no more than five hundred meters; he worried that its leisurely pace might be lulling him into complacency. More frightening were the steady branch-fall and tree-fall reverberating through the forest. He wondered what his men were thinking. Did he have any right to keep them here? He knew it was dangerous to push them too far: they were loath to challenge him openly and might just abandon him if they grew too frightened.

He walked back to camp to greet them. Bleary-eyed from another sleepless night, they accepted his decision to stay without any sign of approval or disapproval. His plan was to stay another day, and if on the next morning the fire showed no signs of withdrawing or fizzling out, they would leave together for the kampong. The trip would take nine to ten hours and they would reach the kampong before sundown. Despite the men's impassive expressions, Van Groot sensed that they were relieved. As he worked in the forest that morning, he kept thinking of their worried families in the kampong: all those brothers and sisters, aunts and uncles, cousins and nephews and nieces, not to mention wives and children—and not one of them would miss a call to prayer until the men returned safely. Someone might even come upstream to fetch them. By noon he feared that he was courting disaster by putting the men and their families under so much pressure. He decided to leave for the kampong at daybreak the next morning, regardless of the state of the fire.

They did not have to wait that long. At midafternoon the bamboo on the opposite bank caught fire and within seconds it was a crackling, hissing mass of flame. Camp became an oven; burning cinders rained onto the house thatch. Drenched with sweat, Van Groot carried his pack into the forest and bounded to the top of the ridge nearest camp. Cupping his hands tightly around his lips, he summoned the men with a *hoo* call. Minutes later they emerged from the forest, blinking as they entered the sunlight. "It's in the bamboo!" he shouted over the roar of the fire. "I've had enough! Let's go!" The prahu was waiting downstream at a grove of *baleo* trees entwined by leafy climbers. The men had already loaded their rice, cooking utensils, and cartons of cigarettes. Van Groot was getting in when he suddenly remembered Mitzi. Johan snatched a burlap sack from the prahu and raced back to fetch her.

The men were lighthearted, grinning and joking as they steered the prahu through the maze of rocks and logs. On his way through the forest to the prahu, Van Groot had already wondered if he wasn't giving up on Mentoko too easily. Seeing the men giddy with relief dispelled his doubts. Below the Bendili Stream there would be smooth sailing, but by dusk they still had not reached it. They stopped to spend the night on an exposed rocky section of riverbed.

While Johan gathered firewood for cooking rice, Nurdin hauled the prahu's floorboards out onto the rocks for Van Groot to sleep on. Mitzi was ecstatic to be free again. After dinner, as Van Groot lay on the hard planks waiting for sleep, he could see her in the underbrush chasing giant cockroaches at the margin of the firelight.

In the kampong Van Groot caught a Pertamina sky van to Balikpapan, where he stayed with Dutch acquaintances in the Union Oil compound on Pasir Ridge. For ten days he enjoyed the air conditioning, ate heaping platefuls of good food, drank cold Dutch beer, took two hot showers a day, and relaxed by the pool reading light novels from the recreation center's paperback lending library. Although he still had several days' worth of raw data to transcribe into his notebooks, he made no move to fetch them from his pack. He didn't think of Mentoko at all for a week.

His men expected him back in the kampong in ten days. Left alone in the house one evening as his hosts viewed a new American movie at the rec center, Van Groot bravely peeled off the outermost of the protective layers that had grown around his emotions since the fire. He pulled the bundle of correspondence from his pack and stood with it in the middle of the living room, holding it as if it were some dusty artifact from a long-dead civilization. He looked down at the first letter—the one from David Cairns-Smith—and the phrase "Maligara Man" caught his eye. The nickname, too, seemed to belong to the distant past. The implications of what had happened hit him then with the force of lightning. All at once he sloughed off the remaining protective layers like a snake's dead skin. His hands trembled. The floodgates opened and he fell across the couch, sobbing. After a while he wiped his eyes on his sleeve and sat up, ignoring the babu peeking in at him from the kitchen. He leaned forward and covered his face with his hands. He realized that when the fire had come, the need for immediate action had blocked any reflection on the future. At the same time, his love for the forest had infused him with false optimism. Since arriving in Balikpapan he had been in a state of shock, numb. As the numbness faded he imagined the worst. He recalled hearing in the kampong that a second wave of fire was moving steadily upstream on the Mentoko side of the river. Even if the first fire had failed to jump the river, the second was sure to hit home. Mentoko would be devastated.

He shook his head miserably. He was too old to start over. Finding and establishing a new site would be a crushing amount of trouble. But, no, it wasn't really that. He might curse and rage at the trouble of starting over, but it would never reduce him to tears. The truth was that he didn't have the slightest desire to live and work anywhere but at Mentoko. He loathed the very idea of working in some strange forest. A new site would only remind him of Mentoko, continually dredge up the pain of his loss. He thought of the destruction there, of the graceful little maligaras scorched and lifeless. He felt hopelessly lost.

Idly he reread the Cairns-Smith letter. It didn't seem so evil now. Had he been reading too much into it? He thought back to his own years as a young and reckless graduate student: had he never criticized his elders in order to impress his peers? At any rate, the incident at Leiden was already fifteen years old. He was sick of it. If Cairns-Smith still thought the way he had then, it was to his discredit as a scientist.

"Let him think whatever he likes about me," Van Groot mumbled to himself. "I won't stoop to that level."

He sat at the dining table and composed a letter to

Cairns-Smith pledging his assistance. Even as he wrote, he felt his hatred for the Englishman dwindling. It didn't matter anymore.

In the kampong, news that the second wave of fire was still burning left little doubt in Van Groot's mind that Mentoko had been hit. The unaccustomed smoothness of the ride upstream belied the turmoil in his heart. It had rained heavily several nights before, the first significant rainfall in more than sixty days, but the fresh flow had not yet forced the intruding seawater back to the river's mouth. The prahu passed boatloads of villagers paddling upstream to bathe and fetch drinking water. A kilometer below the Bendili, the boatmen would stop paddling, and their saronged passengers, clutching bars of soap, would jump laughing and squealing into the shallow water. At least a dozen motorized prahus came downstream filled with gasoline drums of drinking water for sale.

During the ride Van Groot dared to hope again. Had Mentoko been spared the worst? As the truth drew nearer, the ache in his heart began to burn like the forest he had fled. He trained his gaze on the relatively healthy riverine forest, for his spirits sank whenever he glimpsed distant ridges cloaked with leafless forest the color of mud and charcoal. Nurdin and Johan, afraid for their livelihoods, reacted with forced cheerfulness and gallows humor. Johan pointed at a blackened tree stump and joked that it was what was left of his Mentoko hut. When at last the men's camp swung into view, Nurdin and Johan leapt to their feet, hooting and hollering at the sight of their undamaged homes. Van Groot joined in a second bout of cheering as they pulled up to the crescent of sandy beach at Mentoko Camp. His house, framed by charred bamboo groves on either side, stood untouched by fire. The absence of dry leaf litter in the clearings had been enough to save both camps.

The first week at Mentoko dampened his spirits, however. A fair portion of the canopy was still alive, but the entire understory was dead, clogged with dreary stands of heat-killed poles and saplings. The forest floor was a vast carpet of ash. With the gentlest breeze the ash would sift through camp like dirty snow, dusting newly washed clothes on the line, notebooks lying open on the table, cooking utensils, dinner. In many places the trails had vanished on a forest floor laid bare. There were moments, standing in the intense sunlight of yawning gaps in the canopy or gazing at the blackened remains of a favorite kelinsai that had flowered so beautifully only months before, when Van Groot felt oppressed by the destruction. Plagues of insects deepened his gloom. The forest was dense with flies until the rains returned in full force; then clouds of mosquitoes arose, hatching by the billions from ephemeral pools. At work in the forest he coated his exposed skin with repellent, but the mosquitoes bit through his heavy fatigues. In camp he sat imprisoned within a ring of smoking mosquito coils. He felt left behind. Most of the forest animals had migrated in search of food. For days at a time he saw only wild pigs, stringy and listless, and at night he heard the clatter of cans in his garbage dump and the screams of piglets being devoured by boars.

With the aid of field maps Nurdin and Johan set about relocating, remeasuring, and re-marking the trails. Meanwhile, Van Groot censused his vegetation plots. Some of them were nothing more than bare earth and rubble. He scribbled a depressing set of new categories onto his checklists for individual plants: present or absent; alive, dying, or dead; drought- or fire-killed; burned or heat-killed; totally or partially defoliated. He noted singed buttresses, shattered crowns, burned-out roots. Kerwings and merantis, all but one or two of their roots eaten away, teetered menacingly on ridge crests. Around them lay the charred hulks of fallen giants in shrouds of lianas. The volume of recent tree-fall was enormous. One of Van Groot's first tasks was to examine all standing trees within reach of his and his men's houses. Finding no immediate danger, they rested easier in their camps. But in the forest they never felt safe. During that first week Mentoko was shaken again and again by the roar of tree-fall. Van Groot told the men that the site would have to be abandoned if the rate of tree-fall didn't decline soon. Unconcerned, Nurdin and Johan nodded and smiled. They knew he would find reasons to stay.

And before long Van Groot did find them. Even amid the horror of that first week there were striking signs of beauty and continuity. He would stand near the river, enveloped by lush green glades the fire had missed, and feel transported to the old Mentoko. Many small tree species appeared healthy, even some of the riverine lianas. The omnivorous primates were still present, foraging for insects and new shoots. Within twenty minutes of entering the forest on the day of his return, he encountered the common *kra* monkeys feeding on charred pelawan fruit that still clung to the little trees. Later in the week he found orang-utans and leaf monkeys and surprised a small group of rare pigtail monkeys, which dropped from the low crown of a nyatoh and fled along the forest floor. Meanwhile, the gibbons chorused as if to welcome him home.

And there were the maligaras. He roamed the forest checking them off on his list one by one. They were all alive! Not even their foliage had been affected. He felt humbled by their perseverance. A month later, to his great joy and amazement, every one of them flowered on the same day as if in celebration. There had been a few good rains; he'd thought the maligaras might respond, but this was astonishing. When he came across the first grove and saw the warm splashes of yellow dotting the subcanopy, he became light on his feet. He ran from tree to tree and grove to grove. He grew giddy; head spinning, he shouted in triumph each time he found a flowering maligara. The forest seemed to be speaking to him through the maligaras. It was urging him to stand his ground, promising him a second chance at Mentoko.

A week later he sent a letter to Cairns-Smith informing him that the maligaras were alive and well, and suggesting that he visit Mentoko in December after Van Groot's customary autumn in Leiden. He no longer felt the generosity he had earlier when he'd thought the maligaras were dead, but he was satisfied that there was no way to oppose the Englishman's visit. He looked forward to it with stoic resignation.

爲

When Van Groot left camp for Leiden at the end of August, the forest already sported two months' growth of seedlings like a vast meadow under the remaining canopy. He knew that Mentoko was changed forever. The regeneration would produce a new species-poor forest to compete with the remnants of the old. Nevertheless, he felt that some ultimate good must come from this rebirth, and it was with a light heart that he rode the prahu to the kampong. He gave Nurdin and Johan a month's wages in advance, along with a letter to his bank in Samarinda authorizing them to receive two months' additional pay after a specified date. A Pertamina sky van carried him to Balikpapan, where he caught a Garuda flight to Jakarta.

The capital was in the throes of an especially harsh dry season. Dark clouds teased the populace before dispersing as suddenly as they had gathered. The alternating sun and shade reminded Van Groot of the new Mentoko as his taxi crested waves of motorbikes and three-wheel *bajai* on its way to the LIPI offices. LIPI was the government agency that approved and monitored research by foreign scientists. He was headed there to hand-deliver his annual research report. For the sake of maintaining good relations with Pak Masinambo, the official under whose jurisdiction his project fell, Van Groot made an effort to visit LIPI whenever he passed through Jakarta. The current visit was particularly important, for the agency had recently moved into new offices on Jalan Gatot Subroto, and he felt obliged to put in an admiring appearance.

The slate-colored office building's reception area resembled a plush parking garage. A swath of marble fronted the bank of offices, but the floor and exterior wall were of bare concrete. The wall was oddly tiered with strips of open space that let traffic noise and fumes into the building. Van Groot was greeted by the head secretary. Soon Masinambo appeared, beaming, and led his guest into his private office. Van Groot took a seat in a comfortable modern chair that was a far cry from the battered classroom-style ones at the old office. Masinambo moved to the leather swivel chair behind his desk. He looked unusually trim and cool in a light-blue safari suit. Van Groot had just noticed the coolness of the room when his host, grinning proudly, gestured at the window. Van Groot turned and saw a brand new air conditioner humming along, depositing the product of its labor onto the courtyard below with a steady drip.

"Marvelous!" Van Groot exclaimed in Dutch. "Congratulations, Pak."

"It's been a long time in coming, hasn't it?" Masinambo said, also in Dutch.

The official was a Menadonese from northern Sulawesi,

a Christian who as a teenager had attended one of the Dutch academies in the final years before independence. His fair knowledge of Dutch, along with Van Groot's fluency in Indonesian, was a major reason for the rapport they now enjoyed. An outsider in Java, Masinambo had spent a long career in uncomplaining service to his country, far from the halls of power and influence in this city of endless Javanese political intrigue. He was a man who knew his limitations, and for that Van Groot respected him. He was not a hard worker, however, and though this failing had given Van Groot ample opportunity to ingratiate himself through personal favors, Masinambo had an irritating habit of taking favors for granted.

After tea, they eased from social chitchat into business. To his written report on the effects of drought and fire at Mentoko, Van Groot added a verbal summary, knowing that Masinambo would appreciate the personal attention as a gesture of respect and esteem. He also knew that his summaries were useful to Masinambo in reporting to superiors. In the same spirit, Van Groot always submitted his written reports in Indonesian so that Masinambo could crib passages from them without having to go to the trouble of translating them from Dutch. Though years had passed without Masinambo reciprocating in the least, Van Groot clung stubbornly to the belief that such attentions would bring some ultimate reward.

Masinambo jotted down notes as he listened, his expression polite and bemused. The notion of living in the jungle was to him only slightly less bizarre than that of living on the moon, and he regarded Van Groot's returning to the fire-damaged study site as sheer insanity. He waited patiently for his guest to finish. When Van Groot at last rose to say good-bye, Masinambo raised a hand to stop him.

"Just a moment, Doctor," he said, putting on his reading

glasses. He reached for a manila folder. "I have something here of interest to you."

Van Groot sat down. "Yes, Pak?"

"I have just received three weeks ago a proposal from a Dr. David Cairns-Smith of the Cambridge University, concerning an idea for research at Mentoko. It involves . . ." and here he leaned forward to scrutinize something in the folder, ". . . maligara trees." He read on, nodding. "Ah, yes—Dr. Cairns-Smith claims to be a friend of your director at the Rijksherbarium. I think you must know about this already?"

"Yes, Pak," Van Groot answered.

Being reminded of it was very annoying. He looked distractedly out of the window at a palm tree with gleaming fronds fanned out like a peacock's tail. Why hadn't it occurred to him that even the great Cairns-Smith would have to obtain formal LIPI approval like any ordinary "hack"? His mind's eye formed an image of the arrogant young graduate student with his condescending smile. He could hear the nasal, aristocratic voice: "herbarium hacks," it said, then "precious specimens," and finally a spate of algebraic gibberish blurred by the pounding of Van Groot's heart. Masinambo's voice broke his reverie. He struggled to gain control of his emotions.

"I'm sorry, Pak—what did you say?"

"I asked what you think of the proposal. I'm ready to approve it, but I thought I should get your opinion first."

Drawing his notepad and pen toward him, Masinambo waited for his guest's reply. But at that moment Van Groot was gazing past him into a brilliant flash of light that had just burst from a thousand flowering maligaras in his mind. Here was his second chance! He hadn't mentioned the maligaras specifically in his report to LIPI: that was the key to concealing a lie! It was foolproof. He had already invited Cairns-Smith to Mentoko. The Englishman would never in a million years suspect Van Groot's influence on a vaguely worded rejection letter from LIPI. Cairns-Smith would drop the maligara project like a hot potato. His restless intellect would flit off to some other species, some new theory.

Van Groot folded his arms across his chest and said as calmly as he could, "There's one serious problem with that proposal, Pak."

"Oh?"

"The maligaras are all dead."

"*Aduh!* Really?"

"I'm afraid so." With a sigh he looked out at the fan palm again. "Every last one of them burned to a crisp."

"Well. I can hardly approve the proposal then, can I? What a shame. I'll make it very clear in my letter—"

"Oh, don't bother going into details, Pak," Van Groot said casually. "David and I are old friends. As soon as I get to Leiden I'll phone him about our conversation."

"Good," said Masinambo, nodding approvingly. "Personal contact would be best, of course." He picked up his pen. "So . . . no details are necessary?"

"None at all, Pak."

Van Groot smiled faintly at Masinambo, who sat with pen poised to take down his exact words. He thought of all the times he had done the little drone's paperwork for him and waited in vain to be repaid. With carefully feigned nonchalance he continued, "You could just say something like, 'Due to the current situation in the Kutai Reserve, we cannot at this time approve your project.' That should be enough."

"There," said Masinambo, penning a period at the end of the sentence on his notepad. "You've saved me the trouble." He rose with a smile and extended his hand to Van Groot.

"Well, Doctor, have a good flight home. See you in three months?"

# PUSH PULL

"Well, well, look who blew into town," Bill said when he spotted me from the bar. He climbed down from his stool and came over. "Where they been keeping you?" He was trying to seem upbeat but his face sagged as if he'd been sleeping poorly.

"Bangkok mostly," I said. I motioned for him to pull up a chair. I was in Jakarta to cover a regional conference on Cambodia for a Sydney daily and was sorry to have only a few days to spend. A decade in Southeast Asia had failed to weaken Java's strange hold on me. It was a place where people sought escape in ancient, brooding dreams of enchantment. Whenever I was there I sensed those dreams lurking in the clove-scented shadows of rural lanes and city streets, waiting to lure me into the heart of some timeless mystery. Now it was only Bill Silberman materializing out of the clove-scented shadows of the Hotel Indonesia's Ganesha Bar, exposing the folly of my romantic vision.

He looked around for a cocktail waitress but none acknowledged him. With his scraggly beard, faded sports shirt, and scuffed moccasins without socks, he seemed out of place in the Ganesha Bar. He turned to my drinking companion and extended a hand. "Bill Silberman."

The man in the elegant batik dress shirt tilted his head back to look squarely at Bill through his thick black-framed glasses. He wore them with the earpieces high on the sides of his head so that he was always tilting his head back to look at things. He reached out his left hand, leaving the withered right one lying in his lap. "Suprapto," he said with a formal smile. Like many Javanese, he went by only one name.

"Suprapto," Bill repeated. "Not the one who works for the moneychanger here in the hotel?"

"Yes, that one."

"I heard you were some sort of prince a long time ago." Bill's tone was disdainful.

Before Suprapto could respond I said, "Not a prince, a *dalang* trained in the Sultan's court in Jogja."

The disdain vanished from Bill's voice. "A dalang? No kidding? Why did you stop being a dalang?"

Suprapto held up his withered hand and let it fall back onto his lap.

Bill was silent. From his knowledge of Suprapto's prior connection with the Sultan's court and current connection with P. T. Arthra, moneychanger, he had probably pegged my friend as an aristocrat fallen on hard times. Now he was off balance. Suprapto's having been a dalang, the puppet master of traditional Javanese *wayang* theater, impressed Bill Silberman. He loved things Indonesian, at least those not limited to the old Javanese aristocracy or the new state-capitalist elite. Bill had come of age in the late 1960s, an industrialist's son who had renounced his privileged origins to become a self-styled working-class hero. Now in his early forties, his beard and thinning hair peppered with gray, he still wrote exclusively for underground publications. He was working for a Marxist monthly called *Southeast Asia Watchdog*, for which he had filed a steady stream of reports hypercritical of the regime. The postcolonial Javanese elite and the Westerners who associated with them were his prime targets. This caused him all sorts of professional nuisances—he was continually on the verge of being expelled from the country—but Bill was a natural-born martyr, who wore each new nuisance like a badge of truth and decency. Though it was rumored he could afford better, he insisted on living without air-conditioning in a run-down, one-room bungalow on a downtown street frequented by aggressive transvestite hookers. Most of the time he treated us other journalists like sellouts, but every so often he'd stumble under his burden of loneliness and solicit friendship. His rigid views and general unpleasantness made the rest of us shy away.

I didn't like to inflict Bill on my friends, but I knew that a Javanese moneychanger-dalang would confuse him. Suprapto was an ordinary villager, who had been exposed to courtly ways during his training in the Sultan's wayang school in Jogjakarta. The story circulating among expats was that he had already become a respected dalang when his career was cut short by an accident in which his right hand and forearm were severely burned. Afterward he migrated to Jakarta, the nation's center for displaced persons, where he landed a job in what was then Indonesia's only luxury hotel. Strategically placed and speaking excellent English and Dutch, which he had learned at the Sultan's court, he became acquainted with many of Jakarta's Western expatriates. He was now in his early fifties. Though very short and rather ugly, with a long thin face and an incongruous pug nose, he commanded a striking presence. Always dressed in beautiful Jogjanese batik or an immaculate dove-gray safari suit, he embodied the courtly *halus* values of grace, refinement, and self-control in a way that seemed to highlight the *kasar*—the crudeness and excitability—in others. He treated everyone he met graciously, regardless of status or background. I had never heard him make a disdainful remark about farmers or pedicab drivers, on the one hand, or aristocrats or high officials on the other. He was a pleasant contrast to Bill Silberman.

Bill looked particularly bereft that evening. It was part of a familiar pattern: his appearances at the "decadent" Hotel Indonesia always signaled a new bout of loneliness.

"Can I buy you mates another drink?" he asked, affecting an Australian accent.

I told him we were about to leave. Suprapto had been invited to a dinner party at George and Helen Karner's in Kebayoran Baru. Knowing that I was a friend of the Karners, he'd asked me to come along. Bill was noticeably disappointed. He pressed us to stay. Suprapto gave me a sidelong glance, then looked at Bill through his tilted lenses. "Actually," he said, "we're going to a party at the Karners'. Why don't you come along?"

Bill gave a contemptuous snort but his eyes lit up. "Why not?" he said. "To see how the other half lives."

I looked at Suprapto. How could he have made such an error? I knew he had heard of Silberman through the expat grapevine and was aware of the man's reputation. George Karner was a political analyst with the U.S. Foreign Service, precisely the sort of man Bill despised. There were bound to be influential guests for Bill to insult, even an Indonesian general or two.

Perhaps for my own peace of mind, I entertained the thought that Suprapto had seen something in the stars that were beginning to appear through the windows of the Ganesha Bar. As a trained dalang he supposedly possessed mystical powers of insight and control. He was heir to centuries of wayang *kulit,* the Javanese shadow play, in which the dalang, supported by a gamelan orchestra, enthralls his audience from sundown to sunrise by manipulating dozens of stylized, flat leather puppets with movable arms against a back-lit screen. The shadow play instructs onlookers in the halus values of self-mastery and humility through the old Hindu tales of gods, kings, heroes, and villains. Could it be that Suprapto thought the gods were planning something for the Karner affair and that Bill Silberman was their unlikely emissary?

I offered to hire a hotel taxi for the three of us, but Bill insisted on driving us himself in his antique Fiat. Like a native Jakartan he weaved through the laneless morass of rush-hour traffic and hawkers on Jalan Thamrin. The Fiat had no air-conditioning, so we cruised along with the windows wide open, at the mercy of buses, jitneys, and motorbikes spewing gritty black exhaust. The Fiat coughed and sputtered in every gear. I mused that Bill kept it poorly tuned on purpose; to him a smoothly running car was probably sinful enough to keep one from entering the gates of heaven. Suprapto, used to riding the little canvas-topped three-wheel *bajai,* took out a perfumed handkerchief and held it over his nose and mouth.

At last we turned off Jenderal Sudirman and entered the smooth, palm-lined roads of one of Kebayoran Baru's affluent residential neighborhoods. The Karner house sat in a high-walled compound filled with bougainvillea and frangipani. It was a two-story melange of styles: Indonesian, Dutch colonial, Southern California modern. The Indonesian elements were a *pendopo* roof of orange terra-cotta tiles and a heavy mahogany front door with elaborate Javanese carvings. Helen Karner met us in the foyer. Suprapto complimented her on the house and she said, "Yes, I really love the Indonesian architecture." Bill whispered to me, "A roof and a door—is she kidding?" In the living room he rolled his eyes at the sofa cushions patterned with magenta frangipani blossoms and the expensive rattan patio set visible through the Dutch windows. As soon as he had the chance he mentioned to Helen that he lived near Menteng. She said that she didn't know where Menteng was. Bill told her it was downtown. She looked at him warily.

"Actually, it's a very nice old area," Bill said. "The President lives there, you know."

"Oh?" she said. "I thought he lived in the presidential palace."

"He uses that for entertaining dignitaries, but he lives in a big old house in Menteng. Part of his 'man of the people' image. It's a bit larger and has a few more servants and security guards than the average Jakarta residence, though."

Undaunted, she asked, "And how do you like it there?"

"Oh, fine," he said, affecting an upper-crust British accent. "I've got a bungalow, you know. It's only one room with no air-conditioning or hot water, but it has authentic Indonesian architecture just like yours."

Self-satisfied, he strode to the bar, where he proceeded to display his fluency in Indonesian by striking up a conversation with the bartender. The young man looked cornered and mumbled a few responses. I guessed Bill was interrogating him about wages and working conditions.

While I'd known that Bill could be rude and vindictive,

I hadn't realized he was a bully. Helen Karner was an easier target than most, an expatriate who maintained a comfortable Western life-style, rarely if ever experiencing Indonesia firsthand. In Bill's eyes this was a cardinal sin. I knew it wouldn't matter to him if I explained that Helen, having followed George through a string of overseas assignments, didn't really want to be there at all and was counting the days until she went home. Nor would it matter that she was a shy woman who had difficulty adapting to new places and experiences. Bill's sympathy was a scarce commodity reserved for the destitute and hopeless.

I chatted with George, keeping an eye on Helen in case she needed rescuing. Bill seemed content to ridicule her behind her back. He was particularly amused when she got upset over some ants crawling in a bowl of unhusked rambutan fruits. As she called for the babu to destroy the offenders, Bill sidled up to me and said, "Can you believe getting worked up over ants in Java? I'd like to see her come face to face with one of those deer-sized cockroaches at my house." Later I was getting a drink at the bar when I felt a tap on my shoulder. "Look over there," Bill said. He nodded across the room to where Helen Karner was talking with Suprapto. She was showing him her prized wall hanging, a quilt she'd made depicting a rural American landscape: a red barn, a white frame house, cows in a pasture, an apple orchard on a distant hilltop.

"Amazing," Bill said. "She made that damned thing back in Wisconsin or wherever and brought it here like some sort of amulet to protect her from the strange gods of Java."

"Suprapto seems quite taken with it," I pointed out.

"Ah, he's too polite." He made a contemptuous noise and stalked off.

The servants were preparing a long serving table in the den for the *rijstafel,* a kind of Dutch-Indonesian buffet. Just then the babu came out of the kitchen in a panic. Helen went to her and they spoke in whispers. When Helen slipped into the kitchen, Suprapto took the babu gently by the arm and questioned her in Indonesian. Turning to me, he said, "She's burned a batch of fried chicken and is afraid there won't be enough. The driver has the evening off. I think we should ask someone to take her to the *pasar.*" He went into the kitchen after Helen.

I was about to go looking for Bill to ask him to lend me his car when he came up behind me and asked what was going on. While I was explaining, Helen came out of the kitchen with Suprapto, saying, ". . . no, not from one of those filthy pasars—from the Hero, just to be safe. But you'd better take me, instead—the Hero frightens her." She was referring to the Hero Supermarket a half dozen blocks south on Jenderal Sudirman, a vast, sparkling-clean American-style supermarket with shopping carts and labels in English.

Bill stepped forward. "I'll take you, Helen. We'll be back in no time."

I invited myself along. Just as we started to pull out of the driveway, Bill hit the brake. Suprapto was standing right in front of the car in the glare of the headlights. We were all startled; none of us had seen him come out. Bill called to him, "Come on, get in—the more the merrier."

It didn't hit me what Bill was up to until, a third of the way down Jenderal Sudirman, he winked at me and said, "Hey, why go all the way to the Hero?" He hung a sharp right off the broad boulevard into a poor kampong, a packing-case-and-scrap-metal slum. The narrow lane was jammed with pedestrians forced into the roadway by the scores of pushcart peddlers and bicycle repairmen who had laid claim to the plank walkways. I was in front with Bill, and as we began honking and lurching our way into the

warrenlike maze of shacks and stalls, I felt Helen's fingers
clutch at the back of my seat. A profusion of odors assaulted
us through the open car windows: gasoline, rotting fruit,
cloves, palm oil, peanut sauce, raw sewage. Young and old
men in undershirts watched from where they squatted on
food-stall benches in the dim glow of pressure lamps.
Young boys darted to the moving car and thrust at us
cartons of sweet tea, cigarettes, sweets wrapped in banana
leaves. I heard a faint whimper from Helen. Bill glanced
over his shoulder and said cheerfully, "Better roll up your
window halfway. Haven't been in one of these kampongs
lately, have you?" He motioned at a row of makeshift food
stalls where saronged women with grimy fingernails and
scarlet, betel-stained teeth were shooing clouds of flies from
their inventory. "I'll bet you'd prefer a closed store, huh?"
Helen, lips pursed and face glossy with sweat, nodded.

Navigating the roadway was like riding a skiff through
a squall. We lurched across gaping potholes and came to rest
at a shop-house that had been cobbled together from plywood and cinder blocks. The shop portion appeared to be
a combined grocery store and eating place. It was more
prosperous than the standard kampong fare; it even had a
screen door with half of the screen still on it. Rock music
shrieked at us from the photocopy-and-cassette stall next
door.

Bill reached back to open Helen's door and said brightly,
"We're here!" He grabbed my arm when I started to get
out. Helen made some fluttery motions like a trapped mi-
gratory bird, then froze. Finally she got a good two-handed
grip on her purse and stepped from the car. After a few
faltering strides, she stopped in the middle of a mud puddle
where the sidewalk planks were missing. This allowed a
little boy in a peaked cap to catch up to her and start
tugging at her elbow with one hand while holding out his

other hand palm up. Helen was focused on the shop and ignored him. I made another move to get out but Bill grabbed my arm again. "Hey, I'm enjoying this," he protested.

Meanwhile, Helen had turned and with the boy still tugging at her arm was heading back to the car. Bill muttered, "Oh, no, you don't!" and was about to get out himself when I saw that Helen had stopped again and turned back to the shop. The shopkeeper, a wiry, bowlegged old man, was standing in the doorway in an undershirt and khaki shorts. He held the door open with one hand and gestured with the other for Helen to come in. She made her way to the door, where he separated her from the young beggar and escorted her inside. Bill clapped his hands. "I'd love to see her face when she gets a load of the fried chicken in there," he gloated. I pictured the blind, crusty, open-beaked heads protruding from a jumble of pieces warty with flies.

I bought some bottles of sweetened tea from a vendor and we settled back to wait. The evening had turned sultry. Soon there was a tremendous thunderclap. Rain hurtled down in what seemed like a solid sheet of water. The street emptied. People huddled under awnings of leaky plastic and corrugated iron held in place by rocks, bricks, and chunks of sidewalk. Helen was in the shop a good fifteen minutes. I thought she was waiting out the rain, but with the downpour still at its height she emerged clutching a large plastic bag and hurried through the mud to the car. The shopkeeper scuttled along beside her, holding an umbrella over her as best he could. With his dripping charge safely in the back seat, he gave a little bow and scurried back to the shop. Helen blew spray from her lips and brushed at the wet strands of hair plastered against her face. She was grinning, her round cheeks flushed with excitement. She let out a carefree, girlish laugh.

"What a remarkable country!" she exclaimed. "That sweet old man opened up his shop for me!"

Bill said, "How's that?"

She laughed again and let out a sigh. "Well, when I first went to go in I saw it was closed. My driver once taught me the words for *open* and *closed;* I saw the word for *closed* on the door, but the owner must have noticed me and hurried over to open up. Indonesian hospitality! I mean, you expect it at ministry receptions and that sort of thing, but in a place like *this* . . . !"

I looked across at the shop door through the rain. Nowhere did it say *tutup*—"closed." Above the handle was a standard plastic sign that read *tarik,* meaning "pull." I looked at Bill. He gave me a cold smile. He'd seen it too. I didn't like the gleam in his eyes as he turned to where Helen sat beaming in the back seat. With one little remark—a translation of a single word—he could humiliate her so badly that she might never have the courage to venture out again.

I stared straight ahead into the night, waiting for the ax to fall. But it didn't. Bill hesitated for a moment. Then he said, "I see you got your fried chicken."

"Oh, yes," Helen replied, patting the bag on her lap. "Thanks so much for bringing me here. It would have taken ages if we'd gone to the Hero."

Bill restarted the car. I glanced in the rearview mirror and saw Suprapto's thin oval face. His head was tilted back slightly, and through the lenses his eyes were hooded. I was certain it was that look that had somehow stopped Bill from humiliating Helen.

Back at the party, Helen's ristjafel was a great success,

buoying her spirits even more. She told everyone, "It would have been a total disaster without that little grocery store," and "Do you know, he even ran out into the pouring rain to hold an umbrella for me? What wonderful people, the Indonesians!" Meanwhile, Bill Silberman was strangely subdued.

Afterward Bill wanted to go back to the Ganesha Bar, but Suprapto insisted we join him for a beer at his place. It was a modest three-room brick house, with a small yard and flower garden, in one of the kampongs of northeast Jakarta. Suprapto had planted scarlet hibiscus and lavender hydrangeas. I caught a glimpse of a miniature forest of mango and guava trees in back. Inside, there was an eclectic array of Indonesian and Western furnishings and artwork, including Italian figurines, reproductions of Dutch masters paintings, Balinese wood carvings. His collection of wayang kulit puppets dominated the walls of the sitting room. The flat leather figures were set in matrices of finishing nails and arranged in a variety of poses. I recognized Arjuna, with his glittering gold face and multicolored headdress, his hands raised in benediction. There was a black-faced Rama, with his spindly arms hanging at his sides, and a white Hanuman, the monkey god, and the ugly, crippled dwarf, Semar—the pre-Hindu Javanese god who used his halus wisdom to manipulate the Hindu interlopers, playing the fool all the while. The figures were among the finest I'd ever seen, expertly worked and painted. In the orange glow of the lamp's twenty-five watts they imparted an eerie beauty to the plain room.

We sat drinking beer and listening to the restful gongs and metallophones of gamelan music on Suprapto's tape deck. I found myself growing irritated at Bill even before he opened his mouth. Any moment, he was sure to bring up what he'd been brooding over for the last two hours:

Helen Karner's pathetic mistake in the kampong and the ignorance and egocentricity it revealed. It had been unlike him not to rub her nose in it on the spot. Clearly his contempt could not be suppressed much longer. But when he finally mentioned the incident, he did it gently, almost affectionately. He took out a pack of *kreteks,* the clove-spiced cigarettes of the Indonesian poor, and offered them to Suprapto and me. As we smoked, he laughed and said, "Funny about Helen Karner in the kampong, wasn't it? *Push, pull?* " I was expecting some cruel barb to follow, but he let it go at that.

Suprapto drew deeply on his kretek and said, "Yes, quite funny." He looked at Bill. "Very considerate of you, though, not to correct her. Now she has at least one fond memory of Indonesia to take home with her."

Bill added, "I hope she doesn't ever find out what that sign really means."

"I doubt she will," said Suprapto. "They're going home next month, to a place called Minnesota. She mentioned it when she was showing me that—what do you call that thing on the wall?"

"You mean the quilt?" Bill said.

A painting hung on the wall behind the sofa where Suprapto was sitting, a miniature oil painting dwarfed by the surrounding wayang gods and heroes. It was a rural Javanese scene of terraced paddies descending to a stream bordered by banana trees and bamboo. Tiny figures of saronged women walked along the terrace aprons, their heads wrapped in *ikets.* A farmer stood calf-deep in the stream, washing his water buffalo. It was the Javanese equivalent of Helen Karner's quilt.

I was still staring at it when Suprapto said, "Well, what do you think?"

"It's lovely," I said. "Who painted it?"

"An old Jogjanese artist who used to like my wayang shows. It's the village where I grew up. Also where I burned my hand." He paused. "I was pumping up a kerosene lantern at my parents' house and it exploded."

We sat smoking in silence, not knowing what to say.

Finally Bill said, "I'll bet you were a good dalang." He nodded at the walls. "Are these the puppets you used?"

Suprapto pulled his legs into the lotus position and with his good hand took down from the wall the figure of Semar, the wise, crippled dwarf. Holding in one hand all three of the buffalo-horn rods attached to the puppet's body and arms, Suprapto moved his fingers and Semar sprang to life. The dwarf bowed with palms together in the Javanese *salam* and began to speak in a low, resonant, otherworldly voice from deep in Suprapto's chest. Veiled in the smoke of Suprapto's kretek, Semar and his shadow on the wall wheedled, cajoled, persuaded, lamented, to the gonging and tinkling of the gamelan.

I watched, spellbound. I felt drawn into some ancient Javanese dream where human beings were shadows and shadows were gods.

Semar turned to the figure of Arjuna on the opposite wall, the halus hero who led the Pandavas into battle against the kasar Kurawa clan. He addressed Arjuna in English with a few lines from the Bhagavad Gita. He bowed again and was returned to his place on the wall.

After a brief silence, Bill clapped softly. "Marvelous, Pak," he said, using the Indonesian term of respect for an elder. "So you can still do it after all these years."

Through his tilted lenses Suprapto looked from one to the other of us with hooded eyes. "But I can make only one shadow at a time move," he replied. "That's hardly real wayang. Still, one does not stop being a dalang just because one's hand becomes useless."

Bill was looking at Suprapto, his eyes brimming with tears.

On our way back to the hotel we passed a kampong across an oily black canal. Pressure lamps glowed in the mothy darkness. The scene brought to mind Helen Karner's kampong sojourn earlier that evening. I remembered the moment in the car when Bill had turned to her, eager to clip her newly fledged wings. I was sure it was Suprapto's look that had silenced him. A flood of images crowded my mind: Suprapto's unexpected invitation to Bill, Helen's quilt and Suprapto's painting, Suprapto appearing out of nowhere in front of the car, Bill's finally speaking kindly of Helen. Had it all happened in some ancient Javanese dream in which the halus was destined to triumph over the kasar? Had Suprapto orchestrated it? Had he spoken to us through Semar? Had Semar spoken to us through Suprapto?

We pulled into the hotel parking lot. I was very tired and a little drunk, my head spinning from kreteks. Watching the evening's wayang had exhausted me but I still had work to do. Bill parked next to a lamp standard. He turned off the car and headlights. His face, pale in the lamplight, was haggard. He looked bereft again.

"Not ready to go home yet," he confided. "Join me for a nightcap?"

I told him I needed to file a story on the day's conference session. His face fell. He stared out into the warm night. I sensed a terrifying void of loneliness. How many rebuffs like this had he suffered?

"Oh, hell," I said. "I'll get up early tomorrow morning. Come on, I'm buying."

I, too, was one of Suprapto's marvelous puppets, a shadowy figure caught in the web of his clever wayang. And his words came back to me then, the lines of Bhagavad Gita he had plucked from some timeless Javanese dream and put into the grotesque mouth of Semar: *God dwells in the heart of all things, Arjuna: thy God dwells in thy heart. And his power of wonder moves all things—puppets in a play of shadows— whirling them onwards on the stream of time.*

ABOUT THE AUTHOR

LEO BERENSTAIN spent two years, in
the early 1980s, as a field ecologist
in the rain forest in eastern Borneo.
He lives with his wife, Kania,
in Pennsylvania and West Java,
Indonesia.